Unexpected Treasure

CARRIE JACOBS

Cover Design by Qamber Designs & Media qamberdesignsmedia.com
First Edition 2025

for Rick and Evie O'Connell
the ultimate in adventure #relationshipgoals

Chapter One

ALLIE QUINN REEKED.

She heaved herself into the driver's seat of her ten-year-old SUV after a long shift on the Mondayest Tuesday ever. The odd rush of unusually demanding customers had been bad enough, but then there was the barbeque sauce incident that perfectly illustrated her oh-so-glamorous life as manager of a sporting goods store.

She'd been straightening the display of new pre-packaged camping foods when a huge bottle of sauce toppled off the peak of the pyramid and hit the floor with impressive force. The sauce had exploded out of the splintered plastic bottle and splattered a massive brown-red wave in every direction. Across her shoe, up the pantlegs of her tan khakis, and somehow it had even reached her pale yellow Ralph's polo shirt, decorating it with several drips.

The pungent tang of smoky mesquite permeated her vehicle before she'd even had a chance to put the key in the ignition. She rolled her window down the whole way and opened the passenger side a few inches, hoping the cold early-April air would blow the stench out into the night.

Spoiler alert, it didn't.

The drive home was a brutal exercise in mouth breathing and trying not to freeze to death. Or barf. By the time she got home and pulled into the garage, she was sure she'd never be able to stomach barbeque sauce again. She hit the remote clipped to the visor to close the garage door and grabbed her bag from the passenger seat, ready to be done with this day.

The pale glow from the dome light illuminated a lovely brown streak across the worn leather seat as she slid out of the vehicle.

"You've got to be kidding me," she muttered. She pondered the physics of how the sauce was able to somehow splatter her on both the front and back as she dropped her bag onto the concrete floor and rummaged on the shelves to find a container of disinfecting wipes.

Thankfully, the barbeque sauce wiped off with minimal effort, unlike the sauce that had splattered onto the grooved metal shelving at the store and caused her an extra hour of work.

She eased open the door that separated the garage from the small ranch house and let herself into the mudroom that doubled as a laundry room. She toed her sauce-splattered shoes off and kicked them into the tiny powder room to be dealt with in the morning.

Her plan to tiptoe to her bedroom was thwarted as soon as she stepped into the living room and saw her grandfather on his recliner, still watching tv.

"Papi? What are you still doing up? It's almost eleven."

His weathered face split into a grin. "Did you get my message?"

"No, sorry." She fished her phone out of her bag and there it was, a stack of message notifications from several hours ago, half from him and half from the group text with her besties. "I haven't had a chance to look at my phone. What's up?"

"I have news. Sit." He reached over and patted the couch.

She hated to put him off, but the tangy smell was making her nauseous and she didn't want to get sauce on the furniture. "Do you mind if I grab a quick shower first?" She held out her arms so he could see the sauce splatters.

He chuckled. "You look like one of those Rorschach tests. Go, go." He waved a hand toward the hallway.

She turned the shower on full blast and stripped out of her barbequed clothes. A glance in the mirror revealed a stylish sauce highlight streaked in her shoulder-length hair and a bonus dried blob on her ear. On the upside, she'd come straight home instead of stopping somewhere along the way, so at least no one had seen her. She hurried to scrub all the remnants of the sauce away, but not even her favorite cucumber melon body wash could erase the tangy scent from her nose.

A quick twist of a towel in her hair, a full body rubdown, a cozy set of sweats, and she was back through the living room in under fifteen minutes, carrying a basket of laundry. She held up one finger in a "wait" gesture and took a minute to spray stain treatment on her clothes and throw them in the washing machine.

With that done, she dropped onto the couch. "Okay, I'm all yours. What's the big news?"

Papi's fingers drummed on the arm of his hideously ugly threadbare recliner that had long since faded to an awful shade of probably-used-to-be-green. "It's the news I've been waiting for."

Allie perked up. "Oh? Did they approve more physical therapy sessions?" His stingy insurance had only approved ten sessions after his recent hip surgery, so she'd been on the phone for weeks, fighting to get more sessions approved.

"No." His face scrunched like it was a ridiculous suggestion. "Rupert called me. Wants to see me first thing tomorrow."

Rupert Cresswell, museum director at the Marian P. Franklin Museum of Natural History and lifelong friend of Papi's, was always calling with random facts and obscure discoveries he read about, or to invite Papi to see some new thing they'd gotten to display.

This was not great news to Allie. "Define 'first thing.'"

"Eight o'clock sharp."

"Papi..." She ended the word with a tired sigh. A trip to the museum meant she'd have to chauffeur since he wasn't cleared to drive. "I was really hoping to sleep in a little bit tomorrow. I just worked fifteen days in a row." Those crazy stretches with no days off hit a lot different in your early forties than they did as a kid with endless energy.

"I know. And I wouldn't ask you if it wasn't important."

Allie rolled her head, trying to ease the knots in her neck. "What's it about?" She asked mostly to be polite, because the Venn diagram of things she and Papi found interesting and important had very little overlap.

Papi's eyes shone with excitement. "M'yxnih."

She jerked to attention. "What?"

"He thinks they found something." His voice caught on the last word.

She slid to the edge of the cushion so she could reach over and squeeze his hand. Breathlessly, she asked, "Did he say what it was?"

Papi shook his head and pinched the bridge of his nose with his eyes squinched shut. His chin trembled.

"That's amazing." It truly was. M'yxnih was his lifelong passion, and one of the few interests she was excited to share with him.

He pulled in a loud sniffle and blew out a breath, then gave her hand three quick squeezes – their super-secret way of saying "I love you." He wiped his eyes and said, "I'm sorry, Allie-gator. We don't have to go first thing. You need your sleep. I'll let Rupert know we'll be in later. I got excited and didn't even think about that."

"I can take a nap afterwards. This is important." She glanced up at the clock. The museum was a forty-minute drive away. "We'll head out by seven fifteen. But that means we need to get to bed now. Both of us."

Allie snuggled under the covers and was transported back to her childhood in this very room. The walls were the same – covered in pale gray wallpaper with delicate silver stripes and watercolor birds perched on silver-white branches. When she was only eight, she moved in with her grandparents and this became her permanent bedroom. Every night with them was a ritual of Noni giving her a bath and tucking her in with her stuffed monkey tucked in the crook of her arm, then Papi would handle the bedtime story.

Instead of the traditional stories, Papi always regaled her with tales from his archaeological digs. His explorations had taken him all over the globe. Egypt, Jordan, Belize, Mexico, Scotland, China, you name it, odds were good he'd been there on at least one expedition.

The dig that stuck with him, though, even though he hadn't touched a shovel or brush in more than three decades, was M'yxnih, home of the M'yxnihan people. His small team had discovered the previously unknown civilization in Mexico, dating back to the 1500s, in an area that was once part of the Aztec Empire. The artifacts they'd found were a fascinating blend of Aztec, Mayan, and Incan cultures, similar to each, but identical to none.

They'd unearthed an entire village. So much was intact that it seemed the inhabitants had left – or been removed – practically overnight.

Two years of backbreaking work.

Two years of Papi's heart and soul.

And all that remained was what fit in one small display case at the museum.

It was the early nineteen seventies. Papi's six-person team had just secured funding for another year of excavation. Everything was going their way.

Until one day the ground violently shook and split open, reclaiming the entire village. The devastating earthquake robbed them of everything. It took the ruins, their equipment, and nearly their lives.

All they were able to salvage was a handful of pottery shards and their memories.

In the decades since, Papi's discovery was scoffed at and his peers largely insisted he'd merely discovered another Aztec village. Interesting, but hardly remarkable.

He'd gone back to the site that was now a crater half a dozen times, but was never able to find a single shred of evidence that M'yxnih ever existed.

One by one, Papi's teammates gave up and moved on.

Allie burrowed deeper under her covers and drifted into that weird space between memory and dream.

She was eight years old, wriggling down into a flower-print cocoon that smelled of lavender and Old Spice. It was the safest and most comfortable place in the whole wide world.

"Tell me again," she insisted.

Papi chuckled. The bed shifted as he sat down. "Five hundred years ago, there was a princess."

"Princess K'nih," Allie said.

"That's right. Princess K'nih."

"From the city of M'yxnih."

Papi tucked the comforter under her chin. "Why don't you tell me the story, Allie-gator?"

"Okay, Papi-dile. The Spanish drove their ship to Mexico."

"That's right."

"The boat crashed and they walked for a long, long time until they found M'yxnih instead of the place they wanted to go, but the M'yxnihan people welcomed them. The captain convinced the king to let the princess go with them back to Spain to marry the prince." She stopped reciting for a moment and scrunched her face into a confused frown. "Why wouldn't the king go and meet the prince first? How come he'd just let Princess K'nih go to Spain with strangers and get married?"

"Well, things were done differently. Kings and queens and

princesses and princes lived for their kingdoms. Sometimes that meant doing things they might not want to do."

"That's dumb."

He nodded his head. "I'd never let my princess go to Spain without me."

Allie giggled because she knew he meant her. She was his princess. His granddaughter and the apple of his eye.

"Let's finish this later."

"Noooo," Allie argued. "Tell me again."

Papi obliged, as he always did. "When the second ship came to rescue the men—"

"The Santa Anna-Maria." She imagined an opulent, luxurious ship rather than the bare-bones merchant vessel it likely was.

"That's right. When the Santa Anna-Maria arrived, the captain took Princess K'nih and a treasure chest – a gift from her father – and they set out for Spain. Along the way, there were rough seas and bad storms that blew them far, far off course. The men thought it was bad luck to have a woman on board, so they blamed Princess K'nih for the storms and threw her overboard. One of the men—"

"Fernando de Cabra," she sighed dreamily.

"Fernando had fallen in love with the princess. He grabbed her treasure chest and stole a tiny cutter – a little rowboat – to save her. Somehow they made it to shore near Philadelphia. From there, they paid people to take them miles and miles inland. When they reached Central Pennsylvania, they settled on what is now Hauser Mountain, part of the Allegheny Mountains, where they decided to stay and make a home."

"That's near where we live," Allie murmured. Her eyes

drooped with the heaviness of imminent sleep. "And they got married and lived happily ever after."

Papi chuckled again and kissed her forehead. "Good night, Allie-gator."

"After while, Papi-dile." She drifted into dreams of Princess K'nih, her hero Fernando, and a treasure chest full of sparkling jewels.

Chapter Two

ALLIE WAS wide awake before her alarm. Not because she was excited, even though she kind of was, but because Papi had thumped up and down the hallway past her bedroom half a dozen times already. His cane rapped on the hardwood floor with each step. The halting cadence let her know he was trying to be quiet but not having much success.

She threw the blanket back. Might as well start the day.

Allie knew Papi was anxious and excited and feeling all the feelings when they got to the museum and he didn't make a single grumpy comment or even give her a side-eye when she pulled the wheelchair out of the back of her SUV.

He despised the thing, and she couldn't blame him. He didn't need to use it much, but the walk to the museum and through the building was simply too much for him to do with his bum hip. She also suspected he didn't fuss this time because, like it or not, riding in the wheelchair was much faster than making the walk, and this morning he was more interested in getting to Rupert's office than loudly defending his pride.

Allie pushed him through the large double doors into the round marble-tiled lobby.

The security guard hurried over as if he'd been expecting them. "Good morning, Charlie. Rupert asked me to escort you to his office right away." He barely gave Allie a glance, which was fine with her. He might be nice to look at, as her friends had pointed out more than once, but the man was obnoxious.

Papi's fingers gripped the armrests. He nodded once. "Thanks, Jake."

Allie pushed the wheelchair through a side door that led to an employees-only hallway. From there, Jake swiped his badge and they took the service elevator to the fourth floor at the top of the museum, where the offices were located.

Rupert stood in his doorway, anxiously awaiting their arrival.

Inside, two strange people waited. A tall, slim, pale woman with jet black hair slicked back into a severe bun at the nape of her neck, a black turtleneck, black pants, and black boots looked like she'd stepped out of a spy movie. The man with her was also tall and slim, with a similar outfit, but his included a black jacket, and he held a worn briefcase. It was brown, a stark splash against all the black, which irrationally annoyed Allie. It totally destroyed the mysterious spy vibe.

"Dr. Scheffler. Allie. Come in, come in. We have much to discuss."

Whoa. He'd used Papi's title instead of calling him Charlie. She'd been anticipating some small but exciting update, like a newly discovered piece of pottery or something, but the vibe in the room suggested this must be a lot bigger news than she'd assumed.

Allie pushed the wheelchair over to a semi-circle of plush office chairs facing Rupert's desk. The two strangers waited until Allie sat down beside Papi to take their seats.

Rupert went around to the tastefully elegant leather chair behind his desk. He tented his fingers and looked very serious. "Charles, I'm so glad you were able to be here. I'd like you to meet Selena and Chip Anderson. They're here from ARASNAC." He looked at Allie and clarified. "The Agency for the Rediscovery of Ancient Societies on the North American Continent."

The woman leaned toward Papi. "I'm Selena. It's so nice to meet you, Dr. Scheffler."

"Likewise," Papi answered.

"I don't know if you've been following our work?" The woman's voice was clipped and precise, totally matching her stiff presentation.

"I'm sorry, no. I know of the organization, of course, but I haven't been keeping track..." He trailed off and spread his hands.

"Understandable. We're very small. A tiny fish in a massive pond of similar organizations. One of our areas of focus are shipwrecks. More specifically, European shipwrecks that were lost near the Eastern Seaboard during the fourteenth, fifteenth, and sixteenth centuries."

Allie looked around at everyone's faces. Papi listened intently to the woman. Selena focused solely on him. Chip stared out the window. His fingers drummed silently on the handle of his briefcase. Rupert also focused on Selena. Jake stood behind them at the door, his hands clasped in front of him in a familiar security guard stance.

That tripped her up. If they had a security guard in attendance, this must be really, really important.

Selena continued. "Last year we were finally able to track down and positively identify the *Santa Anna-Maria*."

Papi gasped.

"After several dives, we were able to recover the captain's logbook."

"What?" Papi's voice was an awed whisper.

Whoa. Allie sat perfectly still. Even as a mostly-disinterested party, she knew that was huge. Massive. Epic.

"While it's very exciting, a few centuries underwater didn't do it any favors. Our archivists weren't able to salvage much, but what they did recover led us here. To you."

"Me?"

Selena turned to Chip, who reanimated. He popped the clasps on his briefcase and produced a small glass box. Or maybe it was acrylic.

Allie wasn't sure, but she guessed it was hermetically sealed to preserve whatever was inside.

Chip passed the box to Selena, who handed it to Papi.

His hands trembled as he inspected the box.

Allie leaned close to his shoulder. Inside the box were two tiny, dark bits of paper with faded, nearly illegible writing in a foreign language. One piece was roughly the size of a tea bag, the other maybe a quarter that size. She knew it was important. It was historical. But why— She suddenly leaned closer. Tall, narrow, faint letters made a familiar word on the smaller piece. Squinting, she tried to make out the words. Her heart skipped a beat as her eyes made sense of the letters. "Papi! Does that... does it say what I think it says?"

Tears shimmered in his eyes as he nodded vehemently.

"M'yxnih. Oh, my." Allie was at a loss for words. She'd always believed it existed, but to see tangible, original, historical proof was overwhelming. She couldn't imagine what Papi must be feeling.

Selena leaned over and put a hand on his arm. "Yes. M'yxnih. The second bit has three words our team was able to decipher. 'Storm,' 'red,' and 'treasure.' You were right, Dr. Scheffler. And from our research, we believe, as you did, that the trail leads to Hauser Mountain. It appears the entire mountain is private property. We've tried getting in touch with the owner, but so far we haven't gotten any response."

Shaking from Papi's shoulders drew Allie's attention away from Selena's face. Was he was crying? For joy, maybe? A burst of laughter erased any confusion. He let out deep, loud belly laughs until he had tears in his eyes.

Everyone looked at him with the same expression of confusion mixed with concern.

"Papi?"

Rupert slowly shook his head. At the same time, they said, "Estelle."

Papi's laughter subsided and he leaned back in his seat. "Estelle Hauser," he explained. "The mountain has been in her family for, oh, two or three hundred years. They're an eccentric bunch."

Rupert added, "Very private people, to put it lightly."

"The odds of Estelle letting us dig around on her property are slim to none."

Selena cocked her head. "We could always bring out the big guns and force an eminent domain situation."

"Won't work. They tried that back in the eighties and not only did Estelle's family bring out a lot of little guns, quite literally, they also brought a whole team of expensive lawyers who fought the application and won."

"Oh?" Selena's perfect eyebrows arched upward.

"I'll try calling her," Rupert offered. "Maybe appeal to her sense of history and legacy." He didn't sound confident.

"Good luck with that," Papi scoffed.

Allie looked back and forth between Papi and Rupert. "Who's Estelle Hauser?"

Rupert sat back. "I'll let your grandfather handle that one."

"It's a long story. The short version is that back in the day, we traced Princess K'nih and Fernando de Cabra's trail to Hauser Mountain. Rupert worked on distracting Estelle with his irresistible charms while I snuck onto their land. His wooing was unsuccessful, to put it kindly. Her father and brothers were rather displeased with the whole situation. Shots were fired, police were involved, and Estelle never forgave either one of us."

"Oh, boy." It wasn't a stretch to imagine Papi coming up with a scheme like that, or to imagine Rupert going along with it.

"Indeed."

Selena reached over and pulled a piece of paper out of Chip's briefcase. She slid it across Rupert's desk. "When you speak to her, please tell her this is what we're willing to offer in exchange for limited access to her property."

Rupert let out a low whistle. "I'll see what I can do."

Allie watched as Papi cast one last longing gaze at the fragments of paper sealed in the box in his hands. Reluctantly, he gave it back to Selena.

She smiled and patted his arm. "We're so close, Dr. Scheffler. With your help, we can find the red treasure and you'll finally get the recognition you deserve for your discovery of M'yxnih."

Chapter Three

A WEEK AFTER THE MEETING, Jake O'Malley sat in his office, staring at the bank of security monitors. Okay, "bank" was overselling it. He had one big screen with nine squares, a la *The Brady Bunch*, that showed him a rotating carousel of videos from every conceivable angle throughout the museum. The separate monitor for his computer blinked off because he hadn't moved his mouse for at least twenty minutes.

He watched the camera angles flipping through the whole museum, not paying particularly close attention. It was a busy but uneventful Wednesday, and his mind was still preoccupied with Charlie and the people from the Alliance or Agency or whatever of... whatever. Rupert seemed confident about them, but Jake wasn't so sure. He'd checked their website, and they were legit, but there was just something about them that made his spidey senses tingle.

It was easy to see why Rupert was excited about a project like this, though. Hauser Mountain was local, it was being partially funded by that organization, and it would be a massive boon for the museum, not to mention how much this would help his friend Charlie validate his claims. If they found something significant, it would be huge for everyone involved. Not only would it mean a fresh exhibit, which always boosts attendance significantly, it would mean a notation in the history books as being a part of the discovery. It was big a deal, but he couldn't help but feel wary.

Then again, he was generally suspicious of everyone. Part of it was the nature of his job as Head of Security for the museum. Impressive title, but in reality, the entire security staff consisted of Jake, one other full-time guard, and four part-time retired police officers.

The Marian P. Franklin Museum of Natural History was a small, four-story museum in an historic building. It had some important exhibits and artifacts, but it wasn't exactly a Smithsonian-level operation. All in all, it was a pretty cushy job and best of all, he got to know great people like Charlie Scheffler.

Charlie was a fascinating guy. He had a million tall tales from his expeditions all around the globe. He was also a little bossy and had some firm ideas about the exhibits and how the displays should be set up. Particularly the tiny display containing a handful of pottery shards and a chunk of stone with a partial carving from M'yxnih, the village Charlie and his team had discovered decades ago. Those artifacts were Charlie's prized possessions, on loan to the museum in perpetuity. Charlie was not pleased, however, that they were part of the Aztec display.

Rupert had partially soothed his ire with a small card referencing the village of M'yxnih, but Charlie insisted there should be more information educating visitors and explaining that M'yxnih was its own entire civilization.

Jake wasn't sure what to believe, but he wasn't the expert, so he kept his opinions to himself. He believed that Charlie believed his version of events, and that was good enough.

Movement on one of the video feeds caught his attention. He pressed a button to keep that camera live on his screen instead of scrolling to the next view. A boy from a visiting third-grade school group veered away from the rest of his class and was casting suspicious looks at Ella, a velociraptor, and Levi, a Tyrannosaurus rex, the two dinosaur skeletons that guarded the entrance to the prehistoric display.

Jake grabbed his walkie. "Tom? You copy?"

The guard on duty responded immediately. "Go for Tom."

"Ella and Levi have some company."

"I'm on it." Before he closed the communication, Tom sighed and muttered, "Always with the dinosaurs."

Jake watched the monitor closely. Tom casually strolled into view, moving toward the dinosaurs. The wayward boy spotted Tom and skedaddled back over to the other students before the guard even looked in his direction.

A few minutes before five, closing time on Wednesdays, the school group assembled in the large lobby rotunda. One of the adults did a head count and ushered the students outside to their waiting bus.

Jake watched the remaining stragglers exit the museum. All except two.

On the third floor, video showed Charlie and Allie standing in front of the M'yxnih case. Allie shifted back and forth impatiently, gesturing to the wheelchair. She lifted her arm and tapped her wrist and pointed toward the exit. The video had no sound, but Jake could see her mouth moving as she clearly told her grandfather it was time to leave.

Tom was at his station at the now-locked front doors waiting to let the last visitors out.

Jake saw nothing out of the ordinary, so he left his office and hurried down the hallway that would let him out into the Aztec display.

He cleared his throat. "Sir? The museum is closed."

"See? I told you. We have to go," Allie said.

Jake rolled his eyes. "Relax. I'm kidding."

She gaped at him. "Did you seriously just tell me to relax?"

He didn't know why she was always so impatient with Charlie. It irked him to witness. "Yeah. I told you to relax."

"Well how about you—"

"You're right, let's go," Charlie interrupted.

"*Thank* you," she said, clearly exasperated.

Jake frowned. "You know he's an adult, right? You don't need to talk to him like a child."

She fired back, "You know it's none of your business, right? You don't need to insert yourself like a child."

"Now you listen—"

"To you? Absolutely not. Papi, we need to go before Pall Blart, Mall Cop here shines his flashlight at me or something." She tapped the back of the wheelchair. "Let's. Go."

Jake noticed Charlie cast an unhappy look at the chair.

"I hate that thing," Charlie grumbled under his breath.

He could clearly walk, so obviously the wheelchair was just for her convenience because the old man probably slowed her down. "He doesn't want to ride in the wheelchair. Let him walk."

She whipped out her phone and tapped on the screen. "Do you have a pen?"

"What? A pen for what?" What the heck was she talking about?

"So you can write down this number."

"Number for what?" This woman was making no sense.

"His physical therapist. That way you can call and explain that, in your *expert* opinion, *Doctor* Blart, Papi is completely healed and perfectly capable of walking the entire distance from here to the car. You can also explain that you personally guarantee that he absolutely won't fall and reaggravate his injuries, and that, in your expert opinion, he definitely wouldn't need the additional surgery those *morons* say he would need in the event of another fall."

Surgery? He didn't realize Charlie had recently had surgery. Okay, maybe he had overstepped a little bit.

"And unless you plan to be the one handling his around-the-clock care during recovery, I'll kindly thank you to butt your stupid face out of our business."

Jake wasn't sure what to say to that, and her tirade erased any urge to apologize, so he decided the best course of action was to ignore Allie and focus on Charlie. "Rupert mentioned there's going to be a meeting with Ms. Hauser soon."

The old man's face brightened. "Tomorrow."

Allie said, "Yeah. We'll be back here tomorrow, so let's *go*." She patted the wheelchair again, with more force this time.

Charlie huffed an annoyed sigh, but he sat.

Jake felt bad for him. It wasn't right that his grand-daughter was forcing him to ride in a chair when he didn't want to, or force him to leave the museum before he was ready. With some patience, surely he could walk a bit before being forced into the chair he obviously hated. Sure, it was closing time, but he was a friend of Rupert's and had certain privileges, especially with his artifacts on loan.

It was a shame she couldn't be more flexible and under-standing.

Chapter Four

ALLIE GOT Papi situated in the passenger seat and stowed his wheelchair in the back of her SUV before jumping into the driver's seat.

"Sorry," Papi mumbled. "I just wanted to see them a while longer."

"Yeah. Buckle your seatbelt." Allie tried not to stew in irritation. Papi knew she had a split shift, and he still insisted on going to the museum for half the afternoon. He'd promised to be quick, but he'd been anything but.

"What time do you have to be back to work?"

Her gaze flicked to the clock on the console. It was already five thirty. "I was supposed to be back at five. I had to text Ralph and let him know I couldn't get back until at least six thirty."

Papi winced. "I'm sorry."

She reached over and patted his hand while they were stopped at a light. "It's okay. I mean, it's not okay, but I'm not going to fight with you about it." She bit her lip before continuing. "But I'm also not going to be doing this again. It's too much for me to open and close the store and spend the after-noon running you to the museum in between. Especially when you throw a tantrum when I tell you we need to leave."

"Tantrum," he huffed.

"Yes, Papi, a tantrum. I know you hate being reliant on me. I know you hate using that wheelchair when we've got a lot of distance to cover. I know you hate not being able to come and go as you please. I'm trying to bend over backwards to give you as much freedom as I can, but now it's costing me two hours of work, just because you didn't want to leave. I'm lucky Ralph is so flexible and was able to cover me on zero notice. A lot of other managers would fire me, and then where would we be?"

Papi crossed his arms and glared out the window. "At least you'd still have a place to live. Don't forget, you live for free. No rent, no mortgage payment."

Allie stuffed down the urge to slam on the brakes and pull over so she could scream into the void. Instead, she took a deep breath and let it out slowly. If not for her leaving her job in Tucson and wiping out more than half her savings to get his house out of foreclosure, neither of them would have a place to live. Very calmly, she said, "I moved home because you needed me to, remember? I was glad to do it then, and I'm glad to be here now, but don't act like I'm mooching off you."

His shoulders drooped. "I know. I'm just... I don't even know."

He might not know why he was being a brat, but it was obvious to her. "You're anxious about what's going on with Estelle and the Andersons and all the M'yxnih stuff. And I know you want to be able to be in the thick of it yourself. As you should be. It was your discovery, and you deserve all the credit even if you can't be the one traipsing into the mountain, and you're taking all your frustration out on me."

He deflated back against his seat. "You're right, Alliegator. I wish I could be there to make sure everything is done properly. These Anderson people seem nice enough, and ARASNAC is a legitimate organization, but..."

Allie glanced up at the rearview mirror, then back to the road. "I get it. I'm not sure I totally trust what they're saying, but I don't have any reason for that."

"Yeah." He drummed his fingers on his thigh. "Maybe I could ask Jake to look into them."

Allie rolled her eyes. "Jake's a chauvinist butthead who doesn't know how to mind his own business."

"I like him."

"And you are free to do so."

"He's a good guy."

She answered with a noncommittal grunt. Papi thought he was great because he listened to all Papi's stories and validated his tantrum.

As far as she was concerned, Jake's only redeeming quality was that he was nice to look at, but no one was good-looking enough to make it worth putting up with that judgmental attitude.

Thursday morning in Rupert's office, Allie glanced over at Papi. He sat up very straight in his chair, wearing his nicest jacket over a crisp white shirt. He'd even put on a tie and carefully combed his silver hair neatly.

The chairs were in a semi-circle again. Selena and Chip didn't seem nearly as anxious as Papi and Rupert did.

Allie was tense, too, feeding off the vibe of the room. Over the past week, Papi had told her stories of Estelle Hauser and her family and their odd ways until Allie's vision of her was something akin to a hunched, cackling witch from a fairy tale, selfishly guarding access to a treasure.

A quick rap on the door pulled everyone's attention, but before Rupert could round his desk, the door swung open. Rita, the administrative assistant, announced the arrival of Mrs. Hauser.

Allie almost laughed. The woman in the doorway looked more like Betty White than a wicked witch. She was petite, dressed in a sharp hot pink pantsuit with a white blouse under the jacket. The string of pearls around her neck were the same slightly off-white color as her perfectly coiffed hair.

Low, smart heels clipped sharply against the tile with each step as Estelle Hauser crossed the room. She exuded authority without saying a single word.

Rupert met her and extended his right hand to shake hers while his left gestured to an open chair. "Estelle, welcome. It's so good to see you."

Papi rose to his feet. "Estelle."

Estelle fixed him with a withering glare.

Allie stood as well, and finally noticed the young man accompanying her. A grandson, maybe? Probably in his early twenties, she guessed. He walked a few steps behind, wearing dark jeans and a navy button-down shirt. He faded into the periphery next to her commanding presence, like a secret service agent. Behind him, Jake closed the door and took his post beside it.

"This is my great-grandson, William," Estelle said, then turned her sharp gaze on Allie. "You must be Charles's granddaughter."

Before she could answer, Selena and Chip jumped to their feet. Selena grasped Estelle's right hand and pumped it as she gushed, "It's such an honor to meet you, Mrs. Hauser."

Estelle snatched her hand back. "Relax, girl, you're not meeting the Queen." She turned her attention back to Allie.

Chip wisely sat without uttering a word.

Allie offered a smile. "Yes, I'm Pa—Charles's granddaughter, Allie. It's nice to meet you."

They stood too far apart to make attempting a handshake anything but awkward, so Allie didn't try. She slowly retook her seat.

Estelle gave her a nod, then sat in the chair next to Papi. Even her posture demanded respect. She looked across the desk to the director. "Let's get on with it, shall we, *Rupert?*" Venom carried his name from her lips.

William stood silently behind her chair.

Rupert cleared his throat. "Certainly. We... aahh, we'd like to ask your permission to do some exploring on your mountain."

Selena jumped in. "We don't believe it will be a particularly invasive project as far as bringing in heavy equipment. From what we've been able to ascertain, the evidence we're searching for is likely in a cave or cavern. We expect minimal digging and disturbance of your property. You'll hardly even know we're there!" She finished on a slightly-too-loud and false, far-too-chipper note, then continued. "The initial stage of the project will take about six weeks. Perhaps eight. And then we'll have a better idea of how long we'll be on site for the next stage. We're looking to begin in... well, today is, what, the nineteenth? So we'll be onsite on or about May first to begin the first phase."

Allie felt Papi cringe. Rupert was an expert at keeping his face neutral, but the way he looked down at his desk suggested he did not approve of Selena's speech. Allie herself had only known Estelle for three minutes, and she was quite sure this was *not* the way to approach the situation.

She glanced back at Jake, who caught her eye and slowly shook his head like he couldn't believe how Selena was speaking, either. For once it seemed they were on the same page. Small miracles, right?

Selena plowed on, nudging Chip to open his briefcase and produce a folder. "We have the agreement here. It outlines everything. You'll just need to sign here," she tapped the page, "here, and here." She held a pen out to Estelle and kept talking. "We have a fair idea of where the cave might be located, thanks to satellite imaging and mapping."

Estelle took the pen and papers and laid them on the desk. Her voice was sharp. "You seem to be under the impression that I've agreed to any of this."

Selena's eyes widened, then she quickly adjusted her face. "I'm hopeful we'll come to an agreement, Mrs. Hauser. This is of extreme historical significance. We certainly want to go the route that's most beneficial for all of us without needing to exert any sort of eminent—"

Estelle flicked her hand, dismissing Selena's threat like a pesky mosquito. "Organizations far larger and more important than yours have tried and failed." She fixed a meaningful gaze on Selena. "And gone bankrupt in the process." She waited a beat for her words to sink in, then added, "It would be a shame if all your organization's resources were tied up in lengthy legal battles you stand no chance of winning. Instead of, you know, focusing on your work of extreme historical significance."

The silence in the room was a tangible presence.

Rupert cleared his throat and tented his fingers. "Mrs. Hauser. Estelle. I'm sure Selena wasn't trying to threaten—"

"I'll admit my hearing isn't what it used to be, Rupert, but I'll thank you not to mansplain what was very clearly stated." Her direct expression dared him to disagree.

Allie couldn't help but be impressed. This woman was taking zero garbage. She definitely wasn't some sweet little old lady who could be manipulated or cowed. She glanced over at Papi and sucked in a concerned breath. His face was pale and he stared, unblinking, at the desk. His shoulders drooped like he was already admitting defeat, that whatever existed of M'yxnih on Estelle's property would remain a mystery that he would never see a resolution to in this lifetime. His Adam's apple bobbed above the knot of his tie.

He knew this could be the end of the line. He'd come to terms with Hauser Mountain being a dead end until the Andersons showed up and resurrected all his hopes.

She hadn't seen him so excited in years. The door couldn't close like this.

"Mrs. Hauser?" Allie spoke quietly, almost timidly.

Estelle's sharp gaze swiveled to her.

"I don't know anything about archeology. I don't know much about history. To me, M'yxnih has always been like a wonderful fairy tale or a myth. But Papi was there. He crawled on his knees and dug with his hands and he saw it. He touched it. He smelled it and tasted it and it became a part of him. And he watched the ground open and swallow it whole right in front of him." She cleared her throat, not quite sure exactly where she was going. "I don't know much about you, Mrs. Hauser, but I'd be willing to bet that you could close your eyes and make your way over every inch of your mountain. It's in your blood, in your heart, in the legacy that you're leaving for your family. For Papi, that's M'yxnih. And there's a good chance there's a little piece of M'yxnih hiding in your mountain."

One of Estelle's eyebrows quirked upward.

"I'm asking you—I'm begging you. Please. Let the team come onto the mountain and see if there's anything left of M'yxnih. If your mountain was swallowed up tomorrow and I held the last remaining blade of grass, I swear I'd let you have it." She took a deep breath. "I can't blame you if you say no. Coming in hot and threatening eminent domain was foolish and shortsighted and if I were in your shoes, I might tell us all to pound sand and go home to my mountain and never accept another call about it. I'm hoping you're a less petty person than I, and that you'll consider allowing this project to move forward."

Allie looked over to Papi. He was silent, but a few tears made a wet trail down his cheek.

Estelle let out a sigh and sat back in her seat.

Allie's fingers dug into the arms of her chair. All she could do was hope Estelle Hauser didn't hold too much of a grudge against Papi for whatever he and Rupert had done to tick her off all those years ago, and that Selena's audacity didn't kill the project before it even began.

Chapter Five

JAKE HELD his position by the door. In the past thirty seconds, he'd developed a whole new respect for Allie. It's possible that respect was only in contrast to the sheer obnoxiousness of Selena's speech, but it was nice to see a side of Allie that wasn't annoyed at Charlie.

He waited at his station beside the door, right where Rupert had asked him to stand. Rupert never explained, but Jake was frequently invited to stand "guard" during meetings of all sorts. He assumed it was to underscore the museum's importance, despite its small budget and frequent oversight in favor of bigger institutions.

He clasped his hands behind his back, waiting to see how this was going to play out. He wished there was something he could do to help Charlie. He knew the man's hopes and dreams hinged on whatever Estelle said next. Hopefully Allie's impassioned speech swayed her toward allowing the project to move forward.

"This project is very important to many people, Mrs. Hauser," Selena added.

Jake wanted to tell her to shut up, that she was doing the opposite of making a compelling argument. Estelle Hauser was clearly not someone to be motivated by a heavy-handed approach.

"Charles," Estelle began. "I realize many years have passed, but I believe I am still owed an apology."

Charlie nodded without hesitation. "You are. I lied to you, and I'm sorry for that. I treated you poorly, and I was disrespectful to you and your family and your family's property. I thought my goal of chasing my M'yxnih was more important than being a decent person, and I apologize. I should have come along when Rupert made his amends back then, but I was too much of a coward to apologize to you and your family face to face like I should have. However this works out, Estelle, I sincerely apologize and I hope you'll forgive me."

Now Jake was even more curious as to what had happened. Rupert alluded to it, but hadn't shared any details.

"I'm just glad your father missed when he shot at me," Charlie added.

For the first time, Estelle's stiff demeanor cracked and she laughed, letting her head tilt back. She reached over and patted Charlie's arm before putting her hand back in her lap. Her eyes sparkled as she said, "My daddy never missed. He wanted to scare the daylights out of you and make sure you never came back."

"He succeeded. I've never run so fast in my whole life." He sobered. "I have a handful of regrets, Estelle. I do wish I'd treated you differently. And I wish I'd have been able to get in those caves and see if there's anything left of M'yxnih. I know it's a longshot. Even if there was anything there, it's probably been degraded. I just..." His voice cracked. "I just need to know for sure. It's been eating at me for decades."

Jake wasn't particularly superstitious, but he crossed his fingers behind his back, hoping Estelle had been persuaded.

Selena jumped in again and Jake mentally groaned. This woman could not read the room. "We're confident there's something on your mountain, and we have a fairly small search radius. It's true that whatever might have been left behind could be degraded or long gone, but if it's still there, you'd receive a lot of recognition for the discovery."

Estelle quickly turned to look at Selena. Her lip ticked up in an Elvis-like sneer. "I have no interest in that sort of recognition."

Selena tried another tack. "I can personally assure you—"

"I don't know you. Your personal assurances mean nothing to me." Estelle shook her head like she was tired of Selena.

Jake couldn't really blame her.

Estelle eyed Selena for another moment before turning away. "It's true that we don't let many people onto our property, let alone give unfettered access. My mountain is my sanctuary, and I'll not have it disturbed." She looked at Charlie. "I'm afraid there's no possible way for you to get back in those cracks and crevices."

Jake's hopes fell as he watched Charlie look down at his hand, resting on his cane.

Estelle continued. "I am not without sympathy, Charles. This is your life's work. So, with some non-negotiable restrictions, I will allow extremely limited access for this project, within a very, very narrow set of parameters."

Rupert and Charles both sat straighter in their chairs.

Jake's own stance straightened as he waited to hear more. This was incredible news. Whatever her parameters were, surely they'd be able to meet them.

Estelle continued. "I am well aware of my family's *eccentric* reputation. Some of it deserved, some of it not. We have some requirements that most people find odd. We do not allow unmarried workers on the property, namely to avoid any improper fraternization. Yes, this applies to both men and women. No, I will not explain further, nor will I waive this requirement."

Rupert nodded as he said, "Selena and Chip are married. I'll make sure they select the rest of their team accordingly, even though the requirement is..." He waved his hand, trying to pluck the right word out of thin air.

"Unorthodox," Estelle supplied.

"Yes. Unorthodox."

Selena interjected, "That's not a legal condition for you to have. Marital status is a protected class in many states."

Her sharp tone was a bucket of cold water on Jake's relief. She was going to keep pushing until Estelle decided to peace out of the whole thing.

Estelle snapped, "That would only be relevant if I were *hiring* you. Rest assured, that is something I would never do. I am permitted to set any requirements I wish for an invited guest." She turned her attention back to Charlie and Rupert. "Other nonnegotiable rules are as follows: guests must not, under any circumstances, interfere with the wildlife. Neither flora nor fauna is to be bothered. We have several nesting and breeding areas for a handful of threatened species, and they absolutely must not be disturbed in any way. In that vein, there will be no photos or video allowed outside the cave system. Inside, you are free to video or photograph anything you wish."

Chip touched Selena's arm, like he was trying to keep her from speaking again.

"You will be allowed access to the property for precisely four weeks. There will be no work performed on Saturdays or Sundays. A maximum of eight persons will be allowed. Since you are unable to attend, Charles, I must insist that one of those people be your granddaughter. We will have four of our own experienced guides join your eight-person team."

Allie shook her head. "Oh, but I don't know anything about excavating or archaeological stuff."

Jake swallowed hard. It was awful, being helpless to fix the situation. Allie couldn't meet Estelle's requirements even if she wanted to, unless she was prepared to pull a husband out of thin air.

"I expect you'll be more of a go-between for your grandfather, the team, and myself. Relaying necessary information. I assume, Charles, that no one else could decipher symbols and carvings as accurately as you? Allie can send you photos and you can be part of the process, even though you're unable to personally hike to the site."

Impressive. Jake was really starting to like Estelle, despite her antiquated requirement. Clearly nothing got past her.

"But... I'm not married," Allie said quietly.

"Oh." Estelle frowned. "Well. That's disappointing."

Jake stepped forward as the germ of an idea took shape. Maybe there *was* a way to move forward. Was it a good idea? Absolutely not. But it just might help Charlie. Because even if Estelle let the project continue without Allie, that would probably mean Charlie never truly finds out what's left of

M'yxnih, if anything. This was a mess. But maybe, just maybe... "Excuse me for interrupting." He walked over and put a hand on the back of Allie's chair.

She looked up at him with one eyebrow raised.

Jake smiled down at her confused face, hoping she'd roll with his crazy plan, then looked at Estelle. "We're engaged."

Chapter Six

ALLIE'S INSIDES screamed bloody murder. What the heck was Jake doing? Estelle was never going to believe this nonsense, not in a million years. She managed a bit of a smile and said, "I didn't think that counted." This performance deserved an Oscar. Or an antacid.

Estelle shook her head. "It doesn't. When's the wedding?"

Jake's hand moved from the chair to her shoulder. "September."

If she turned her head far enough, she could probably bite his hand. Maybe that would be strong enough to convey her disapproval of this ridiculousness.

"Well, then. We'll talk in the fall." Estelle moved to stand.

"Wait!" Selena jumped in. "We don't need them. She said herself she's got no experience, and I'd bet he doesn't either. There's no value to their presence."

Ouch.

"The value is that there is no moving forward without Allie."

Being the rope in this tug of war didn't feel great.

Selena didn't look happy, but she pressed on. "What if they get married now? The legal part? And then you can still have the actual wedding later. That could work, right?"

Estelle shrugged. "I don't care about the pomp and circumstance, I care about the union itself."

"What do you think, sweetie?" Jake asked.

It was the most bizarre, absurd, ridiculous scheme she'd ever heard. But it was the only way she could be Papi's eyes and ears. Her being onsite was the next best thing to him being there himself. That was the obvious upside. But there were some pretty big downsides. She'd already lied to Estelle's face, which made her stomach a little queasy. She'd have to keep lying, and Estelle would one hundred percent figure them out. Then what? She looked over at Papi. His eyes were full of hope. Telling Estelle the truth would extinguish that hope, maybe forever. She pulled in an unsteady breath and chose the lesser of two evils. "Sure. We'll have to see what we need to do." It was the most noncommittal thing she could think of to say with everyone watching.

Selena changed the subject. "Mrs. Hauser, about the four weeks. I'm afraid that won't be enough time to pinpoint the location, conduct our search, and explore the target area. That's an impossibly short timeline."

"There's no need to pinpoint the location. We know exactly what you're looking for, and we know exactly where it is." Estelle looked to William, who was patiently standing behind her chair. "William?"

The young man pulled a folded sheet of paper from his shirt pocket and handed it to Estelle. She unfolded it and gave it to Papi.

He sucked in a long breath as he studied the page.

Allie leaned over to see better. "What is it?" It didn't look like much to her. Dark scribbles on a piece of paper.

"A charcoal rubbing."

"What?" Jake asked as he leaned over her shoulder to get a better look.

Papi explained. "The Scouts do it all the time on nature hikes. You put a clean sheet of paper over something, say, tree bark or a fossil in a stone. Then you rub a pencil or piece of charcoal over the paper and you'll get an image of the texture or carving."

Allie couldn't figure out what it was supposed to be. The black smudge showed an oval with short lines spiking out from the outer side of the oval, and longer lines drawn across the inside of the oval.

After a moment, Papi nodded. He handed the paper to Rupert. "It's a beetle."

As soon as he said it, Allie could see it. An oval beetle with short legs and lines across its back, which could be stripes or segments. "Does that make sense to you that it could be a M'yxnihan carving?" she asked.

He nodded. "It does."

"Do you remember that tiny earthquake we had back in 2011?" Estelle asked. "It originated somewhere in Virginia and we felt it up here? There was no damage, but we believe that earthquake caused some already-unstable rocks to shift, which exposed a cave entrance that led to a handful of carvings like this."

For several long minutes, the only sound in the room was the crinkling of the paper as it was handed around for everyone to see.

Estelle handed it to Papi again. "You can keep that." She

stood. "Your dig can begin after I have a legitimate marriage certificate in my hand and not before."

Selena said, "What if we proceed without Allie? We can be ready to go as early as Monday."

"No."

"But—"

Estelle huffed an irritated sigh. "I'll make this clear enough that even you can understand. My land, my rules."

Rupert jumped up and rounded the desk. "Thank you, Estelle. I'll be in touch as soon as we have something for you."

"Yes, Estelle, thank you so much," Papi said as he struggled to his feet. "You won't regret this."

"We'll see. William?"

The young man offered his elbow. She put her hand in the crook of his arm.

Jake hurried to open the door. "Thank you, Mrs. Hauser."

She fixed him with a sharp gaze.

Allie was certain she saw straight through him and knew he was lying. *They* were lying.

That was bad. But what if she believed them? That was even worse.

After Estelle left, they sat in silence for a few moments until Rupert clapped his hands and said, "Well, Selena, Chip, we'll let you go so you can assemble the rest of your team while we iron out some details."

"But what—"

"We'll be in touch very soon," Rupert said, cutting her off and urging her toward the door.

Allie stood, but Rupert closed the door behind the Andersons.

"I have a few ideas. Jake, have a seat."

Allie sank back onto her chair. What the heck had they just done? And what was Rupert up to?

Jake sat in Estelle's seat, on the other side of Papi.

"What were you thinking?" she shouted.

"I don't know," he shouted back. He shook his head and lowered his tone. "She was talking about her requirements and all I could think was that I wanted to help Charlie and it just came out. At least it bought us a little time."

"Time for what? She wants me there, but I'm not married, so this isn't going to work. She's not going to relax her weird rules, and I'm not going to get married. Which means we're stuck."

Rupert interjected, "There's another option. A compromise of sorts."

Allie shook her head. "What compromise? You're either married or not. There's no such thing as 'a little bit married.'"

"But there is."

"Huh?" Her head was starting to ache.

Jake said, "You're going to have to explain, because it's doesn't make any sense to me, either."

"I'm an ordained wedding officiant," Rupert explained. Not the religious sort, but we've had enough requests for couples to marry here at the museum that it made sense for me to become ordained, so I'm quite familiar with the process. We apply for a marriage license. The two of you will sign it, then I will sign it as the officiant. It will be a one hundred percent legitimate document. We will provide it to Estelle, and after the project is complete, we shred it. For a marriage to be valid, the license must be filed with the county. In our case, the license will expire without ever being filed. We give Estelle the legitimate document she required, because she's too savvy to accept a fake. She'll be able to see that the application was processed, because that's public record. We simply... fail to complete the transaction and allow it to expire."

Allie pinched the bridge of her nose. "You want us to actually get a marriage license."

"Do you see an alternative?"

Jake asked, "Isn't that fraud? Couldn't you get in trouble?"

"With whom? The three of you aren't going to turn me in, and it's not unheard of for licenses to expire for any number of reasons. That's not suspicious. The entire process is above-board and ultimately for the greater good."

Allie bristled at the phrase. It was practically her mother's tagline to explain why she breezed in and out – mostly out – of Allie's life. She shoved those thoughts aside. What Rupert said made sense.

She looked over to ask Papi's opinion. His weathered finger traced the lines of the charcoal beetle. His expression was vacant, like he was traveling back in time to when he was excavating M'yxnih.

"It just... expires?" she asked. "We don't have to get a divorce or annulment?"

"Correct."

That made it slightly more palatable. "What do we say if someone asks why it wasn't filed? Don't they follow up on things like that?"

"Nope."

"What about witnesses?" Jake asked. "I thought you needed two witnesses?"

"In Pennsylvania, if you have a certified officiant, which I am, you do not need witnesses. You only need witnesses if there is no registered officiant."

"Oh."

Rupert waited a beat, then resumed his explanation. "You'll need to begin the application process on the online portal, and then appear in person, together, with valid identification. You'll also need court documents pertaining to any legal name changes, divorces, or in the event of being widowed, a copy of a previous spouse's death certificate." Rupert continued, "After you appear in person, there is a three-day waiting period. If we get the application filled out online now, you can appear as a walk-in at the courthouse tomorrow. Then you'd be able to pick up your license next Wednesday."

Papi sniffled and looked up from the drawing. He folded the paper without looking and slipped it into his shirt pocket. "I appreciate all this, I really do. But I can't ask either of you to go through with this. There are a lot of ways it could go wrong, and I don't want that on my conscience. And you can't take off work for a whole month, Allie. Even if Ralph approved, you don't have that much time off coming." His voice was sad and resigned.

Rupert leaned forward and clasped his hands together. "There is a discretionary budget I can tap for the project. The museum will gladly pay Allie a reasonable salary for the four weeks, since she'll technically be working for us for the duration."

"I bet Ralph would approve if he got some free advertising out of the deal," Allie said, mostly thinking out loud. "We'll be caving, so we'll need ropes and lights and hardhats and whatnot. If I approached it as asking Ralph to be a sort of sponsor, I bet he'd be on board."

"How will this work?" Jake asked.

Rupert explained. "Since it's a joint project between ARASNAC and the museum, and with Estelle's odd parameters for the project, I think it's best if we send you two as the museum's representative team. Your job will be mostly to observe and report. Photographs, notes, et cetera. The ARASNAC team will handle the actual digging and collection of artifacts, if there are any. They'll do the cataloguing, and then everything will come here and we'll eventually create a display."

"So it'll be the two of us and six of them," Jake said. "Do you think they're going to let us actually see what they're doing?"

"I don't see any issue. ARASNAC has done a lot of joint projects, this is old hat for them."

Allie wasn't sure about this whole scheme. She said, "I don't know. What if something goes wrong with the paperwork?"

"Once the project is done and we meet for debriefing, you and Jake can destroy it yourselves." He pointed to a small shredder beside his file cabinet. "The paperwork will never leave this office, and no one comes in here aside from myself and Rita. It will be perfectly safe."

Chapter Seven

JAKE SHARED ALLIE'S TREPIDATION. This might be a terrible idea. Then again, it might be the best thing ever. It was basically a free vacation out in nature that he didn't need to use PTO for. Jake used to love camping, but he hadn't gone for years. Surely this would be similar.

Additionally, Rupert's plan made perfect sense. The project couldn't move forward without Allie. And because of Estelle's rules, that meant it couldn't move forward without him, either.

Surely they could tolerate each other for four weeks. It wasn't like they had to be affectionate or pretend to be in love. They could easily explain any lack of affection by saying they're both uncomfortable with PDAs.

His biggest hesitation was the fact that they would need to lie to Mrs. Hauser. He hated that part, but it was either lie or not have a project. Both options stunk, but letting the project go was a far worse scenario.

He glanced over at Allie, then followed her gaze down to

Papi's hand. The tip of his index finger was black from the charcoal on the drawing.

A wave of nostalgia came over him. Seeing Charlie's finger was like watching his own grandfather leaning over the sink, washing hands that were blackened from grease or garden dirt or whatever messy project he'd just completed. He could feel his grandfather's presence in the room. That sealed the deal.

Yes. He could easily tolerate Allie for four weeks to help the old guy out.

Charlie sighed. "You're sure there's no way this plan can go wrong?"

"I honestly don't see how," Rupert assured him.

It was a simple scheme, really. Legitimately give Estelle what she asked for, then just quietly let it expire. The little lie was a better option than abandoning the whole project. "I'm in," he said.

Allie slowly nodded. "Me, too."

Rupert beamed. "Perfect! Let's get the application started."

The following Wednesday afternoon, Jake stood on the sidewalk outside the courthouse. Allie was beside him, holding the envelope that contained the marriage license they'd just picked up.

"This is crazy, right?" he said.

"It's the craziest thing I've ever done." She put the envelope in her leather messenger bag. "Can I ask you something?"

"Sure."

"Why are you doing this?" She held her hand over her eyes to shield them from the sun as she looked up at him. "I'm doing it for Papi. But why are you?"

Jake stuffed his hands in the pockets of his jeans. "I'm doing it for him, too. I like him. I like listening to his stories. He's a great guy."

She didn't seem convinced. "Yeah, but I bet you know lots of great guys with interesting stories that you wouldn't give up a month of your life and get fake married to their grand-daughter for."

He couldn't argue with that.

"And I know it's not because you're trying to get close to me."

He snorted. "Definitely not."

"Wow."

Contrite, he said, "Sorry." That hadn't come out the way he'd intended.

"No, it's fine. I'm not thrilled about being stuck with you, either. But I do want to know what's so special about Papi that you're willing to do this?"

What kind of a question was that? Wasn't it obvious that her grandfather wasn't just another patron? "If you have to ask me what's so special about your grandfather... that's just sad."

She rolled her eyes. "Don't be ridiculous. I'm asking why you're so invested in a complete stranger. He doesn't have any money, if that's what you're after."

He took a step back and nearly tripped off the curb. That accusation came out of left field. "Money? You think I'm after money?"

"I just have my doubts that you're doing it out of the good-ness of your heart. You don't seem like the selfless giving type." She delivered her assessment with a matter-of-fact tone that didn't sit well with him.

Who did she think she was? "Hypocrite much?" he snapped.

"What?"

If she was going to go after his character, he could return the favor. "You're the one living in his house for free, mooching off the guy's social security or whatever."

"Wow."

"Wow? That's not much of a defense."

"Defense? So you admit you're attacking me. Nice."

"Attack? Oh, please." He rolled his entire head and put his hands up. "You didn't deny it, so you're all but admitting that your grandfather supports you. Let me guess. You're a 'strong independent woman who doesn't need a man' or something like that." He made air quotes around the words.

"Better than being a clueless bozo who can't stop spouting nonsense out of his facehole."

"I see why you're still single."

She laughed. Actually *laughed*. "You wanna be the pot or the kettle? You should probably be the pot because kettle is kind of a big word for you." She enunciated each word carefully.

"Why are you being so hostile?"

"You're the one coming at me. Don't expect me to just accept it."

He couldn't remember who came at whom, or when the conversation devolved into insults. He was pretty sure she started it, but it was possible it had been him. "I'm not coming at you. Let's just call a truce or start over or whatever."

"Fine."

"Fine."

She adjusted the shoulder strap of her bag. "We should get this to Rupert. The sooner we get this started, the sooner we can be done." The last word carried a lot of emphasis.

"Okay." He opened the passenger door of his truck for her.

She mumbled thanks and climbed in.

Jake rounded the front of the truck and silently reminded himself he was doing this for Charlie. Allie's question niggled at the back of his brain, though. Why? Why was he willing to go through all this, and put up with her, for Charlie's sake? Was it because he reminded him of the grandfather he missed so much, or was part of it actually for *him*? Maybe he craved a little adventure away from his steady but mostly boring day to day life.

Not that his reasons mattered much at this point. He was committed and what's done was done.

He backed the truck out of the parking space and headed for the museum. A few times during the twenty-minute drive, he glanced over at Allie. She was pretty, he grudgingly admitted. He always did a double take when he saw her on the monitors. Now though, he only saw the back of her head because she was facing the window, pointedly ignoring his existence.

Her hair was dark brown, cut in a straight bob that skimmed just above her shoulders. Today she had on tan pants and a light blue t-shirt with the Ralph's Sporting Goods logo emblazoned across the front and the words, "ASK ME

ABOUT RALPH'S OUTSIDERS CLUB" written on the back. Yeah, right, like he was going to ask her about *anything*.

Half an hour later, he pulled into the employee parking lot at the museum, where Allie'd left her car before their field trip to the courthouse. They hadn't exchanged a single word during the drive, and they maintained their silence for the walk across the parking lot. He swiped his badge to open the back door and led her to the elevator, which they rode in silence.

Jake rapped once on the open door to Rupert's office. "Hey, we have the... paper."

The director stood and gestured to the chairs in front of his desk. There were only the two usual chairs instead of a semi-circle. "Excellent. Come on in. Sit."

Allie sat down, pulled the envelope out of her bag, and slid it across the desk.

Jake sat in the chair beside her and watched Rupert pull the license out of the envelope. He read the paper, then pushed it back across the desk toward them, along with a pen. "Allie, you'll sign here." He tapped a blank line. "Then you'll sign here, Jake." He tapped a second line.

Jake heard Allie whisper, "It's for Papi," under her breath just before she grabbed the pen and signed her full name.

They were going to be in this for at least a month, so he decided to lighten the mood. Maybe it would help get them on better footing. "Your middle name is Genevieve? Like from King Arthur?"

"That was Guinevere."

"Oh. Close but no cigar, huh?"

She put the pen on the paper and slid it toward him. "Nope, no cigar."

He scrawled his signature across the line Rupert had indicated.

"Marvin is your first name? How did I miss that when we filled out the application?"

He shrugged one shoulder. "No wonder I go by Jake, huh?"

"Marvin the Martian was always one of my favorite cartoon characters. Papi and I watched him all the time when I was a kid."

He wasn't sure what to say to that. It didn't feel like she was teasing or being snarky, which was a nice change. Maybe it was her own little olive branch. He gave her the benefit of the doubt and stuck with the subject of characters. "I had a Transformers obsession back then."

"I loved the Transformers."

Rupert glanced to the calendar on the wall. "April twenty-fifth," he said, mostly to himself, as he dated and signed the license. "Congratulations, I now pronounce you temporarily husband and wife until the expiry on May twenty-fifth." He put it back in the envelope, sealed it shut, and slid it under the outbox on the corner of his desk. "A month from now we'll put it in the shredder."

Allie checked her watch. "I need to get going. I'm closing tonight."

"I'll walk you out. Thanks, Rupert."

Jake rode the elevator with Allie and walked with her to the exit. "We should probably iron out some details."

"Like what?"

This was going to be awkward, but he said it anyway. "Like are you going to use my last name while we're on the project? I'm guessing people will default to that."

"Absolutely not."

Geez, she didn't even hesitate. "I don't mean officially."

"Jake. Say it out loud. *Allie O'Malley?* Not happening, even if we were married for real." She fished in her bag for her car keys.

He winced. Yeah, that didn't sound great, did it? "What if someone calls you Mrs. O'Malley?"

"Then I will answer, and I will probably correct them. We're a quarter of the way through the twenty-first century. It shouldn't shock anyone that a woman would choose to keep her own name." She paused, then said, "I'm guessing it won't come up much, though. It seems like a small, casual group, so I'm sure they'll just call me Allie."

"You're probably right."

She grinned up at him. "Practice that phrase. You're going to use it a lot." She pushed the outside door open and walked out before he could think of a suitable retort.

Chapter Eight

LATER THAT NIGHT, Allie engaged the lock on the front door and hit the button to change the electric sign's scrolling message from "COME IN, WE ARE OPEN" to "CLOSED, PLEASE COME AGAIN."

One by one, she typed codes into each of the three cash registers. They began spitting out long tapes with a tally of the day's sales, divided by cash and credit so she knew exactly how much cash should be in each drawer. While the slips printed, she clicked off three-quarters of the overhead lights.

After each machine finished printing, Allie folded the long slip, tucked it into its respective cash drawer, then she stacked the three drawers and carried them back to the office. The empty registers were left ajar, per protocol, so that if anyone broke in, they could see drawers were empty and would hopefully move on instead of damaging the expensive machines.

She sat at the second desk in Ralph's office and began counting the cash.

Ralph was at his own desk, poring over a catalog and making a list. "How'd we do today?" he asked.

"Pretty good for a Wednesday. I think we got cleaned out of pickleball supplies."

Ralph shook his head. "Good thing there's more coming in tomorrow."

"Don't forget we need to get stuff in for the new cornhole league, too." This was a much easier conversation than the one she needed to have with him.

"Already on it. I'm ordering a bunch of boards with our logo."

Allie shook her head. "Why would people want cornhole boards with our logo?"

Ralph peered at her over the wire rim of his glasses and smirked. "Because they'll be significantly cheaper than the other boards."

"I suppose we're getting branded beanbags, too."

"Of course."

It was a silly question. Of course they were. She looked down at the cash drawer and couldn't miss the giant "RALPH'S" emblazoned across her shirt. It was also written across the back of nearly every sports jersey in town, from preschool soccer to adult softball, as well as Ralph's not-subtle custom wrapped van that always seemed to be coincidentally parked near any community event.

The over-the-top branding might be obnoxious if Ralph wasn't such a great guy.

She finished counting the drawer and steeled herself to ask for the time off. Ralph was not going to be happy about her suddenly being gone for an entire month. Yes, he was a great guy, but he was running a business and needed employees he could count on.

The totals of all three drawers matched within the five-dollar tolerance, hallelujah. She double-counted the money, signed off on the slips, restocked the drawers with starting money, and bagged the rest of the money in the bank bag.

Unfortunately, finishing the task meant she was out of reasons to put off this awkward conversation.

"Hey, uh, Ralph?"

He looked at her over his glasses. "What's up?"

"Umm..." Well, this was off to an outstanding start.

Ralph's hands dropped to the desk and he sat up straight. "You're not quitting, are you?" He pulled his glasses off.

"No, no, nothing like that."

He leaned back in his chair but still looked concerned. "Everything okay?"

Allie made herself smile. "Yeah. It's nothing bad, just awkward." He'd known her grandfather for years, so the back-story should be easy enough to explain. "You know about Papi's discovery of the lost village and that he was sure the trail led to Hauser Mountain."

"I remember. Good luck breaking into that fortress," he said with a chuckle.

"Well, funny story. There's some research team that does shipwrecks or something. ARASNAC, but don't ask me what it stands for. Anyway, they found the ship that was involved in the whole thing, and they retraced Papi's steps and came to the same conclusion that there's something in Hauser Mountain. They're working with Rupert Cresswell at the Marian P. Franklin Museum, and of course they got in touch with Papi.

Long story short, Estelle Hauser is allowing a small team to have limited access to her land."

Ralph's eyes bugged. "Whoa. She is? That's a golden opportunity right there. Your grandpa must be so excited."

"He is. But." So far, so good, but she wasn't sure how he'd take the next part. "There's no way he can accompany the team with all the hiking and going through caves and stuff. He's only a few months out from his hip surgery and it's just not possible for him to go."

His mouth drooped in sympathy. "I suppose not."

"They want me to go in his place."

Immediately he perked up. "Really?"

"Yeah, so I'd need some time off—"

"Hauser Mountain, huh? You'll need hiking gear and yeah, probably lots of caverns back there. You say caves? That makes sense. I haven't been through Hauser Mountain, not many people have, but it's gotta be similar to the other mountains around here." He rocked in his chair and tented his fingers, staring at a spot on the wall across the room, a familiar position when he was puzzling out details in his mind.

Allie wasn't sure he'd heard the bit about needing time off. "The dig or project or whatever the technical term is will last four weeks. I'd need to be off work a whole month. And they want to start really soon."

He nodded absently. "You're going to need a lot of equipment." He sucked his lip against his teeth as he continued to nod. "How many people on the team?"

"Oh. Um, two of us for the museum and I think six from the other organization. And Mrs. Hauser said something about a few people from her family joining as well."

"When is this?"

"I don't have an exact date, but I think next week." She left off the part about getting fake married.

"You'll be needing some time off, then."

"Yeah," she said, relieved he'd gotten the point.

"It'll be fine. Better than fine. It's good timing, actually. Most of our big sports are already underway, and if you're starting next week, you should be back in time to help with the Memorial Day sale. How much press coverage do you think this'll get?"

"Press?"

"Sure. Big discovery, crazy location, it'll be big news for a small town."

"I mean, maybe local coverage?"

He nodded some more and drummed his fingers on the desktop. "I wonder how much equipment the other outfit's team has?"

"They do a lot of exploring, so I'd say they have most of their own stuff. Why?"

He finally looked directly at her. "So I know how much stuff to pull out."

"You don't need to equip us." Sitting here, in front of him, the idea of pitching it as a sponsorship opportunity felt icky. Even though he'd just brought it up himself, she didn't want to take advantage of his generosity.

"Of course I do."

"I really can't afford much."

An incredulous look screwed up his face. "Allie, don't worry about that. I'll take care of everything."

"Ralph, you can't. It's too much."

"Nonsense. It's good advertising."

"Advertising?" Okay, it made perfect sense that would be

his line of thinking, but it was a tiny group who'd already been warned not to photograph anything outside of the caverns. Caves. Whatever. "I really don't think there's going to be anyone to advertise to. Especially if we get there and find out it's a dead end."

"Even if that's the case, you could grab some selfies for our social media, right? Who's your other teammate from the museum?"

"Jake. Jake O'Malley. He's one of the security guards."

"Sounds familiar. Get me his sizes – shirts and boots – and bring him in over the weekend so I can get you both outfitted. And find out if anybody else needs anything."

"I really appreciate it, Ralph. I know this is really short notice."

He shrugged one shoulder and put his glasses back on. "Things come up when they come up. When's the last time you practiced your knots?"

"I don't think I'm going to need to make knots."

Ralph made a stern face at her over the rim of his glasses.

Before he could start one of his famous safety lectures, she held up a hand. "Okay, okay, I'll practice my knots."

He scowled. "Grab some of that nylon rope on your way out. I want you to bring me twelve good knots when you bring Jake in."

"I've taught knot classes, Ralph, I don't—"

"Twelve. Good night." He flicked a hand toward the door and turned his attention back to his paperwork.

Allie grumbled all the way through the store, but she did grab a bundle of nylon rope to practice knots. Brushing up wasn't a bad idea. She had no idea what the terrain was like, or if there was a possibility of sliding down an embankment or needing to climb a steep incline. So fine, Ralph won that round.

After she got in her car, she texted Jake for his sizes and to see when he'd be available over the weekend. Then she sent an email to Rupert asking if the other team needed anything. That done, she headed for home to update Papi on the eventful day.

Chapter Nine

WHEN SATURDAY ROLLED AROUND a few days later, Jake parked in front of Ralph's Sporting Goods and checked the time. He was supposed to meet Allie at three when her shift ended. At two fifty-five, he went inside and spotted Allie right away. She was straight ahead, in the middle of the aisle, straightening the endcap display.

"Hey," he said as he approached.

"Hey." She pushed a box of campfire s'mores in line with the other boxes on the shelf.

"Those look good."

She shook her head and quietly said, "It's much cheaper to just buy the stuff at the grocery store."

He matched her low tone. "You aren't supposed to discourage customers, are you? I might have bought one of those kits." He tapped the front of the box. "It even comes with skewers, Allie. *Skewers*."

She laughed at that. "Fine. If you really want one, I'll let you use my employee discount."

A short, husky man came around the back of the aisle and

waved. "You must be Jake." He stuck his hand out. "I'm Ralph Riggle, the Ralph in Ralph's Sporting Goods."

Jake took his hand and tried not to wince as Ralph squeezed and pumped his whole arm with enthusiasm.

"Come on back. I've got a bunch of gear laid out for you guys."

"I'll clock out and be right there," Allie said.

Jake followed Ralph through a maze of aisles, holding all manner of sports, fitness, and outdoor gear. "You have a huge variety of stuff here."

Ralph grinned over his shoulder. "We pride ourselves on that. Our mission is to encourage everyone to get outside and get active, no matter what you're into."

"That's great."

"What do you like to do outdoors, Jake?" They'd reached the back corner of the store. Ralph pushed open a door that led to a short hallway and through another door that opened to a massive storeroom full of skids of merchandise.

"I used to go camping, but it's been a while since I've gotten out there." A while. Probably a decade.

"Where'd you go?"

"My grandparents had a cabin way up Licking Creek."

Ralph nodded appreciatively. "One of the most beautiful areas in the world, if you ask me. Well, this whole area is. Don't like the terrain? Walk fifty yards and you've got something brand-new."

Jake chuckled. Ralph sounded like his grandfather, who pretty much only came inside to eat and sleep. And sometimes not even that.

A square of tables was set up in the middle of the room,

probably for sorting stock. One long set of tables was covered with an assortment of... things.

"I didn't miss anything, did I?" Allie asked from behind them.

Ralph answered, "Nope, I was just getting ready to show Jake what I pulled out."

Jake shifted as Allie came alongside him and looked at the table. He said, "This can't all be for us."

"It just looks like a lot when it's spread out like this," Ralph said. He walked to the left end of the table and put his hand on a large dark blue backpack. A bright yellow Ralph's logo stood out from the front flap. "We've got your packs. Military grade fabric, waterproof, lots of pockets for organizing your gear, and there's a nice sturdy loop on the side to clip your water bottle to." He moved on to two massive metal water bottles with engraved Ralph's logos. "Check this out." He picked up the dark blue water bottle and turned it around. "JAKE" was laser-engraved on the side. A bright orange bottle had "ALLIE" lasered on one side, and, of course, the store logo on the other.

Jake's gaze slid along the table as Ralph excitedly went over everything. They were both outfitted with their own compass, flashlights, extra batteries, rubber-soled boots, helmets with headlamps, waterproof matches, safety vests, rope, carabiners, gloves, socks, and a myriad of things Jake didn't pay much attention to. He was distracted by the way every single thing, down to the smallest carabiner clip, was engraved, stamped, or printed with RALPH'S SPORTING GOODS. Including the stack of t-shirts at the end of the table. They were going to be walking advertisements.

The only things Ralph had a single set of was the hand

drill with a weird looking hammer and small set of various nuts, bolts, and anchors.

Allie picked up the drill. "I think this is overkill."

"Better to have it and not need it," Ralph said, dismissing her comment.

"Um, Ralph? What's all this going to cost?" Jake asked.

"Nothing for you. I explained to Allie that it's an advertising opportunity. Basically a write-off."

He didn't know much about the pricing of outdoor equipment, but he'd seen a couple tags and knew this was not a small amount of money Ralph was giving them. "So we just... bring it back when we're done?"

Ralph snort-laughed. "What am I supposed to do with used equipment? After the dig, expedition, whatever, it's all yours. To keep."

"That's really generous. Thank you."

Ralph winked. "Use it to get back to camping." He snapped his fingers like he'd just remembered something, then walked away.

Allie was at the table, picking up one of each thing and making a pile at the end of the table.

"This is a lot of stuff," Jake quietly said to her.

She nodded. "It is. And get this. Ralph offered to outfit the whole group."

"Wow." He picked up the other backpack and hovered as he watched her.

"Yeah. I got a snippy 'no thanks' to the offer."

"From who? Why?"

Allie unzipped all the compartments on her backpack. "From Selena. I emailed Rupert to see if their team needed anything. He forwarded my message, and she sent back a super rude response. She basically said they've been doing this a long time and they don't need any cheap junk that I could get, and I wouldn't know what I was looking for anyway. So rude."

"What the heck? That's really unnecessary."

"I know, right? I was – well, *Ralph* was – just trying to be nice. How was I supposed to know if they might need anything? Aren't most of their projects shipwrecks and stuff like that? Wouldn't that be completely different equipment?"

"I'd think so." He got his backpack and followed her lead, unzipping the compartments and packing his gear the way she was packing hers. He held up a small silver square wrapped in cellophane. "Emergency blanket. He thought of everything, didn't he?"

"You know it." She grinned and shook the pack of water-proof matches. "He said something about camping. Do you go?"

"Not for a few years."

"Are we talking deep woods camping in a tent or a cushy modern cabin with all the amenities?"

"Something in the middle. My grandparents had a cabin, but there was no electricity or running water, so we were stuck with an outhouse. I'm pretty good at starting a fire and catching fish, but I don't think we'll need either of those things."

"Probably not. Speaking of not – knots. How are you at knots?"

He pointed down to his sneakers. "I can tie my own shoes, but beyond that I don't know anything fancy."

"I'll teach you a couple basic knots. Probably not necessary, but I have no idea what the terrain is like, so you should know a few just in case we have to get down an embankment or something."

"Okay." He put the first aid kit into his pack. Learning some fancy knots seemed like a useful skill to have.

"Here's what I was missing," Ralph said, opening a box as he walked back toward them.

"What is it?" Allie asked.

"Air quality meter. I don't know how far underground you'll be, or what the airflow is like, so this'll monitor the oxygen levels and alert you to carbon monoxide and other unsuitable conditions." He tested the device, then wiggled it at Allie. "Yes, it's overkill. No, I don't care. I want you to be safe."

"Thanks, Ralph." She took the meter and clipped it to her backpack.

"If you need anything else, you be sure to let me know and I'll get it."

"I think you've got us covered," Allie said with a big smile. She reached over and gave Ralph a one-armed side-hug. "Thank you so much. I'll keep you posted."

Ralph squeezed her shoulders, then reached over to give Jake another bone-crushing handshake. "Speaking of posting, be sure to put pics on our social media."

"I will," Allie promised and walked toward the door.

Jake quickly retrieved his hand and slung his backpack over his shoulder. The water bottle smacked against his hip.

Allie sped through the store, weaving around aisles and disappearing out of sight twice. By the time they exited, he was a little out of breath trying to catch up with her. "Where's the fire?"

She shot a look over her shoulder. "I'm starving."

"Shouldn't we talk about some of this stuff now?"

She stopped abruptly and turned to face him. "Yes. We should. I'm going to the diner up on the hill, because if I don't eat, I'm going to start getting mean. I've been on my feet since six, all I had was half of a stale granola bar on my way out the door this morning, and I didn't get lunch today. I'm beyond hangry, so it's best for both of us if we just talk at the diner, okay?"

He bit back a snarky comment and instead settled on, "I'll meet you there." He took his time putting the backpack in the back seat of his truck and getting himself situated as he watched Allie cross the parking lot to a row of cars at the far side. Presumably employee parking.

After she pulled out, he followed her out of the shopping center, through a traffic light, and up the hill to the diner. It might be a good test to see if they were able to spend more than five minutes together and have a regular conversation without devolving into an argument.

Chapter Ten

ALLIE SLID INTO A BOOTH. The waitress rounded the counter and came over just as Jake arrived. She didn't need to see a menu, because the diner had the best roast turkey club sandwiches in the whole county. Slow roasted actual turkey, not deli meat fake turkey. Quite possibly it was the best in the whole country.

"I'll have a turkey club, French fries, and a Pepsi, please."

Jake said, "Just a coffee for me, please."

"You got it."

She smoothed her hair back from her face. Her sleek bob was a flyaway hot mess after a full shift of moving boxes and stocking shelves and leading customers to items they couldn't find on their own.

The waitress brought their drinks. Allie drank half her soda before Jake was done adding sugar and creamer to his coffee.

"What's on the agenda?" she asked.

"I don't know how you want to handle this whole 'married' thing."

"There's not much to handle. Everybody knows we got married quick for this excursion, so we can just act like we're not actually changing anything until the big ceremony in September."

"But we should have the same story about our relationship, right?"

The waitress set a plate of food down. Allie thanked her and attacked the sandwich, snarfing a massive bite before she gave Jake's question any thought. She wiped a spot of mayo off her lip and finished chewing. "Ohmygosh this is so good."

He raised an eyebrow.

"Sorry, I told you I'm starving." She shoved some fries into her mouth.

"Half a stale granola bar doesn't go too far."

"You're not kidding," she said around another mouthful of turkey sandwich.

"I wonder why Selena was being so snippy about the gear."

Allie swallowed and said, "She doesn't want us there, is my guess."

Jake sipped his coffee. "Yeah, but she wouldn't be able to get on the property without you, so she should be a little nicer."

She shrugged one shoulder. "Maybe that's why she's mad. She's got all the expertise and experience and she can't leverage it. I can see where that would be annoying."

"Back to the... marriage. What's our cover story? I think we should keep it as close to the truth as we can. Like we met at the museum and got together from there?"

She agreed completely. Simple was best. "Yes. For sure. No specifics. And we can be very open about how much we both hate PDAs, plus we're being respectful of Mrs. Hauser's clearly puritanical views, blah blah blah." She turned her attention back to her sandwich. Thankfully it was helping a lot. The sharp edge of hunger was abated, and her mood was definitely improving.

Jake stared down into his coffee cup. "Do you... do you think there are going to be a lot of, like, tight spots or places we'll have to crawl through?"

His Adam's apple bobbed. Why did he sound so nervous? She asked, "Are you claustrophobic?"

"No," he answered quickly. "I just don't want to get stuck."

"I really, highly doubt we'll have anything like that. I've hiked a lot of caves and caverns in the mountains around here, and haven't had an issue with getting stuck. Besides, if these people were living there and hiding stuff and making cave drawings, you'd think there must have been fairly easy access."

"You're probably right."

She grinned at him. "There's that phrase again. Good job."

"Ugh," he said, returning her smile.

"Are you sure you're up for this? We'll probably be under-ground all day, every day."

"As long as I have room to move, I'll be fine."

"If you need to, you can always blow your Ralph's Sporting Goods panic whistle."

He laughed. "I have never seen so much branded stuff in one spot. Even the little clips have 'Ralph's' engraved on them. And I'm a little blown away they had water bottles in stock with our names on them."

"They probably weren't in stock, exactly." She finished

the last of her fries and took a drink of the fresh Pepsi the waitress had recently brought to the table. "Ralph is one of the best promoters I've ever seen. He and his wife actually bought a laser engraving machine. Thousands of dollars, because he knew he could buy stuff wholesale, engrave it himself, and the machine would pay for itself. He was right. It did. That's how they did the water bottles with our names so fast."

"That's impressive."

"The next time there's a local event – any kind of event – look around. Ralph's van will be parked nearby. Mark my words. The Memorial Day parade through town? I promise you the van will be in a visible location. Jazz festival? Trout derby? Huge family reunion? Doesn't matter."

"Smart."

"It's brilliant. He gets the name out there everywhere." She leaned across the table. "You want to know one of the craziest things he did?"

"What?"

"He bought thousands of bookmarks and stuck them in a ton of books at the library. He put them in all the books in the grocery store, and even got a few dozen stuck in books at the bookstore before he got caught and told to knock it off. So then his wife spent a whole day driving around to those little free library stands and put bookmarks in all those books. It was a whole campaign."

"Is that what those blue box things are that have been popping up? I wondered what they were."

"Yeah, I see them everywhere lately. What's your favorite book?"

"I don't know that I have a specific favorite. I like historical books. Nonfiction mostly, but I like a good mystery novel, too."

That was a pleasant surprise. "I read fiction pretty much exclusively. Mysteries and thrillers. Geneva Rose is one of my favorites."

"I haven't read any of hers. Maybe we should swap books sometime."

"Yeah, if we have any downtime, that could be fun." Not that she expected much downtime. She assumed Selena would probably have them doing the worst of the grunt work.

"I'll add a book to my packing list."

"Me, too."

"How's Charlie? I bet he's excited as all get out."

She sat back against the booth. "I feel bad. He's got a whole bunch of emotions about the whole thing. He's excited, but he's kind of depressed about not being able to be there himself. And he's not thrilled that I hired someone to come in twice a day to check on him."

"Shouldn't that be his choice?"

Allie immediately bristled. Jake seemed to think he knew more about Papi's situation than he actually did. It was bad enough that Papi fussed and carried on over every little thing, she did not need a virtual stranger questioning her, too. "No." She didn't like overriding the wishes of a grown man, but no, Papi couldn't make all his own choices all the time. His decisions were what necessitated her moving back home.

"No? He's an adult. If he doesn't want a stranger coming in, why would you go ahead and hire someone? You're not his mother, Allie. Consent should mean something."

His verbal dart landed on its bullseye. She snatched the bill from the edge of the table and grabbed her purse. As she got out of the booth, she snapped back, "So should minding your own business." She handed the waitress the bill and enough money to cover it with a generous tip, then went out the door.

Footsteps hurried across the parking lot behind her. "Allie. Allie, wait."

She got to her SUV and turned to look at him. Maybe he was going to apologize. "What?"

"I get that you think it's none of my business, but maybe you get so defensive because somewhere deep down you know I'm right."

Her brain glitched. Was this moron serious? "I—What?—That's—No!" she sputtered. "Who do you think you are? You literally see him for five minutes twice a month and you honestly think you have a clue – a single *clue* – about his life? His health? Trust me, Jake, there is nowhere, deep or shallow, where I have considered for a nanosecond that you might be right, because you are so colossally, incredibly, absolutely, yet confidently *wrong!*"

She jumped in the vehicle and slammed the door shut.

Jake tapped on the window, so she cranked the radio. How the heck was she going to survive almost a month with this guy?

She slowly backed out of the parking space, careful not to hit him with her car, no matter how tempting the idea was.

Chapter Eleven

JAKE WATCHED Allie pull out of the parking lot. There was a chance, a very small chance, that he might be projecting his own experience with his grandfather onto the situation. It was true that he didn't know Charlie well, and he'd never seen him outside of the museum. But there was also a good chance Allie was treating him like a child and shouldn't be. It was his obligation to point that out and help her do better, for Charlie's sake.

He went home and got busy packing his duffel bag. He assumed they'd be able to leave on the weekends since Estelle had said there was no work on Saturday or Sunday, so he packed for a week. If he was wrong, oh well. He'd leave and go back if he had to. It's not like they were prisoners.

He didn't hear from Allie again until she texted him Sunday evening.

Meet at my house at 6AM.

He debated a dozen different responses, but settled on texting back a single word.

OK

He hardly slept. Part of it was anticipation. This was going to be an interesting adventure, however it turned out. He was excited to be a part of following Charlie's path and hopefully finding some more evidence of the village he'd found so many years ago.

He also dreaded seeing Allie again. They were going to be stuck together for a whole month, so he'd decided to keep his opinions about Charlie's care to himself, however hard that might be. Unless he saw something with his own eyeballs. Then he'd speak up for sure.

After a long, hot shower, because there probably weren't great facilities on the mountain, he slowly dressed and put his stuff in the truck. He pulled into Charlie's driveway at five minutes before six.

Allie let him in without actually looking directly at him, and led him to the kitchen. "You should see some of this before we headed to the Hauser compound. Selena told me we should be there at eight."

"Okay." He looked at the pile of books and papers in the middle of the table.

Allie sat down, so he followed suit.

"Papi will be out soon. He wanted to show you his research."

"Oh." She sounded subdued, but he didn't know her well enough to accurately gauge her mood. Maybe she was still annoyed at him, maybe she was nervous about the project, maybe she just wasn't a morning person. He had no idea.

"Jake, my boy, good morning!" Charlie came into the kitchen, his cane clomping on the floor as he walked. His exuberance lit up the whole kitchen.

"Good morning, Charlie. How are you?" Jake couldn't help but grin in response.

"Good, good. We don't have a ton of time, but I figured I'd show you some of why this is so important."

While Charlie gave him some backstory on his expedition back in the seventies, Allie got up and made some bacon and eggs and toast. She set a plate in front of Charlie, then said to Jake, "There's more on the stove if you want some."

Jake hesitated, but it was bound to be a long day, so he fixed himself a plate and sat back down. While they ate, Charlie showed him some of his notes and sketches of the carvings he'd seen in M'yxnih. They were all from memory after the village was destroyed.

He tapped a page. "This is how I know for sure we're on the right path. I mean, I always suspected it, but this proves it. To me, at least." His finger trembled a little as he pointed to a sketch of a beetle.

Jake recognized it immediately. "It's the same as the charcoal thing Estelle's great-grandson had." No wonder he'd been so excited to see it.

"Exactly."

He showed him a few more sketches and some journal entries.

"And this is the only photograph that survived. All our equipment, our gear, everything, got sucked under. We were lucky to make it to the jeep and get out with our lives."

The black and white photograph was of a much younger Charlie, grinning at the camera with six other men. All of them were holding up pieces of pottery with intricate designs etched or painted on the clay.

"None of that pottery survived?"

"The pieces on display at the museum are the only things left. When we went back it was all gone except one piece of one bowl. Everything else was crushed to dust."

"I'm sorry."

Charlie stared into the pile of his notes, but he was clearly back at M'yxnih. After a few moments, he snapped back to the present. "Well. Anyway. I just wanted to share with you why this is so important to me."

Jake nodded. "I wish you could come with us." The time had flown by as Charlie captivated him with his tales of M'yxnih. He was sorry they had to leave, but now he had a new level of excitement for being involved in this project. It was more than a vacation. This was *important*.

Allie stood and took her plate to the sink. "We need to get going. I'll be home Friday night."

Good. It seemed like she had the same schedule in mind.

She gave her grandfather a big hug. "I'll check my phone as often as I can, but we probably won't have service. If you need something, leave a message, or call Trista. It will *not* be a bother."

He waved her away. "I'll be fine. You be careful. I love you, Allie-gator."

"I love you, too, Papi-dile."

Jake stepped back and looked away, trying to give them a little privacy.

"Call me or Trista if you need anything," she repeated.

"And do *not*, under *any circumstances*, take off your alert button. I mean it."

"Yeah, yeah." Charlie shuffled over and patted Jake's arm. "Be safe."

"We will."

Allie picked up her backpack and another bag and headed for the door.

Jake followed her, his eyes fixed on the shiny white ASK ME ABOUT RALPH'S OUTSIDERS CLUB lettering across the back of her red shirt.

Once they were in the truck and on the road, Jake cleared his throat. "Um, I know we're eschewing all the regular newlywed stuff—"

"Eschewing? Nice."

He bristled. "I do know some big words. I'm not stupid."

"I didn't think... Oh. Because I said kettle was a big word. Yeah, sorry. We were both being really obnoxious."

He remembered it a bit differently. "I didn't insult your intelligence."

"You insulted my integrity."

The details of the argument were fuzzy, but he'd been so annoyed with her that he couldn't exactly remember every word he'd said. "If I did, I apologize."

"Yeah, okay. Back to the eschewing."

What seemed like a good idea over the weekend now seemed kind of silly, but he pressed on. "It occurred to me that it would probably look really weird to not have any kind of rings."

Her eyebrows shot up in surprise. "I didn't think of that."

At least it didn't seem like she thought it was totally stupid. "It's your lucky day. I got rings. They're in the glove box."

She popped the compartment open and pulled out the pack of silicone rings. There were a dozen black and white rings in different sizes. "A variety pack. How romantic."

He caught her amused tone and teased, "Sorry, your imaginary six-carat diamond is on backorder."

She laughed at that. "Six carats? I wouldn't be able to lift my hand."

"Good thing it's on backorder, then, or you wouldn't be able to dig," he joked.

The cellophane crinkled as she picked a ring out of the package.

His own word sparked a question. He asked, "Do you think they'll actually let us dig?"

She huffed. "I highly doubt it. I think we'll be given some random busy-work that means essentially nothing. Our tagging along will be tolerated only because we're the admission ticket to Estelle's property."

"So cynical." He agreed, though. They didn't exactly bring any expertise to the table, except Allie's secondhand familiarity with M'yxnih. He wasn't sure how that would help them, anyway.

"Realistic."

"Yeah, probably."

"My main goal in this whole thing is to photograph every

detail so Papi can see what's here. As long as I can do that, I'll consider it a win."

"What do you think the red treasure is?" He glanced over at her.

"Honestly? Nothing." She tried a different ring. "Ah, this one fits."

"There are so many references to it, though. In your granddad's notes, in the journal piece from the shipwreck. It's an odd thing to keep popping up."

"I think there *was* a red treasure. Rubies, maybe? I can't think of anything else that's a treasure that's red, can you?"

"Garnets, red topaz, there are a few," he said, even though he also assumed it would be rubies.

"Huh. I guess I never thought about it that deep. It always seemed like a legend, so I didn't go much beyond red treasure must equal rubies."

"It's a fair assumption, and a definite possibility."

"Even if there was a treasure trove of rubies and garnets and a million other red gemstones, I'm sure it's long gone. Even if it made it aaaaaaaaaaall the way from Mexico to Central Pennsylvania, which I highly doubt, there's no way it sat undiscovered for five hundred years, preserved and just waiting for the right person to uncover it."

"You're probably right."

It didn't take long to reach Hauser Mountain, which was only a twenty-minute drive from town. He put his turn signal on and followed the lane up an incline through a thick grove of trees. Beyond the grove, they came to a stop at a gate across the road.

William, Estelle's great-grandson, waved and pushed the gate open. He motioned for Jake to roll the window down.

"Good morning," he said pleasantly. "The other team got here a bit ago. You'll go up the hill and go right at the fork in the road."

"Thanks." He drove forward and rolled his window back up. "Did you catch that?"

"Him calling it the 'other' team? Yeah. Interesting."

A few minutes later, they veered to the right at the fork and after another steep incline, they arrived at a large building. Not quite a barn, not quite a garage, definitely not a house. It was a huge rectangle pole building with aluminum siding and two rows of matching square windows along the long side. The short side had a concrete slab as a sort of patio, and a set of doors. The building was surrounded on three sides by trees and a large gravel parking lot on the fourth, where they'd driven in.

"It's big," Allie said, leaning forward to peer out the windshield.

"I wonder where they live?" Jake said, mostly to himself.

"There's a path over there." She pointed to the left. "Maybe that's where the house is."

"Maybe." Jake took the package of silicone rings and put a black one on his finger. "You ready, Mrs. O'Malley?"

"Ready as I'll ever be, temporary husband."

They grabbed their bags and headed for the building. The door opened into a huge room set up with rows of tables and folding chairs, like a community room that did a lot of spaghetti suppers. There was a big industrial kitchen on the far side of the room. To the left was a sitting area with four large sofas arranged in a square, surrounding a large coffee table. There were two staircases, one on each side of the room, that disappeared into the ceiling.

Selena came over to them. "Nice to see you finally showed up."

It was seven thirty, half an hour before they had been told to arrive. Jake had a feeling she was going to be a pain in the backside for the next four weeks.

A few curious strangers looked at them, but before they could introduce themselves, Chip walked over and pointed to the stairs. "Rooms are up there. Might as well stow your stuff and we can get started."

He followed Allie upstairs. The stairs led to the center of a long hallway with at least ten doors on each side. A handful of doors were closed down the left hallway, so without a word, they headed to the right. All the rooms they passed seemed to be outfitted with a double bed and two sets of bunk beds.

They picked the room at the end of the hallway and dropped their bags on the double bed.

"What the heck goes on here?" Allie asked.

"Family reunions?" Jake looked around. Everything seemed normal. The doors had knobs with locks that flipped from the inside and each knob had a set of two keys dangling from it. He unclipped one key and gave it to Allie, who looked at it thoughtfully.

She asked, "Does your truck have a keypad to unlock the doors?"

"Yeah, why?"

"Will you tell me the code? We should keep one key in your truck and keep one with us. We don't want to lose them somewhere out there and not be able to get into our room."

"You're a genius."

"I am," she said with a laugh. "What's your code? I'll put it in my phone."

It was good she was laughing with him. They were going to be a team within a team for the next month. Getting along with each other was imperative, especially since it didn't seem like they'd be getting along with Selena very well. Hopefully the rest of the team was friendly or this month was going to feel like a decade. He looked around, pretending to make sure no one was listening, then in a very serious voice he said, "I warn you, it's super complex."

She opened the notes app in her phone. "I'm ready."

He cupped one hand at the side of his mouth and whispered, "1-3-5-7-9."

She laughed again. "At least it's not 1-1-1-1-1."

"Doggone it, you just guessed the PIN for my debit card."

Chapter Twelve

Downstairs, they picked seats at the table where the rest of the team was already sitting. Selena looked irritated, Chip looked vacant, and the other four people looked like they were anxious to get going.

Allie dropped her pack and sat down across from a woman who looked to be in her mid-twenties. "Hi."

The woman's blonde ponytail swung as she turned to look at Allie and smiled. "Hi, I'm Bess. This is my husband, Toby."

The pleasant-looking young man beside her nodded once. "Nice to meet you."

"You too. I'm Allie, and this is Jake, uh, my husband." Her tongue tripped over the word.

The couple on the other side of Toby leaned over. "I'm Piper," the woman said, "and this is Aaron."

They exchanged a round of handshakes and pleasantries until Selena cleared her throat. "Now that we've introduced ourselves, let's go over the plan. Once we arrive at the target location, the six of us—" she pointed to herself and the other members of the team, "—will take the lead. The two of you will bring up the back and stay out of the way, basically. For safety reasons," she added, although Allie knew the concern was definitely not safety. She just didn't want them around.

The front door swung open at eight o'clock sharp. Estelle Hauser entered, her heels tapping the floor with each step. She wore a pale lavender pantsuit.

William, another man, and two women came in with Estelle.

"Good morning, explorers," Estelle said. She settled herself in a folding chair William quickly placed at the head of the table. "You've already met William. This is his wife, Kylie. And this is my daughter Delia and her husband, Shane. They'll be assisting you on your project."

Selena balked. "We—"

"Since your time is limited," Estelle continued, ignoring Selena, "a few members of my family will assist you in reaching your destination, and will be available for any questions you may have. Delia?"

"Good morning." Delia, a tall woman who looked to be around fortyish, addressed the group. "The entrance to the caves is a two-hour hike from here."

Allie looked at Jake, doing the math in her head. Four hours of hiking. She wondered if they were going to sleep in the caves? Ugh. Not ideal, not what she'd been expecting, but then again, she'd never been on a proper dig, either.

He also looked taken aback, but didn't say anything.

"Good thing we have four-wheelers available," Delia added with a grin. "The trails are dry right now, so it should only be half an hour to get up to the entrance. Once we're inside, it's fairly straightforward. We have copies of a map

William drew to give you an idea of the layout. There are lots of little offshoots, but most of them are too small for a fully grown human to navigate. We've never found anything as far as artifacts, but there are lots of carvings and drawings, and in Caves One and Two, there are dirt floors that will probably be the focus of your efforts."

Selena rolled her eyes and muttered to Chip, "We'll decide what our focus will be."

"There's not a lot in Cave Three, but there are some carvings that will be of interest."

Selena tapped her nails on the table impatiently.

Delia raised an eyebrow. "Is there a problem?"

"We have a lot of work to do, and we're burning daylight," Selena answered.

"I'll take this opportunity to remind you that you are guests here. If you find our hospitality lacking, you may avail yourself of the exit."

Allie sat stock-still, only moving her eyes back and forth between Delia and Selena. Delia had obviously inherited her mother's no-nonsense attitude. Allie smiled on the inside, even though her face was perfectly neutral. It felt like Selena didn't get put in her place often. At least the rest of her team seemed surprised when she'd spoken out.

"Anyone? No? As I was saying, we want to get as much information as we can to Dr. Scheffler, so we'll let Allie's team go in first to get photographs in Cave One. When they move on to Cave Two, we'll head into Cave One so you can get your preliminary investigation done. Then, when they go to Cave Three, we'll move to Cave Two. Then we'll have Allie's team exit and Team Two can get into the third cave. This evening, Selena, you'll be able to divide your group among the three caves as you see fit in order to begin working tomorrow." Delia didn't wait for a response. "Let's do our last bathroom break and head out in ten."

Allie deliberately looked far away from Selena, whose jaw had clenched even harder after Delia's announcement. She already didn't want them there, so having to wait while Allie and Jake went in first? Yeah, she was probably ready to scream.

Everyone headed toward the bathroom beside the kitchen, so Allie went upstairs and used one of the two communal bathrooms on that floor. Two bathrooms. For eight people. This was going to be fun when everyone wanted a shower at the same time.

A few minutes later, she and Jake went outside. He secured their backpacks to the rack on their four-wheeler with bungee cords while she came to terms with the fact that she was about to be squashed up close and personal with her fake husband for the ride. William and Kylie got on a matching ATV and led them into the forest.

Allie tried to focus on their surroundings or the directions they were traveling, but the only thing that registered was Jake sitting in front of her. His t-shirt was stretched taut over the muscles in his back. He smelled nice, like laundry detergent, but she bet the ride at the end of the day would be a much different experience.

The four-wheeler bounced over bumps and potholes in the steep trail. It was uncomfortable, but much better than hiking on foot, which would have taken them forever.

Her watch showed it only took seventeen minutes from the time they left until they stopped the ATV and climbed off.

Jake un-bungeed their backpacks and held hers up so she could slip it on.

"Thanks."

From there, it was only a quick stroll over a small hill until they stopped at a smallish clearing in the trees.

"Here we are," William said.

Allie looked around and turned in a slow circle, trying to figure out what he was talking about. She saw tall brush, some rocks, and tall trees surrounding them. "I don't see anything."

Kylie playfully nudged his arm. "Don't tease them." She waved a hand to Allie and Jake. "It's over here."

Allie followed her to a large rock. Beside the rock, on the ground, was a hole the size of a large manhole cover, hidden by brush and some flowering weeds.

William used his booted foot to swish the brush aside and tamp it down. "This is what opened up in that 2011 earthquake."

"I remember that," Jake said. "The museum had a few things fall over in the display cases and everybody wondered what was going on, but no damage."

"We figure this wasn't terribly stable in the first place, just some roots and dirt accumulating over the years, and then a good shake was all it took to open the hole back up. Once we get inside, you'll be able to see that it was originally a much bigger opening."

Allie buckled her helmet under her chin.

"I'll go first," William said. "Then Allie, then Jake. Kylie will bring up the rear."

"Sounds good," Allie said.

"It's straight down," Jake said suspiciously.

William switched his helmet light on. "It's not too deep. You'll see." He sat at the edge of the hole and shimmied down, disappearing into the ground.

Allie followed suit, turning her light on and sitting at the edge. Seated there, it was a lot more obvious that the drop was only a few feet, then the tunnel curved downward. She slid down into the darkness. "Oh!" she said as she realized there was room to stand up as soon as she got past the initial entrance. "This isn't bad at all."

Bits of dirt tumbled onto her feet as Jake gingerly made his way into the hole.

They moved forward, giving Kylie room to enter.

The tunnel was about four feet wide, with the ceiling a little more than six feet above, if the sounds of Jake's helmet scraping the rock was any indication.

William started walking. "Most of the tunnel is easy, like this. A few places it gets short and we'll have to crawl through, but there's plenty of room."

He'd no sooner said the words than the floor jutted upward and they had to scramble over it and slowly crawl for a few yards to keep from getting their packs stuck before it opened up again and they could walk upright. Every step took them deeper into darkness. The light from their helmet lamps cast four distinct beams into the tunnel. Allie had forgotten this was the worst part of caving. It seemed to take forever for her eyes to adjust to the complete lack of natural light.

"Right up here, you'll see a skinny offshoot to the left. It doesn't go anywhere. Stay in the main tunnel."

The opening was so narrow Allie wasn't worried about

accidentally going that direction. Likewise for the crevice on the right-hand side a few yards farther ahead.

After ten or fifteen minutes, the tunnel suddenly widened and forked. William turned and said, "Caves One and Two are to the right. This narrow path on the left goes to Cave Three. It's a lot tighter to get back into." He headed into the right fork.

Goosebumps popped out along Allie's arms. The cool air smelled stale and earthy.

They reached a second fork.

"Cave One is to the right, Cave Two is to the left," William explained.

The path to Cave One was short. A few steps and the walls suddenly expanded to a huge room that looked to be the size of a basketball court with a ceiling that was probably seven or eight feet high. Very comfortable to move around in. Allie stepped forward and nearly stumbled into William's back. The ground changed from a rock surface to more of a dirt-packed floor.

"Watch your step," she warned Jake.

The beam of light from her headlamp swiveled as she turned her head. It took a few moments to adjust to the lighting, but when she did, she gasped. The walls were covered in ancient doodles and carvings. She walked to the wall and studied a beetle carved into the wall. Her fingers traced the lines.

She was no expert in archaeology or geology, but almost immediately she recognized the walls were comprised of very different types of rock. Some were incredibly smooth. Others were grainy and rough. It made sense that certain places would have been relatively easy to carve, and others would be near impossible.

Tears stung the backs of her eyes. Papi should be here to see this. He'd likely be able to handle the ATV ride, but there was no way he could climb down into the tunnel. It was too bad ARASNAC didn't find the *Santa Anna-Maria* ten years sooner.

"You okay?" Jake asked.

Allie nodded and wiped her face. "Yeah. I just wish Papi could see this with his own eyeballs."

"Hey, at least he gets to see pictures of every square inch, right? That's more than he has now."

"Yeah, you're right."

"I'm sorry, what? Could you repeat that?" He joked and put a reassuring hand on her back.

Kylie and William joined them in laughing. Allie dropped her backpack to the ground and got the camera out. "I hope I have the right settings. I'll need some steady light, please."

Jake got one of the small LED lanterns Ralph provided and held it up, moving around the room with her as she snapped pictures and stepped to the side. It took half an hour to get the initial pictures taken of the room.

As they made their way out of Cave One, she snapped several pictures of the whole area from the entrance.

William led them back and took the left fork and up a steady incline to the next room.

Cave Two was massive. It could easily fit a football field. An oddly-shaped football field, to be sure, but that was the amount of space in the room. The ceiling was odd and uneven. At the entrance and front part of the cave, it was about six feet high, then slowly sloped upward until it was probably nine or ten feet high at the far side of the room.

Even though it was much larger, there were fewer markings, and it took the same amount of time to take all the initial photographs. She'd check with Papi and see what he wanted more detailed pictures of. Again, she took photos of the whole empty room as they made their way back out to the tunnel.

At some point, Kylie had left to bring the other team into the first cave, but Allie was so focused on taking pictures of every inch of the cavern she didn't know how long ago she'd gone.

When she was done, William led them back out. "This is a bit tighter," William warned as he slipped into the tunnel that would take them to Cave Three.

He wasn't kidding. They had to take off their backpacks to squeeze through the hallway.

Cave Three was tiny compared to the others, maybe half to three-quarters the size of a tennis court.

Allie was able to photograph the whole room in under fifteen minutes.

"Ready to head out?" William asked.

"Yup." She donned her backpack and followed William to the exit. Just a few steps in, she had to turn sideways and side-step her way along the path.

Her headlamp didn't seem to shed much light, and William's was quickly too far away to help. She gingerly inched along. The tunnel narrowed more until her backpack scraped tightly against the wall. Moving in this direction, the angle of the walls was against them, making the passageway feel much smaller than it had on the way in. She wriggled and shimmied her pack off and tossed it as far ahead of her as she could. It gave her some breathing room and made it much easier to pass.

She turned her head back toward Cave Three, but couldn't see Jake's light. "Jake?"

He didn't answer.

"Jake?" she called, then held her own breath to listen. She heard heavy breathing from his direction. Either he'd been eaten by a bear and the bear was now following her, or Jake was possibly stuck. She side-stepped back toward Cave Three. A few yards around a curve in the tunnel, she saw Jake's light.

"Hey, you okay?"

"Nope," he managed with a gasping breath.

She hurried awkwardly over to him. "Jake? What's going on?"

His light swung back and forth, blinding her as he shook his head.

"Are you stuck?" She deliberately kept her voice calm, because he was most definitely not. His breaths were short and quick.

The light bobbed up and down.

"Breathe, Jake."

He sucked in some air.

She found the strap of his backpack. "Can you shimmy a bit? We'll get your backpack off and that'll give you room."

"I can't," he wheezed.

"Baloney. I bet you shimmy all the time in your living room. Radio up, dancing around in your tighty-whities. Don't even try to deny it."

He managed a panicked sort of laugh.

"I knew it. Let's get this arm out." She touched his arm, which was so tense his muscle felt nearly as hard as the rock walls all around them. The strap easily slid down. Allie helped him maneuver his arm out. "Good job." She felt around his backpack. The bulk of it was on the side nearest to her. "Shimmy back the way you came in and I'll wiggle the backpack."

He obeyed, but his breathing was rapid and shaky.

It only took a few seconds to relieve him of the backpack and set it on the ground between them.

"There you go. Better?"

His light bobbed up and down, but he didn't sound much calmer.

She looked the other way, but William was out of sight.

"We're heading out, okay? You're good."

He audibly gulped.

"Come on." She slid away, but he remained in place. She moved back and put her hand atop his, which was pressed against the wall. His fingers were so tight they felt like claws.

He was breathing so fast she was afraid he might pass out.

She forced her own voice to stay perfectly calm, which wasn't easy. Even though she'd been in similar situations, it was unnerving to feel trapped in the pitch blackness underground and easy to panic. It would do no good to let him know she was freaking out a little bit. "Jake? Listen to me, okay? I need you to not hyperventilate, okay? You're going to close your eyes and breathe with me, okay?"

His eyes squeezed shut.

She rubbed her thumb across the back of his hand. "Nice and easy, Jake. We're going to breathe for a count of five.

Breathe in, two, three, four, five. Out, two, three, four, five. Good job. In, two, three, four, five, out, two, three, four, five. That's better. You've got it." She repeated the breathing count several times until she felt his hand relax, just a fraction.

She stood with him for a few more minutes before suggesting they start moving. "Ready?"

His light bobbed up and down above his tightly pinched eyes and puckered mouth. He croaked out, "Yeah."

"I got your bag." She grabbed the strap of his backpack and pulled it with her as she slowly eased toward the exit.

They inched along the hallway until it tightened at the narrowest point. Allie slid through, but Jake stopped again.

"Jake?"

His voice was loud and panicked. "TELL ME ABOUT THE OUTSIDERS CLUB," he yelled.

"The Outsiders Club?" What was he talking about?

"ON OUR SHIRTS." His breathing ramped up again. His voice echoed off the walls.

Oh, boy. They were three yards from the widest part of the tunnel and Jake was freaking out. "Why don't I explain it to you outside?" she offered.

"I don't fit. I can't move."

"You have to move, Jake. You don't want to be stuck down here all night."

"I can't. It's too tight." His voice wobbled.

She tried a different argument. "We got in, Jake. We can get back out. We're almost there."

"I'm trapped, Allie. Go on without me."

"I'm not leaving you."

Chapter Thirteen

JAKE KEPT his eyes squeezed shut. The walls were quite literally closing in, inch by suffocating inch. He knew rationally that they were close to the spot where the path would widen, but it felt like he'd never make it there.

He opened his eyes but the darkness just outside the beam of his headlamp made the walls feel tighter.

"I'm not leaving you," she repeated.

His mind raced, trying to picture outside things. Birds, the sun, the sky, the grass... anything except the horrible slabs of rock he was wedged between. "Outside," he said, hating how pitiful he sounded, but he couldn't make himself sound strong any more than he could make himself take one more step from this spot.

Allie's hand found his arm. "I'll tell you about the Outsiders Club, but only if you promise to move with me." She wrapped her fingers around his wrist and gently pulled.

He tried to let her move his arm, but it was fused to the wall.

"I've got you," she encouraged.

He forced his arm from the wall and it moved an inch in her direction.

"Good job. Technically, it's 'Ralph's Outsiders Club' because you know Ralph – everything gets branded, even the tagline."

He struggled to focus on Allie's voice.

"It's another promo avenue to get people in the door and turn them into loyal customers. There's an actual punch card, but we can also keep track in the system if a customer signs up. I guess it's really two different reward systems under the same name, or different paths to the same end. Once a punch card is full, or once you've acquired enough points in the system, you're entered into a drawing."

She pulled his arm again.

Even though he'd squeezed through once without issue, he was convinced he'd never fit back through to get out. He could feel his heart rate going up again. "What drawing?" he gritted out as he slid an inch or two toward her.

"We do lots of drawings. There's a monthly drawing for a store gift card. It's usually twenty-five bucks. We give away lots of product, too. You know that s'mores kit we saw the other day? We had those in a huge camping-themed drawing last summer. I think it was for Fourth of July. Maybe Memorial Day? Heck, it might have been Labor Day, I'm not sure."

He visualized the s'mores kit. Open space, campfire, starry skies, firelight, roasting marshmallows. "Skewers," he whispered. His breathing calmed as he slowly shuffled toward Allie's steady voice. He was almost glad for the closeness of the walls because he didn't think his shaking legs would support him.

"You're obsessed with the skewers, Jake. I promise I'll buy

you a set when this is over." She gave a little laugh, then continued. "There was the s'mores kit, a really nice tent and two premium sleeping bags. Of course they were all branded. I swear Ralph would have branded his kids' foreheads if he could have. Anyway, there was that one, and then another drawing we had one of those super nice YETI coolers and we filled it with tailgate stuff to kick off football season."

The heavy packs scraped along the wall as Allie dragged them both. Embarrassment came more sharply into focus, edging through the panic. He prided himself on being strong and capable, but instead of carrying his own weight, a woman half his size carried it for him. If – *when* – they got out of here, he'd work double time to prove to Allie that he was a worthy partner for this adventure.

She continued speaking, calm and steady. "The punch cards are pretty cool, though. Ralph's main goal, other than getting people to shop, is to get people outside. He gives out punches for purchases over twenty-five dollars, but he – we – also give punches for activities. If you go camping, you get a punch. The kids get punches for every game they play in an organized sport, or outdoor activities with family or friends. He's super liberal with punches. If you go to a family reunion and play tag with your cousins, you get a punch."

Outdoor activities. He thought about running. Fields, meadows, wide open spaces. Fishing. Canoeing. Hiking. Outside. Which is exactly where he needed to be, and there was only one way to get there.

The walls were inching apart again, and he could feel the panic release its hold on his chest, just a fraction, but it was a start.

"He even worked with the library and if a kid is reading a

book outside, that counts for a punch. They just have to tell us the title of the book and where they were reading it. You'd be surprised how excited the kids get when they get a punch on their card. The adult punch cards are all white, but the kids get colored ones. Those go in a separate drawing for prizes that are way more interesting to kids than a YETI cooler."

"I'd love a YETI cooler." His voice still trembled.

"Me, too. But kids prefer cheap plastic junk."

"Branded, of course." The grip on his chest loosened another fraction now that they were moving into the wider tunnel.

"Absolutely. I drew the line at putting brand stickers on every pack of gum we had at the register."

He managed a laugh at that. "He didn't really try to brand gum, did he?"

She chuckled. "No, but the fact that it's completely believable should tell you something. Oh, look, we're at the fork."

Voices echoed out from Cave Two, but he couldn't make out what they were saying. And frankly, he didn't care. He just wanted to get outside.

Allie moved forward, hauling both packs. Every few yards, she asked him, "You doing okay?"

"I'm good," he answered back each time. The only time he wasn't particularly good was when they had to crawl through the smallest part, but he knew that meant they were almost out, so he pushed onward. The daylight streaming down into the tunnel was the most beautiful thing he'd ever seen. He pushed toward it.

Allie made hefting the packs out of the hole look easy. She climbed up the incline and out into the wide-open space.

Jake scurried to get out of the hole. His plan was to look casual, like it was no big deal, but his shaking legs and weak knees had other ideas. He crawled a few feet away from the hole and rolled onto his back like an upended turtle.

Allie sat down beside him and unscrewed the top of his water bottle. "Here. Get some water in you."

He sat up and gratefully took several long swigs.

William hurried over. "Are you okay? I thought you were right behind me."

Jake screwed the lid back on his bottle. "I'm okay. Got a little stuck for a minute there." He waited to see if Allie would say anything, but she was busy with her own water bottle.

When she did look up at William, she started a completely different topic. "How is this supposed to work? Are we sequestered here, or can we come and go?"

He looked a little surprised. "Of course you can come and go. Why couldn't you?"

"I mean, there's a gate to get in and out."

William cocked an eyebrow. "Yeah, we had a problem with hunters trespassing and poaching a few years ago, so we installed gates."

"At the risk of offending you, can I ask what the big building is for? I kind of assumed it meant when people came here they had to stay."

William smirked. "We certainly have a crazy reputation around town, don't we? I'm afraid the truth is boring. We have a huge extended family that likes to get together. We're the most central location, so everyone can stay here and not worry about hotel fees. We also have a bunch of different conservation groups that do work on the mountain and it's easier to stay at a basecamp when they're here for a few weeks at a time. That's why Grandmother asked that no one take photos outside of the caves. It might be overly cautious, but we don't want to risk accidentally exposing a protected plant or something."

Jake watched the exchange. He had been under the same impression – that Hauser Mountain was some kind of super secret installment that was hostile to outsiders, but William's explanation made sense.

"Should we wait here for the other team, or can we go back to the basecamp so I can start organizing these pictures?"

He hoped William would agree, because he wanted to put as much distance between himself and the tunnels as he could.

"We can head back. I'll go in and get Kylie." He put his helmet back on and disappeared down the hole.

"Thanks," Jake said.

"For what?"

He fidgeted with the strap of his backpack. "Not telling William I had a panic attack."

"First of all, that's not something I would tell someone without a good reason, and second of all, I wasn't categorizing it as that until you put a label on it yourself." She put a hand over her eyes to shield them from the sun and earnestly asked, "Do you think that's going to affect the rest of the project? I mean, are you going to be able to go in and out of that tunnel, or is it going to be a problem?"

"I don't know," he answered honestly. "I think it'll be okay as long as I take my backpack off before we go through there.

That's what tripped me up. I tried to push through and kind of wedged myself with the pack, and the more I tried to force myself to keep moving, the more stuck I got." His heart pounded, reliving the experience.

Allie reached over and patted his knee. "That's a solid plan. But you don't have to force yourself, you know."

"Didn't it bother you at all?"

"No. I've done a fair amount of cave exploration, in much tighter quarters than this. Comparatively speaking, this was a cakewalk compared to some of those places you have to slither through on your belly."

He shuddered. "No way." Definitely not his idea of a good time. "You did that on purpose?"

"Yes," she said while laughing.

"What other crazy stuff have you done?"

"Let's see. I've bungee jumped. Did not love that, would not do it again. I've done rappelling, which was pretty awesome. White water rafting, which is a rush. I've also been skydiving a few times."

"A *few* times? I guess I'm not as adventurous as I thought."

William popped out of the hole like a whack-a-mole and scrambled to his feet before turning to offer Kylie his hand.

Jake and Allie got up and put their backpacks on.

"What did you think?" Kylie asked. "There are a ton of markings."

"There really are," Allie said as they walked back to the ATVs. "I didn't expect so many."

"I can't wait to find out what they mean."

"Same."

Jake secured their packs to the ATV rack.

"I'd like to drive, if you don't mind," Allie said.

He wouldn't have argued any other time, either, but he was grateful she'd offered. He was still feeling shaky and it was probably safer if he not operate a motor vehicle.

Allie slid to the front of the seat and Jake climbed behind her. His hands rested on her hips for the trip back to the basecamp.

When they got back, William said, "If you need anything, let us know. We'll come back this evening for the debriefing." Then he and Kylie continued past the basecamp building.

Jake waited for Allie to get off the ATV, then he climbed off. He put a hand on his pack and hesitated. "Thanks again."

Allie held up a fist. "We're a team, right?"

He bumped fists with her and nodded in agreement. "We're a team."

Chapter Fourteen

Since they were alone in the building and no one was waiting for the bathroom, Allie took her time in the shower. She encouraged Jake to do the same. The hot water would be good for him.

It was almost two thirty when she settled back downstairs at the end of one of the long tables. She popped the SD card from her camera into the slot on her laptop when Jake came down the stairs. "I'm excited to see what these look like." Allie clicked to open the picture files.

"Me, too." He sat in the folding chair beside her and scooched closer to see the screen better.

She clicked on the folder and a zillion little squares populated the screen.

"How many pictures did you take?" he asked.

"About a thousand, according to the number of files."

"Wow."

She enlarged the thumbnails. "I'm going to sort them into folders first." She then selected bunches of pictures and moved them into one of three folders, one for each cave.

"Okay, here we go." She clicked onto the folder for Cave One and double clicked on the first picture to enlarge it on the screen.

They looked through hundreds of photos. There were drawings of people, seemingly random shapes, and a few symbols Allie guessed were religious in nature. The carvings were more crude – several beetles, and lots of shapes like circles and wavy lines and straight lines.

The folder for Cave Two held more of the same.

Cave Three's folder was much smaller. There were a few beetle carvings the size of her fist, and one large carving, the size a pineapple, that was an upside-down U with a circle in the middle.

"I have no idea what any of this means," she said. She didn't want to give voice to the fact that going through the photos was almost a letdown. Maybe it was because this wasn't her area of expertise or particular interest. Maybe it was because she'd had the tiniest inkling of a silly childhood fantasy of walking into a cave and seeing a treasure chest overflowing with rubies.

"Me, either. I'm sure Charlie will love seeing all these, though."

"I can't wait to show him." It crossed her mind to leave now and go home to show Papi the pictures, but she didn't want to give Selena any more reasons to be annoyed. Besides, she didn't want to miss the recap so she could have some professional information to share with Papi along with the pictures.

"Maybe we should do some of those rubbings," Jake suggested.

Allie's brow furrowed. "Why? We have clear photos."

He shrugged one shoulder. "Maybe the size is significant?"

"Oh. That's a really good point." She thought over the things they'd brought. "I wonder if William has paper and charcoal we can use."

Jake nudged her arm with his elbow. "What, no Ralph's Sporting Goods charcoal rubbing kits in our packs?"

She chuckled. "I'll have to let him know he dropped the ball on that one."

"By next week, there'll be a huge branded display of charcoal rubbing kits right when you walk into the store."

"You kid, but that actually happened once. We had a customer come in and mention to Ralph they had to buy skateboard wheels somewhere else. You better believe he was in the office placing an order before they left the store. We had plenty of boards but not replacement parts."

"I absolutely believe that."

Allie sent William a text.

Almost immediately he replied that they did indeed have supplies on hand to do rubbings.

Around four o'clock, the door burst open and Delia led the other team into the building. She looked annoyed.

Behind her, Selena barked orders to her people about where to sit, how to organize their notes, and the importance of sticking to the plan, which was clearly *her* plan.

Allie and Jake exchanged a look that clearly said they were glad to not be an integral part of Selena's team.

Everyone filled the seats at the same table Allie and Jake already occupied. Allie closed the lid of her laptop.

Selena stood at the head of the table and crossed her

arms, scowling until everyone was seated and not rustling anything.

"It's a shame we essentially wasted an entire day," she began.

Allie wished she hadn't picked the seat at the end of the row, putting herself closest to Selena. She sat as still as possible, hoping it made her invisible.

"I suppose going directly to the correct location is a time-saver overall, but I don't normally operate with so many nonsensical restrictions, so you'll forgive my testiness because I'm frustrated by the constraints." She huffed, then pulled in a deep breath and lifted her face to the ceiling before looking back down at everyone. "That's neither here nor there. Tomorrow, we'll be marking off our grids and hopefully putting the GPR to work."

Allie had no idea what GPR was, but she wasn't about to ask.

Luckily, Delia's husband, Shane, raised his hand. "Would you explain what a GPR is for those of us who may not be familiar with the terminology?"

Allie guessed he'd asked for her benefit, since he was some sort of geologist or something and probably used it in his daily work.

Selena rolled her eyes and held up one finger with each letter. "G – ground. P – penetrating. R – radar. We use it to see voids. That means *holes* or *spaces* under the *ground*."

Oof, this woman was so obnoxious. At least there was an end date to this adventure. It wasn't like they were going to be permanent coworkers or neighbors. Thank goodness.

Selena was in the middle of explaining how the team

would set up a grid when the door opened. William, Kylie, and Estelle came in. Again, Selena rolled her eyes.

"How did today go?" Estelle asked as she sat in the seat across from Allie and waited for an update.

Selena continued. "Fine. Now as I was saying, tomorrow we'll explore the area with the GPR." She flicked a hand toward Allie and Jake. "You two can work in Cave Three."

Allie was going to let it go, but William interrupted. "Actually, we're going to be doing charcoal rubbings of all the actual carvings. It's possible the proportions might be significant when we loop Dr. Scheffler in with the cave markings."

"That won't be possible." Selena's lip curled in an irritated sneer. "You'll be in the way of marking off the grid."

Piper cocked her head. "I was planning to get some measurements myself tomorrow, so Allie and Jake can work with me and Aaron. There's plenty of room for us to stay out of the way."

"If you want to be responsible for babysitting while these two do arts and crafts, that's on you."

Piper's brow furrowed. She looked over at Aaron, clearly confused and annoyed, but said nothing.

"Fine. Start in Cave Two while we set up the grid in Cave One."

"Sounds good," Aaron said.

With one last huff, Selena said, "I guess we're done. Plan to leave here at six."

Estelle's sharp gaze followed Selena as she flounced up the stairs.

"Hopefully this is enough." William put three pads of art paper and two boxes of charcoal sticks on the table.

Piper picked up a box of the charcoals and opened it. "Oooh, these are nice. Does anyone have baby wipes? We should probably take a pack because our hands are going to get super messy."

Jake caught Allie's eye. He gave her a little smirk, and she returned the expression, knowing they were both thinking about packages of Ralph's branded baby wipes.

"Did you get many pictures?" Estelle asked, pulling Allie's attention.

She opened her laptop. "I did. Would you like to see?"

"Very much." Estelle's expression softened.

Allie got up and went around the table to sit beside Estelle. She opened the folder for Cave One.

"Oh, my," Estelle whispered as Allie slowly clicked through all the photos. "This is incredible."

"It is. Thank you so much for letting us in to see it."

She sighed. "Your grandfather and Rupert insulted me and I'm very good at holding a grudge. I suppose I should have let them in all those years ago."

"I have no doubt they deserved your ire," Allie said.

"They did." The corner of Estelle's mouth quirked upward, but her smile quickly faded. "But if I had known all this was down there, I wouldn't have refused. This is much more significant than I expected, and I prevented it from being studied."

William took Allie's original seat across from his grandmother. "None of this was accessible until the earthquake in 2011, so it's doubtful he would have found anything anyway. If *we* couldn't get in there, he surely wouldn't have been able to."

Estelle chuckled and looked at Allie. "My kids have been on and in every inch of this mountain. Climbed every tree, followed every stream, explored every cave and crack and crevice they could find."

"Honestly, Mrs. Hauser, I'm not sure his health would have allowed him to get in there even in 2011. Now he's just so happy to know for sure, even though it has to be from a distance."

"Well." Estelle patted her arm. "I'm glad you're here to see it for him. How is it working with the other team?"

She answered carefully. "I haven't had much chance to talk with them. Everyone seems really nice and excited about the project."

"Everyone?"

Allie wasn't touching that with a ten-foot pole.

"Just remember, Allie. This is *your* expedition. Whatever their expertise, regardless of their own agendas, they're only here to get what you need so your grandfather can complete his life's work."

Allie shifted uncomfortably. "I can't even begin to know what we might need."

Estelle cocked a perfectly arched eyebrow. "Keep your eyes open and figure it out, Allie." She glanced to William, who immediately held the chair for her to get to her feet. "Allowing Selena to control what you see isn't in anyone's best interest."

Chapter Fifteen

JAKE EYED the double bed in the middle of their room. It looked so small, but not as small as either of the two sets of bunk beds. "How are we going to do this?"

Allie sat on one of the bunk beds and pointed. "I guess we'll stash our stuff over on that one. I'll take this bunk bed, you can have the bigger bed." She snickered. "Unless you want a bunk so your giant feet hang off the end."

"I'm not sure they won't hang off the end of this one. I have a California king specifically for that reason." He felt a little pang about taking the biggest bed, but she'd offered, so he wasn't going to argue. There was no way he'd be able to get any sleep curled up on a tiny bunk bed.

"I have a queen, so our downgrades are pretty comparable." She pulled some clothes out of her bag. "How do you feel about white noise?"

"I prefer green noise," he joked.

"I'll see if it's on here." She swiped on her phone.

"What?"

She sat on her bottom bunk and looked up at him, totally serious. "Green noise. My app has all kinds of options."

He sank onto the edge of his bed, facing her, utterly confused. "I was kidding. Green noise isn't a thing, is it?"

A slow smile curved her mouth. "It actually is. There's a whole rainbow of sound."

This was news to him.

She explained. "I think it has to do with the frequency. Like the difference between *sssssssss* and *shhhhhhhh*."

That made sense. Sort of. "Huh. Learn something new every day."

"I always use it if I'm in a hotel or away from home. It helps mask the weird background noises I'm not used to."

"No problem, if you want it on, that's fine by me."

"I also have nature sounds if you like that better."

"Sweet. Do you have something soothing like Manhattan traffic?"

She laughed at that. "Actually, yes." She swiped on her phone and a moment later a steady rumble of engines and horns played. "I tend to stick with gentle rain or babbling brooks, but whatever floats your boat."

"I'll stop making jokes now. I'm clearly out of my element."

Allie plugged her phone in and set it on the nightstand between their beds.

"How do you think today went?" he asked as he climbed under the covers.

"Good, I guess. I keep feeling like I'm focusing on the wrong things, though."

That didn't make a lot of sense to him. "What do you

mean? The carvings and drawings would be the most important things."

"That's what I think, but there's a little voice in the back
of my head telling me that Papi would be looking for other
clues that I'm not noticing even if they're right in front of my
face."

He punched the flat pillow into shape, trying to make it
comfortable. "You can't expect to look at this with the eyes of
an archaeologist because you're not."

"Then it's kind of pointless, isn't it?"

Her lack of confidence caught him off guard. "Not at all.
You're looking at it from the angle of an experienced rock
climber cave hiker person, so you know what's not part of the
natural formation, right? That's certainly good enough for
now. Charlie will get to see the photos at the end of the week,
and you've captured the entire rooms, so if there's some clue
he wants investigated, he'll tell you and we'll work on that
next week."

"You're right."

"Whoa. Say that again," he teased.

She smirked and shook her head. "Not a chance." She
walked over to the door and flipped the light off, then shuffled
back to her bed in the dark.

A moment later, the light from her phone illuminated her
face. "You want Manhattan or nature sounds or plain white
noise?"

He grinned into the darkness. "How about a nice relaxing
Waffle House brawl?"

She chuckled. "White noise with a touch of rain it is."

At first the sound was a little annoying, but the next thing
he knew, it was five o'clock and Allie's phone chirped its way

into his subconscious. He heard her whack the nightstand and the sound stopped.

He tried to catch a last few minutes of sleep while Allie rustled around the room.

"Are you awake?" she whispered.

"Yeah."

"I'm going to the bathroom. Do you want me to lock the door behind me?"

"Nah." He stretched and yawned. "Will you turn the light on?"

"Sure." She flipped the light on and went out the door.

He wasn't particularly excited to go back to the caves, but he jumped out of bed and did some pushups and a few squats to get the blood flowing. Small spaces were not his jam, especially ones that were dark and creepy. The way the air swallowed the light was unsettling. How people went on these sorts of excursions for fun was beyond him. At least with camping there were wide open spaces and you could look up and see stars or the moon instead of the claustrophobic blackness of underground.

When Allie came back, he took his clothes and toiletries to the bathroom. It was five thirty when they went downstairs.

Bess stood at the island, packing lunches in little plastic boxes for everyone. Toby was at the stove, making scrambled eggs. "Good morning."

"Morning, Toby. What can we help with?" Selena had posted a schedule of which pairs were responsible for cooking for the teams. He and Allie weren't on duty until the fourth week of the project.

"Would you mind starting the toast?"

"Sure," Jake said, attacking the twist tie on the loaf of bread while Allie plugged the toaster in.

"What else needs done?" she asked.

"The water bottles weren't filled yet, if you don't mind."

Jake made a stack of toast while Toby pulled a two sheet pans of crispy bacon and sausage links out of the oven.

A few minutes later, everyone was piling their plates full and fueling up for the long day ahead.

"How long have you been married?" Piper asked.

Jake nearly choked on a mouthful of egg. He pounded his fist against his chest and took a swig of orange juice. Despite the black silicone band on his finger, he'd mostly forgotten they were supposed to be married.

"It's kind of crazy," Allie explained. "Our actual wedding isn't until September, but with Mrs. Hauser's rules, we went to the courthouse last week and made it official so the project could move forward."

Piper beamed. "Awwwww, so this is like your honeymoon."

"It was either this or Tahiti," Allie joked.

"Give me a good dig over sitting on the beach any day," Bess said.

"Or a bad dig," Aaron added.

Piper looked at him lovingly. "Aaron and I spent our honeymoon in Sainte-Colombe."

"Where's that?" Allie asked.

"Eastern France. They call it mini Pompeii. It was an ancient Roman city that was destroyed by a major fire. Unlike the actual Pompeii, though, it seems that the inhabitants were able to escape."

"That's so interesting. Will you go back there again?"

"It's probably a parking lot by now," Aaron said. "Or an apartment building."

Piper explained, "It was only discovered because there's a French law that requires developers to conduct an excavation of possible historical sites before they start building. It was all very hush-hush because looters will literally strip a place bare of anything that looks like it might have any value. One of Aaron's old professors was involved and was able to get us included. It was so exciting. But yeah, it's probably paved over by now."

Jake sort of tuned out as Piper, Aaron, Bess, and Toby excitedly told Allie about different expeditions they'd been on around the world. He felt an acute pang of sympathy for Charlie. This wasn't just a job for him, or for the people Jake was surrounded by right now. It was a passion. A calling. He could appreciate the significance. He loved being surrounded by history on a daily basis. But choosing to crawl around in a cave instead of sit on a beach in Tahiti? Not a chance.

"Are we about done with this stroll down Memory Lane?" Selena asked with way too much snark for such an early hour. "We've got work to do."

Chairs being pushed back and the clank of silverware and dirty plates being loaded in the dishwasher took the place of conversation.

The Hausers once again led them up the side of the mountain to the entrance to the tunnels.

Jake helped Allie put her backpack on and watched her disappear into the tunnel. He took a deep breath, gave himself a little pep talk, and followed her into the darkness.

Chapter Sixteen

Much to Selena's obvious annoyance, Jake was invited to help the guys maneuver the GPR along the grid they'd marked on the floor. Allie had expected it to look like a metal detector, but once it was assembled, it looked more like a walk-behind lawnmower, with four wheels and a long handle with a rectangle screen at the top.

She fell into an easy rhythm with Piper. Piper would write down several measurements for each carving and then Allie would follow behind, firmly hold a piece of paper over it, and rub a bit of charcoal over the paper to create an impression of the carved grooves.

She had to admit Jake had been right. The rubbings gave a very different perspective than the photos did. Once she finished a rubbing, she marked it with a number so she'd know its exact location when she showed them to Papi along with the photos.

The work was simple, but largely tedious. *Methodical*, she corrected herself at the end of the week. They'd spent four days going over every square inch of all three caves until Selena declared this phase of the project complete early Friday afternoon. She was so proud of Jake. He'd been in and out of the caves all week without much more than a few moments of hesitation. She, on the other hand, was so over it. Getting home for the weekend could not come fast enough.

Her backpack felt heavier than it had all week as she trudged to the waiting ATV and plunked her pack down onto the rack. Drizzling rain made the trip back to basecamp cold, unpleasant, and longer than usual as Jake had to move slowly to avoid losing traction in the mud. She gripped his middle and wished for earplugs because the whine of six ATVs traveling in close proximity was overwhelmingly loud and obnoxious after a long week.

When they finally reached the basecamp parking lot, she couldn't get off the ATV fast enough. Her heel caught on the seat. Jake caught her wrist and pulled her against him before she toppled over. She muttered a curse and allowed a moment to lean on him before she righted herself.

"Thanks." She forced a small smile in response to his concerned expression.

The group made their way into the basecamp building.

"Here, let me take that." Jake reached for her pack and she let him have it.

Everyone congregated at the tables, but no one sat down.

Selena said a few lines about the GPR and analyzing the results over the weekend, blah blah blah, and finally concluded with, "That's a wrap for the week. We'll get back out there at five a.m. sharp Monday morning." With that, she spun on her heel and walked away.

Allie wanted to leave. Now. She was wet, tired, cranky, hungry, and sore.

"Let's change into dry clothes and then head out?" Jake must have been reading her mind.

She offered to carry her own pack, but he gave a shake of his head and jerked his chin toward the stairs. "I've got them. Go ahead."

Her rubber boots squeaked against the tiled stairs. It was the most annoying sound she'd ever heard. Aside from Selena's grating voice. And Jake's snoring.

As soon as she got into their room, she kicked her boots off. At least her socks were still dry. Nothing else was, though. The cold rain had drenched her from head to almost-toe. Her hair was plastered to her head. Her shirt and pants were heavy from the water, but even in her annoyance she realized something that felt significant.

"Did you ever notice how dry it is in the caves?"

Jake shook his head, sending drops of water flying from his hair. His brow furrowed in thought. "Now that you mention it, I was kind of expecting the walls to be damp and slimy or something and they're not."

"Interesting. I'll have to ask Papi why that might be." She grabbed a towel, a pair of yoga pants and a hoodie and went to the bathroom.

When she got back to the room, she was still hungry and grumpy and tired and sore, but at least she was dry. Except for her damp hair.

While Jake was in the bathroom, she threw her clothes into her bag. Might as well take them home and do laundry while Papi spent hours poring over the pictures and rubbings.

Hopefully he'd be content to go through everything himself and she could sleep. That's what she needed. Food and sleep.

Jake crammed his dirty clothes into his bag and slung the strap over his shoulder. "You ready?"

"Yup." She carried her travel bag and messenger bag downstairs and was relieved to see the place was empty so they could get leaving without any more distractions.

"Do you mind if I grab some fast food?" Jake asked when they approached town twenty minutes later.

"Yes, please. A bag of something hot and greasy sounds amazing right about now."

He swung through the drive-thru and in a few minutes, they were back on the road. Fifteen minutes after that, Jake pulled in the driveway. "I'm anxious to see what Charlie makes of everything."

Allie scrubbed a hand down over her face and sucked a long sip of soda. She felt much better after inhaling her fries and chicken nuggets while Jake drove. "I'm sure he'll have a lot to say. What's your plan? I was thinking of going back Sunday evening since we're starting so early Monday."

He nodded. "That's what I was thinking, too. But I'm definitely bringing my own pillow and blanket. I can't take another three weeks of that."

"Same. It feels like I've been laying in a valley. There's zero support in that bunk bed."

"Would it help if we put the mattress on the floor?"

She thought about it. "I bet that would help a lot. If you want to come over, I don't know, maybe around five on Sunday? Then Papi can give us an overview of what he's found before we head back to Hauser Mountain."

"Sounds good. I'll see you Sunday night, then."

"See you then."

The front door popped open as she climbed out of the truck. Papi stood on the porch waving at Jake while she grabbed her bags and ran up the stairs to greet him with a massive hug.

He peppered her with questions. "I missed you. How was it? Did you get to see much?"

"Missed you, too. It wasn't quite what I was expecting, and I have lots of pictures to show you. Let's go in your office." She waved at Jake as he backed out of the driveway.

It surprised her to note she kind of hated to see him go. He'd ended up being a pretty good temporary husband over this first week, especially when they had to listen to Selena's snark every evening during the daily debriefing. It was starting to feel like they were a good team.

When they got inside, Allie put her SD card in the slot on Papi's computer and copied all the files into a folder on his desktop. While the files transferred, she grabbed a sheet of paper and drew a crude map. "Here's kind of what the layout is. That might give you a little better context."

He straightened his glasses and peered at the map. "There are three rooms?"

"Yup." She described the size of each. "You'll see that Cave One has the most markings, and Cave Three has just a handful."

"Fascinating."

Once the files were done copying, she put the SD card back into her own bag. "Do you mind looking through the pictures yourself while I grab a shower?"

"Of course. Go ahead."

While the hot water soothed her aching shoulders, it occurred to her that she should do a video to give him even more context. She hadn't even thought about using her phone underground because there would be very little to no signal, but she could still take a video along with the stills she'd taken for Ralph's social media.

She dressed in cozy sweats and fuzzy socks and went back to Papi's office.

He stared at the computer screen with silent tears streaming down his face.

She grabbed a box of tissues and carried them over to him. The last photo from Cave Three was on the screen. "You okay?"

He nodded.

Allie pulled a chair over and took the mouse. She clicked back to the first folder and started to describe everything, from the entrance that had opened up during the earthquake, to the GPR equipment, all the way to the way some walls were gritty and some were smooth. "I hadn't even noticed until we were leaving today and it was raining, but the inside is so dry. I've never been in caves so dry, and I don't know why it's like that."

Papi sniffed and wiped his face. "Some stones behave like those little desiccant packets they put in with new shoes. It's not terribly unusual. Well, in this area I'd expect moisture in most caves, but I'm sure there's a geological explanation."

"That's good enough for me. I'm already in way over my head here."

"You look tired." He reached over and tucked her hair behind her ear.

"I am." She wanted nothing more than to crawl into bed

and go comatose for the next fourteen hours, but Papi was having a moment and she wanted to share it with him. "Okay, let's start at the beginning." She got the sheath of rubbings out of her messenger bag and clicked into the folder for the Cave One photos.

"What's all this?" Papi asked.

"Charcoal rubbings."

He snatched the stack of papers from her. "Whoa. Allie, this is incredible."

She had to give credit where credit was due. "It was Jake's idea. He thought having the actual scale might be helpful."

Papi looked at her over the rim of his glasses. "How is your temporary husband?"

"Fine. It's been a little weird. We forgot we were supposed to be married when Piper asked us about our wedding. We had to scramble a little bit and stuck with the story that the wedding isn't until September, but we did the legal stuff because of Mrs. Hauser's rules."

"You've been getting along?"

"For the most part. He thinks he knows more than he does about things he doesn't need to stick his nose into. Other than that, we're getting along pretty well."

"Good. I've been worried about that."

"About what? Us getting along?"

"Yes. I should probably keep my mouth shut, but some-times you can be a little abrasive. He's a nice guy. Maybe don't chase this one off."

So much for coming home to relax. Allie was too tired to get into a whole discourse about how many "nice guys" weren't actually all that nice once they decided a woman owed them some time or attention or a smile or a date or whatever else they had in mind. Like the ex-boyfriend Papi was not-so-subtly referencing. Behind closed doors, he'd turned out to be not nice at all. To Jake's credit, he didn't fall into that category. He fell into the category of guys who just weren't her type because they think they have all the answers when they don't have a clue.

"All the charcoal rubbings are numbered so they're in order with the pictures." She clicked onto the first picture. "I didn't measure the drawings, but Piper did. If the exact dimensions are important, I can get those from her next week."

They slowly went through the photos. Papi explained that the drawings had likely been made with the tips of charred sticks and ink made from local berries. The drawings were simple, and repetitive. "You should have used a better camera so the details are sharp. Did you just use your phone?"

"No, I used the good camera. It's very dark. Not easy to get great pictures."

Allie felt bad for not being more excited as Papi clicked through each photo and explained that the people were probably the artist's family, that the drawings were likely done by the same two or three people over ten or fifteen years, but he'd be able to tell more if he had better pictures.

She zoned out and tried to remember he was only being critical because he was upset that he couldn't be there in person.

"It's a good thing it is so dry. That's what's kept these drawings preserved for so many years."

"That's great." Allie yawned and covered her mouth with the back of her hand.

"Why don't you go get some sleep," Papi suggested.

She glanced at the time. It was just after seven o'clock, but she was ready to crawl into bed. "Don't stay up all night," she warned. She hoped she could follow her own advice. She needed to rest up after a long week of living his dream.

Chapter Seventeen

SUNDAY AFTERNOON, Jake stuffed two pillows into his bag over his clothes. The zipper was barely able to close. Hopefully the pillows, and the blanket he folded and tucked under his arm, would make it easier to sleep. He tossed his things onto the back seat of his truck and headed to Allie's. He couldn't wait to see what Charlie thought about what they'd seen.

Allie let him in the front door. "Papi's still in his office, poring over the pictures and rubbings. I was thinking that tomorrow we could do a video tour to give him even more perspective."

"Great idea." He followed her through the kitchen connected to a small mudroom and into a large home office that was probably originally intended to be a bedroom, where Charlie sat at a desk.

"Jake! Come in, come in. Have a seat. What do you think of all this?" He gestured to the computer. "Incredible, isn't it?"

"It's been really interesting."

"Did you get some rest? Allie slept most of the weekend away."

She rolled her eyes and said, "I'm going to finish packing."

Jake wasn't sure what to make of Charlie's tone, like he was annoyed at how much she'd slept? Weird. "She's been working hard this week. And the beds are terrible for getting any rest."

Charlie snorted. "You should be glad you even have beds." He launched into a description of the various different grounds he'd slept on while out on digs, and once they even slept in trees to avoid predators.

Jake listened and nodded periodically. He didn't point out that he'd been doing it because that's what he wanted to do, not because he was doing a favor to someone.

Whoa. He wasn't sure why he was feeling so protective of Allie all of a sudden. Maybe because he'd been with her all week, watching her do her best to gather as much as she could, and her sole motivation was to do this for Charlie. He knew she'd rather be stocking shelves and punching Outsiders Club cards and sleeping in her own bed at night than hanging out in dark caves all day and dealing with Selena's snide comments.

As much as he might disagree with the ways she treated Charlie like a child, he was her sole reason for doing this, so it didn't feel fair to begrudge her catching up on her rest.

Jake had done the same, opting to sleep later than normal because his own bed was soft and comfortable and he had no reason to leave it.

A soft knock at the door pulled his attention.

"We should probably get going," Allie said.

"Sure." He stood. "Good to see you, Charlie. Keep us

updated if you figure out where the treasure is." He shook his hand and walked past Allie. "Can I take your stuff out?"

"It's beside the door, thanks."

She had a small rolling suitcase this time, with her laptop bag on top, hooked around the suitcase handle. He carried them both to the truck and put them in the backseat.

It was after seven when they got back to basecamp. Toby and Bess sat on one of the couches looking at something on a laptop. They both looked up and smiled.

"Selena wants to have a meeting at eight," Bess informed them.

"Sounds good. We'll unload our stuff and be back down," Jake said.

In their room, he said, "Do you want to get your bed set up?" He gestured to the mattress she'd slept on. "We could use this one and that one—" he pointed to the other set of bunks "—and that one together. Probably more comfortable than just the one."

"That's a good idea. I hope Mrs. Hauser doesn't mind us rearranging the room."

"We'll put everything back. It's not like we're painting the walls or something."

"Yeah." She didn't sound very enthusiastic.

"Everything okay?"

"Sure. Let's do this quick and get back downstairs."

He pulled the mattresses off and stacked them together. "Give it a try." It was one small thing he could do to make her more comfortable. Last week had been hard for both of them, but Allie had carried their part of the team on her shoulders like a champ. This week, he was determined to return the favor however he could.

She sat down and gave him two thumbs up. "Major improvement."

"Great." He unpacked his pillows and tossed them on his bed while she did the same.

She grabbed a notebook and pen. "Just in case."

He held the door open for her. "Good idea."

Downstairs, Bess and Toby had been joined by Piper and Aaron. Delia, Shane, William, and Kylie occupied a second sofa. Chip was in the kitchen getting a cup of coffee.

Jake and Allie took seats on one of the empty couches and waited.

Chip came over with two cups of coffee and took a spot on the fourth couch. A few minutes later, Selena joined them with a folder. She opened it and said, "Our remote team was able to analyze some of the GPR results for Cave One, and we have a couple potential areas to focus on. We should have more results late tomorrow, but we'll be able to start digging."

Jake glanced at Allie, who gave him a little shrug. Apparently there was a remote team? It was a bit annoying to be left out of the loop.

"Since we aren't able to get the GPR into Cave Three," Selena continued, "and we don't believe there's a lot in there that could be negatively impacted by your... *inexperience*, Allie and Jake, you'll work in Cave Three. Hand digging where you're able, visual inspection, that sort of thing. Chip will give you the tools you'll need in the morning."

Jake didn't bother listening to the rest of her speech, monologue, recap, instructions, whatever. It was beyond annoying to be outright dismissed as useless. Especially when Selena wouldn't even be here if it wasn't for them.

He was glad when she stopped talking and the meeting was over.

Allie was off the couch and heading to the stairs like she'd been shot out of a cannon.

"Are you okay?" he asked when he got to their room. She was already sitting on her bed, so he sat on his, facing her.

"Yeah."

It certainly seemed like something was bothering her. "You sure? If you want to talk, I'm right here."

She rolled her eyes. "No, Jake, I can't talk to you. You'll very helpfully mansplain why I'm wrong, and I'm not dealing with that right now."

He guessed she must have had some disagreement with Charlie, and she automatically assumed he'd take his side. He balked at the notion, but when he thought about it, she probably wasn't too far off base. "If you can't talk to your temporary husband, who *can* you talk to?"

That earned him a little smile. "It was a frustrating weekend, that's all."

"Charlie keep you up going through all the stuff?"

"More like he complained about everything. I didn't use the right camera settings, or the right angles, and the rubbings had too much charcoal or not enough charcoal and I pressed too hard or not hard enough. I took too many pictures of things that were unimportant, and not enough pictures of the things that could possibly be the key to the whole project." She angrily swiped at her eyes. "Go ahead. Say whatever you feel the need to say."

Jake felt for her. It wasn't the reaction he'd expected, and surely not what she had, either. "I'm sorry he acted that way. He should be a lot more appreciative of what you're doing for him. I don't know many people who'd put their whole life on hold for an entire month to go wrap up someone else's dream."

She eyed him suspiciously.

"I mean it. I understand he's probably frustrated that it's so close and he can't be here himself, but that doesn't make it okay to criticize you. He's got a lot more than he had a week ago."

Her shoulders relaxed. "Thanks."

"You're doing a great job. Maybe we'll find something important in Cave Three and Selena's head will explode."

She snickered. "That'd be amazing. I'm not surprised she's banishing us out of her way, but my goodness, does she have to be so snotty about everything? Sheesh."

"Maybe that's why she got sent on this gig. Then the other people could dive on a shipwreck without being microman- aged or insulted."

"That feels right."

They reorganized their backpacks and set out their clothes for the morning. Jake turned off the light and climbed into bed.

"You okay with white noise?" she asked.

"Do you have anything with an eagle screech?"

She laughed. "Did you know that most eagle sounds on television are actually screeches from red-tailed hawks because they're louder and sound more powerful?"

"I did not know that. I'm curious how you do."

"It was a fun fact I learned on a bird walk. A local birding group was doing walking tours and of course Ralph thought it would be a great opportunity to sell them a bunch of stuff."

"Was it?"

"I swear we sold more binoculars than ever." She snuggled down into her blankets. "And compact monopods. They *reeeeeeeeally* liked the monopods."

"I assume that's like a tripod, but with one leg?"

"Yup. Great for adding stability when taking action shots."

"Branded?"

"Of course."

"I gotta say. Ralph's a marketing genius."

"He really is."

He was reminded of his grandparents' well-worn logbook of birds. "My grandparents were really into birdwatching."

"It's a lot more interesting than I gave it credit for. Are these the grandparents that have the cabin?"

"Had, yeah. They've both passed."

"I'm sorry."

He stared up into the darkness. "My grandma passed about fifteen years ago. It's been almost two years for my grandpa, but it sure doesn't feel like that long. Charlie reminds me a lot of him." He left off the part where Allie reminded him of Lucinda, his ex. The one who thought his grandfather was a burden. Which was a big part of the reason she was an ex.

Allie softly said, "He must have been a great guy."

"The best."

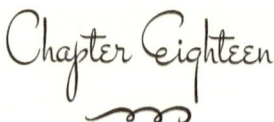

Chapter Eighteen

MOVING the mattress to the floor and bringing pillows from home was a massive improvement. It wasn't as good as sleeping in her own bed, but it was on par with a decent hotel stay. She could live with it for another three weeks. No problem.

They were downstairs and ready with the rest of the crew when Selena reiterated that Allie and Jake were to be banished to Cave Three while everyone else carried out work that actually mattered.

Allie said, "That's fine, but just a heads up that I'll also be doing a sort of video tour of the entire site, including all three caves."

"That's not necessary," Selena said, shaking her head.

"Dr. Scheffler says otherwise."

"Dr. Scheffler isn't here."

Allie was tired of her attitude. "Yes, but without him, you wouldn't be, either." She had no problem deferring to Selena's authority on the project, but for Pete's sake, the woman's unrelenting snark was getting old. Without waiting for a response, she grabbed her pack and headed for the door.

Jake secured their backpacks on the ATV rack. "Way to stand up for yourself."

"I respect that she's in charge, but I'm so over the little comments directed our way."

"I agree."

She took her spot behind him on the four-wheeler and fastened her helmet. Soon her thoughts were lulled by the steady rumble of the pack of ATVs moving toward the caves.

Everyone grabbed their gear and hiked to the entrance. Allie and Jake hung back, waiting for the tunnels to clear so she could video the site.

She held her phone and tapped the red button to start recording. "Here we are, heading into the site. You can see the ceiling is pretty low, but it's fairly easy to navigate." She narrated periodically, trying to be sure to capture everything with a minimum of camera shake. "Here's the first fork. We'll head to the right, and we're at the second fork. Right again, and we're heading into Cave One."

She panned around, then walked the outer edge of the room. "It's hard to tell on the video, but this room is about the size of a full basketball court. Here we have Piper, Kylie, Delia, Toby, and Aaron. Wave, everyone."

Everyone smiled and waved. Piper added a cheery, "Hello, Dr. Scheffler!"

Allie turned. "We're leaving Cave One and going back to the fork. Turning left, we go into Cave Two. This room is about the size of a football field, give or take. And here we have William, Bess, Shane, Chip, and Selena. You can see we've got some more fancy equipment in those cases over there. I have no clue what it's for, but these guys are bona fide experts who know what they're doing."

Chip and Selena ignored her and kept their backs to the camera as she recorded her way around the room while everyone else waved. Whatever.

"Leaving Cave Two. Crossing the second fork, and back to the first fork. This goes to Cave Three, and this passageway is definitely trickier."

She gave up narrating as she squeezed through the tight tunnel. When she came into the room, she continued. "This is Cave Three. Obviously the smallest of the rooms, maybe half a tennis court. You can see Jake over here, getting ready for the day."

He gave the camera a cheesy grin and two thumbs up.

She turned the camera around. "And of course I'm your guide, Allie, and that concludes today's underground tour!" She waved and stopped recording, then grabbed a selfie of her and Jake with their Ralph's shirts clearly in the photo.

"I'm sure Charlie will like that."

She shrugged one shoulder. "I'm sure he'll let me know how I could have done it better." She stopped herself. "Sorry. I'm still a little salty about his reaction to the pictures. I thought he would have been so excited."

Jake passed her a hand shovel. "You did a great job with the pictures. I'm sure he's just mad he can't be here."

"I know, but that's not my fault." She waved the shovel around. "Where should we start?"

"Beats me."

She stamped her foot on the ground a few times. "This feels like solid rock. I think there's loose dirt around the edges. Maybe we just poke around the outer part of the floor and see what happens?"

"Sounds good. I'll start on this side and we can meet somewhere in the middle." He dug around in his backpack and pulled out a pair of kneepads. "I have to admit I was not impressed with how much stuff Ralph made us cram into these packs, but the man knows what comes in handy."

Allie pulled her own kneepads over her pants. "He really does. I'm heading straight to his house when the apocalypse starts, because I'm one hundred percent convinced he won't even bat an eyelash at the zombie uprising."

Jake held his palm flat and pretended to write a note on it with his finger. "Solid plan. I will also be heading to Ralph's. We can fight zombies with Ralph's Sporting Goods branded weapons."

That made her laugh. "Absolutely."

They quieted after that. Scraping and tapping of the metal shovels was the only noise for a couple hours until Allie turned and sat with her back against the wall. She hadn't made it very far. The ground was solid, and chipping away at rock seemed pointless. "Find anything?"

"Nah." Jake dropped his shovel and mirrored her position.

"Maybe we should try over there. From this vantage point, it looks like it might be gravel?" She pointed to a spot in the far corner of the room.

"It does look looser, doesn't it?"

"Or we could save it for tomorrow and go back to the basecamp and get lunch."

"It's only nine o'clock."

"Meh."

"Tell you what. Let's set a timer or something and work

on that spot and when the timer goes off, I'll give you this."
He pulled something from the corner pocket of his pack.

Allie gasped. "Mixed berry! There weren't any of those
left. How did you get one?"

He waved the granola bar back and forth. "There was one
left at the bottom of the bin."

"No fair."

"We get through some more digging, and it's all yours."

She sighed. "You drive a hard bargain, Mr. O'Malley." She
held out her hand for the bar.

"Work first, Mrs. O'Malley." He shook his head and slid it
back into the pack.

"Rude." She rolled her eyes but picked up her shovel and
stood. She stretched and put a hand on her lower back.

They hunkered down together, working on a section of
the floor that was about four feet wide along the wall, and
maybe a foot wide from the wall into the room.

"This is weird," Allie said. "It's almost like there's a seam
between the wall and the floor. Like the wall was just
plunked down on top of it."

"I don't know much about geological formations or
anything, but yeah, this doesn't look natural to me." He poked
his shovel into the crack and scraped out a bit of gravel.

"Look at this." Allie ran her finger up a long thin crack
that went from the floor up about three feet, then sharply
turned right. "Do you think this was put here on purpose?
Like a door? Or to seal off another tunnel?" For the first time,
she felt a little jolt of electricity, like maybe there was a treasure after all.

"I don't see how anyone could lift it or put it in place so

perfectly. My guess is it's a coincidence and it looks like something only because we're looking for something."

He was probably right. "Hmm. Maybe. Let's keep going."

A few minutes later, she scraped out a bit of gravel and stopped. The light from her headlamp glinted oddly on something. "Jake, look." She picked up a triangle-shaped shard. "Is this pottery?"

He took it from her to get a closer look. "Whoa, I think it is. That's incredible."

They resumed digging with a brand-new enthusiasm.

Another hour or so passed, but they didn't find anything else. Jake held out the mixed berry granola bar. "You've earned it."

Allie accepted it with a laugh. "Do you want to eat outside? I'm afraid my skin is starting to turn green from lack of sunlight."

"Yep, let's go get some Vitamin D." He paused at the doorway. "Are you going to do a video of the way out? So we've got a full round trip?"

"Now I am. That's a good idea. I should also grab some stills to post on Ralph's social media." She pulled her phone out and narrated their way from the cave to the exit.

Chapter Nineteen

WILLIAM AND KYLIE were already outside, sitting on a blanket to eat their lunch. Kylie waved them over. "Join us." She patted the blanket.

Jake followed Allie. Two pairs of boots stood neatly beside the blanket, so they both slipped their boots off before stepping onto the blanket and sitting down. While they got their lunches out of their packs, Kylie asked, "How are you guys doing over in Out of the Way Land?"

"Good, actually," Allie said. "There's not much in Cave Three, but we did find one spot of loose gravel and found a pottery shard. Just one, but at least it was something."

"A reward for quietly accepting our banishment," Jake joked.

"That's really exciting."

He watched Allie's face. She smiled and agreed with Kylie. "Not quite as exciting as a treasure chest full of rubies, but it's something."

Before long, everyone else was aboveground and enjoying the warm early-afternoon sunshine.

"I can't believe it's almost summer," Bess said.

Piper nodded. "Any big plans?"

"Toby's been looking into going back to Greenland."

"For vacation?" Allie asked.

"Sort of. There are a lot of archeological digs in Greenland, believe it or not."

"I think Aaron and I are heading back to Australia for a few months." She looked at Allie and Jake. "What about you guys?"

Jake shoved his sandwich in his mouth and made a noncommittal shrug. Allie answered with, "Oh, you know, we're so busy with wedding plans. We probably won't go anywhere over the summer."

"That makes sense," Piper said. "A vacation on top of a wedding would be a lot to deal with. Are you excited? September, right? That's a wonderful time of year, especially in a climate like this. It'll be beautiful."

"Thanks."

Bess asked, "Where are you going on your honeymoon?"

Jake answered, "Bahamas," the same time Allie said, "The Caymans." For a panicked split second, he thought they'd be found out as frauds and the entire expedition would be canceled, but Allie recovered quickly.

She said, "It's a cruise. We leave from Florida and go to the Bahamas and then it loops around Cuba and we stop at the Cayman Islands. You can see which of us is excited about which location." She punctuated the words with a laugh.

He breathed a sigh of relief. At least they'd both picked the same general vicinity and Allie was able to cover for them.

"I've never been to the Caymans, but it's on my bucket list. Have you ever been to Turks and Caicos?" Bess asked.

Piper said, "We were supposed to go there once, but a hurricane derailed our plans so we ended up going to Belize instead."

"Oooh, I *love* Belize," Bess said.

Kylie gave a little laugh. "And I thought our honeymoon to Yellowstone was exotic."

"Yellowstone is so beautiful," Allie said. She nudged Jake. "It's on our travel bucket list."

Jake nodded. Yellowstone really was on his travel bucket list, so he didn't have to fake his enthusiasm. "I can't wait to see the Mammoth Hot Springs and Old Faithful."

"If you want to see some amazing wildlife, be sure to put Lamar Valley on your itinerary," William said. "It was incredible."

Kylie's head bobbed in agreement. "After this we'll have to get together and show you our photos. William is so talented with a camera. We got one of his pictures of a wolf framed for the living room. It looks like something out of National Geographic."

William looked a little embarrassed but pleased with her praise.

Everyone ate in silence for a few minutes. It was Piper who groaned and stood first, brushing at her pants. "Guess it's time to get back to work. How are you guys doing in your secluded cave?"

Allie shrugged. "It's okay. We found a little spot to dig and uncovered one pottery shard, but I think that's about all we're going to find."

"Good job!" Piper said enthusiastically. "And hey, at least you get to spend lots of time together, right?"

"Uh huh," Allie managed. "How are you guys doing?"

"We found a mostly intact bowl in Cave Two, so that's very exciting."

"That's great. Maybe we'll find the rest of whatever pottery we found." Jake got up and put his helmet on. "Ready?"

Allie jumped up and headed for the hole. "See you guys later. Happy digging!"

Jake tried not to heave a sigh as he followed Allie from the warm sunshine back into the chilly, dark cave system. They squeezed and crawled and shimmied their way back to Cave Three.

"I am sooooo not cut out to do this as a job," Allie said as she pulled her kneepads back on. "I don't have the patience."

"Same." Jake settled beside her and they went back to scraping at the hole that was slowly getting bigger. "Charlie is so talkative and always on the go. It's hard to imagine him doing this and being content."

"I'm sure he did a lot of hyperfocusing. When something interests him, he's got one-track mind."

"Has it been a while since he was in the field?"

Allie's shovel slowed. "Yeah. It's been a very long time," she said quietly.

He turned his head and studied her face in the glow from his headlamp. "What's that tone?"

"I don't know. Guilt, maybe?"

He sat back on his heels, curious about her response. "Guilt? For what?"

"Papi went everywhere. He knew everything about everything. Some of his colleagues were strictly into, say, Ancient Egypt, or the Mayans, or whatever. Papi loved it all. His specialty was history itself. He's been on every continent, in a zillion different countries, digging up things from a zillion different time periods." She moved and sat cross-legged. "Okay, I guess he did narrow his focus down to modern man. He was never into dinosaurs or the cavemen sort of history. He's told me so many stories, and I probably know more than your average person, but it's not my passion like it's his."

"And you feel guilty about that?"

"No. Not that." She pulled her gloves off, finger by finger. "When I was eight, he gave up working in the field."

Jake had a hard time imagining Charlie quitting field-work. It didn't make sense. "Why?"

"Because Nancy – my mother – and I were visiting Papi and Noni, and in the middle of the night, Nancy took her stuff and left. We found a note on the kitchen counter the next morning."

He sucked in a breath. "Allie, I'm sorry."

"Papi was scheduled to leave the following week for somewhere. Peru, I think? I'm not sure. Noni was a nurse and couldn't take time off on short notice. My mother promised she'd be back the next week. So we all figure he'll miss one trip, no big deal. Only one week turned into six months, then a year. My grandparents spent a small fortune hiring a PI to track her down so they could at least get her to sign legal papers for them to get me into school and take me to the doctor and all that stuff."

He couldn't imagine for a second either of his own parents just up and leaving him and his sister and disappearing. "I'm sorry," he repeated.

"She inherited all of Papi's wandering spirit, but none of his decency. She showed up on Christmas morning with an armload of expensive presents after she'd ghosted me for eighteen months and had the audacity to be mad that I didn't welcome her with open arms. She'd randomly pop up every now and then over the next few years, and every time... Every. Single. Time, she'd use Papi's words. He always said his work was for the greater good, because the more we learn from history, the better we can be. Every time she left again, she'd try to hug me and tell me that she had to leave because she was doing work for 'the greater good.' Last I heard, she was tagging penguins."

"You have no reason to feel guilty. It's not your fault your mother abandoned you."

"I know," she sighed. "But sometimes I get wrapped up in that whole 'if it wasn't for me' baloney that's hard to ignore. It does a number on a kid when the person who is supposed to love you more than anything in life shows you that measuring corals is more important than you are."

He wasn't sure what to say. It certainly gave a little insight as to why she was a bit of a control freak.

"Don't get me wrong, Papi never made me feel like any of it was my fault. He missed being in the field, but his greater good was his family. He got a job teaching at the university, and he did love doing that, too. When Noni died suddenly, he kind of gave up the dream of getting back into the field."

"He made that choice, Allie. He weighed all the options and made the call."

"I know that up here." She tapped her temple. "Anyway, that's my tragic backstory. What's yours?"

Jake leaned back against the wall. His light shined a beam

on the opposite wall. "I don't really have one. Unless you count the summer I was nine and my sister convinced me that my Superman costume could really make me fly, but only if I was really, really high up. I climbed out my bedroom window onto the roof. She put a bunch of pillows on the ground and I jumped. Needless to say, the costume did *not* give me the power of flight."

Allie gasped. "Oh, gosh."

"I ended up with a broken arm and a gash on the side of my head that required twenty-seven stitches." He chuckled at the memory. "My poor parents. I tried to cover for my sister, but they saw right through it and she was grounded for the rest of the summer. I'm not sure she ever forgave me for that."

"Forgave *you*? How old was she?"

"Eleven."

"Do you have other siblings?"

"No, thank goodness. We terrorized each other. I can't imagine adding another kid to the mix. Do you have any brothers or sisters?"

"One half-sister. She lives in Montana with her family."

"Are you close?"

"No."

Her answer was short, so he let it drop. "Shall we get back to treasure hunting?"

"Sure."

They mostly worked without talking through the afternoon.

After a few hours, Allie said, "I think I'm done for the day."

"Me, too." Jake pulled his spade from the hole, and something caught his eye. "What's that?"

They hunkered close to the floor to peer inside. A small, flat, black triangle was wedged at the back of the hole, under the wall. Jake reached in and gently pulled, making sure it wasn't stuck, so he didn't break it.

He pulled his hand out of the hole and held the triangle in his palm.

"What is it?"

"I don't know. It doesn't look like pottery or stone, does it?"

Allie took off her glove and plucked it from his hand. "Okay, this might sound crazy, but it almost looks like leather."

"It really does," he agreed. He got the handheld flashlight out of his bag and laid on the ground to look as far into the hole as he could, but he didn't see anything except dirt and stones. "I don't see anything else."

"Let's take it outside and see if someone else has an opinion on it. Hopefully tomorrow we can find more."

Chapter Twenty

ALLIE PUSHED through the narrow passageway too fast and nearly got herself wedged. She muttered a curse and forced herself to stop and calm down. Rushing through a tunnel like this was never a good idea. She shimmied sideways and slid between the stone walls. The black triangle in her pocket was a mystery she wanted to solve *right now*.

She hurried past the forks in the path and crawled through the narrow spot to the exit. The burst of sunlight was a welcome sight as she crawled up out of the ground and waited for Jake to crawl out behind her.

"Who do you think—Oh." Allie stopped when she saw Selena climbing out of the hole, followed by Chip.

"What?" he asked.

Allie took Jake's arm and led him over to the ATVs. "I don't want to say anything to them."

"Okay. How about William? We can see what he thinks."

"Or Delia?"

He nodded. "I think either one."

She was glad they were on the same page. As much as she

liked Piper and Bess, they worked for Selena, and Allie didn't know how close they actually were. Best not to make any assumptions.

Soon the whole group was milling around the ATVs. Jake took his time securing their packs to the rack, while other pairs got on their machines and headed for basecamp.

"Everything okay?" William asked.

Allie looked around. They were the only four people who hadn't left yet. She waited until the last ATV was out of sight before she said, "We found something, and we don't know what it is." She pulled the stiff triangle out of her shirt pocket and handed it to William. Seeing it in the light, she was more convinced it was leather.

He and Kylie bent their heads to study it.

"I'm no expert," William said, "but it feels like some kind of canvas?"

"Leather," Kylie said, echoing Allie's initial thought.

William looked at it again, then handed it back as he said, "Oh, I bet that's what it is."

"We should show it to Delia," Kylie suggested.

Allie nodded. "Okay."

Jake put a hand on her back. "I'm not sure I want to tell the others just yet."

"Definitely not," William quickly said. "I know there's been quite a bit of us versus them, which bothers me, but I feel like I need to be up front and say that I don't quite trust Selena and Chip. We've been working near them and something is just... off." He held up a hand. "I'm not saying they've done anything. It's just a gut thing."

Allie breathed a relieved sigh. "I thought it was just me.

Maybe it's just her abrasive comments, but I'm a bit wary of her and it makes it hard to trust her."

William nodded. "Follow us to the house. We'll get Delia and Shane to take a look at your find and get their thoughts."

Allie slipped the triangle back into her pocket and got on the ATV behind Jake. They followed William and Kylie down the mountain and past the basecamp. They slowed, then took a right at the fork to the exit.

The large log house came into view. A stunning wrap-around porch was the main feature. Several rocking chairs would be the perfect seats to sit with a cup of coffee to look over the view and listen to the sounds of nature. Allie could easily see why Estelle and her family defended this property so diligently.

They parked their ATVs beside Delia and Shane's and followed William up the stairs and across the wooden porch.

Allie turned and looked out over the view. "This is gorgeous."

Kylie smiled. "It's one of my favorite places in the whole world."

"I can see why."

William held the door.

Inside, Delia looked surprised to see them. "Allie. Jake. Is everything okay?"

Allie pulled the triangle from her pocket. "We found this in Cave Three."

Delia put glasses on and walked to the window. She moved it around in the light, turning it over and studying the edge for a long time.

Shane bounded down the stairs. "Supper should be—Oh, hey guys. What's going on?"

Delia waved him over to study the piece.

He looked at it for a few minutes, then said, "It's leather."

Allie and Jake exchanged a look. She said, "That's what I guessed it might be. But why would it be in the cave? Does that mean this stuff is from a different time period and might not even be related to M'yxnih?"

Shane's brows furrowed. "Leather has been used for thousands and thousands of years. Back as early as the third century. Off the cuff, I see no reason to assume this is unrelated."

"What do you think it's from?"

He held the piece out and ran his finger along the jagged longest edge. "See how this is torn and the other two angles are straight?"

"Yeah."

"My guess at this point is a book."

Allie felt the air whoosh from her lungs. She sucked in a huge breath. "A book?"

"Sure. Wasn't our guy from a ship? It's possibly he had a ledger or a log."

"Could a book from the fifteen hundreds survive this long?"

He shrugged one shoulder. "Sure, if the conditions are right. I probably wouldn't expect to find much more than this, though. It's extremely unlikely we'd find a whole book."

From the doorway, Estelle said, "Though stranger things have happened."

"Sure. Things are discovered all the time. I just don't want you to get your hopes up." He gave the piece back to Allie.

Delia put a hand on Shane's arm. "But it's a great find. Truly."

"It is," he quickly agreed. "I hope I'm not discouraging you, because Delia's right. This is a great find."

"Thanks, we appreciate you taking a look," Allie said.

William added, "I think we'll keep it between us for right now, though. Just in case."

Jake agreed. "We should head back."

"Why don't you have dinner with us?" Estelle said.

"I'll set extra places," Shane said as he headed for the kitchen.

Allie looked at Jake, but William was already gesturing for them to head to the kitchen so they headed that direction.

A few minutes later, Allie found herself seated beside Estelle.

"How is everything going?" Estelle asked as she passed a plate of garlic bread to Allie.

"It's good. We found a pottery shard and a piece of leather in Cave Three. I'm not sure what's going on in the other two, though."

"There was some pottery in Cave One," Delia said.

They piled their plates with spaghetti and meatballs. Allie's fork split a meatball and she took a bite. "Mmm, this is so good. I can't make a decent meatball to save my life."

Estelle chuckled. "I use a mixture of ground beef and ground sweet sausage. And lots of spices, of course. Gives it a nice flavor."

"It's delicious. Thank you for inviting us."

"Of course. I hope you're enjoying the experience. Is your room comfortable?"

Allie almost mentioned the bunk bed mattress, but

remembered that she and Jake were supposed to be married and presumably sharing a bed. "To be honest, the bed's a little smaller than I'm used to." She felt her face burn. It was technically the truth, but it seemed as though Estelle had the ability to read her mind and see that she was hiding something.

"My nephews tell me that all the time. We couldn't afford to outfit the whole camp with queen-size beds, though."

"Everything else is great. It's a nice building. The living room is super comfortable, and the kitchen is laid out really well. It's been easy for four of us to make meals at the same time without being on top of each other."

"Good. If there's ever anything you need, don't hesitate to ask. I want you to be comfortable while you're here."

"We definitely are. Thank you for everything." She took a sip of water. "When we first talked about the expedition, I kind of assumed we'd either be sleeping in the caves or camping outside, so believe me, I have zero complaints about the accommodations."

From there, the conversation flowed to Kylie and Delia, who talked about the progress in Cave One.

Before she knew it, Allie's offer to help with dishes was rejected and she and Jake were on the ATV headed back to basecamp. Everyone was congregated in the living room, on their phones or laptops or having side conversations.

"We thought we lost you," Piper said.

"We were just visiting with Estelle," Allie said.

"Oooh, we're on a first-name basis now?" Selena said with a smirk.

Allie ignored her. "What time are we heading out in the morning?"

"Five. Of course you have your own personal Hauser family guides who will escort you no matter what time you decide to get up."

Allie wanted to ask Selena what her problem was, but she didn't. "Okay, see you all in the morning. Good night." She headed for the stairs with Jake right behind her.

For once she couldn't wait to get to sleep so the morning would come faster and they could get back in the cave and see if there was anything else in there. The idea that there might – probably not, but *maybe* – be a book that they could possibly find had sparked a brand-new excitement in her that she hadn't felt to this point. How amazing it would be to find a precious journal or ship log or ledger or something to show Papi. He'd be over the moon.

She hoped more than anything that they'd find something more.

Chapter Twenty-One

THE REST of the week didn't turn up anything more than a slowly growing pile of dirt and tiny stones. By Friday afternoon, Jake was ready to crawl out of the cave and never go back.

Allie sat with her back against the wall. Her spade landed with a thump as she tossed it. A few seconds later, her gloves landed near the spade. "I'm so bored." She ran a hand down over her face. "I know I'm not supposed to admit that because this is super important work, blah blah blah, but I'm. So. Bored."

Jake sat on the other side of the hole they'd dug and mirrored her position. He crossed his feet at the ankles and tugged his gloves off. "I'm glad you said it. It might not be so bad if we were someplace with, I don't know, *light*? This is driving me bananas." He flicked a hand to gesture into the darkness that their headlamps couldn't fully erase.

"Same." She lifted her arm and pulled her sleeve up to look at her watch. "Are you serious? It's only one thirty? UGH."

He knew exactly what she meant. "It's been dragging ever since we found that scrap of leather."

"I have a feeling that's the pinnacle of our discoveries."

"Yup." This was definitely not his idea of a good time. A triangle of leather and a shard of ceramic in two weeks did not feel like time well spent.

"And we have two more weeks of this. *Weeks*. We're only halfway into this."

He tried to look at the bright side. "No, we're already halfway done. That sounds better."

"Okay, Mister Glass-Half-Full. Your positive spin isn't helping much, sorry."

He chuckled. "Tell you what. I'll make sure to buy a whole box of mixed berry granola bars for next week."

She reached over and nudged his arm. "You're the best husband ever."

"Can I ask you something?" he asked. He was pretty sure he was about to overstep but he went ahead anyway.

"You can ask. Doesn't mean I'll answer."

"Why aren't you married? For real?" It didn't make sense. Yes, she could be testy, but she was beautiful and intelligent and a darn good partner for this adventure.

"Probably some messed up reasons that I should get therapy for," she answered quickly. "The short answer is that my mother had a brand-new husband every time she popped back into my life. Made it hard to take the idea of marriage seriously."

"Your grandparents were happily married, though, right?"
"Mostly."
"What about your dad?"
"He was definitely married," she said drily. "He was

married the whole time he and my mom were messing around. Of course, their relationship was 'true love' and his selfish wife was holding him back."

"Yikes."

"Yeah, it was a pretty gross situation."

"Is he your half-sister's dad?" Her light danced as she shook her head.

"No, he doesn't have any other kids that I know of. Nancy met a guy in Nepal – they were both backpacking – and a few months after she had my sister, she showed up on his doorstep with Anna and left her with him. She acted like she was doing my grandparents a big favor by not dumping a second kid on them. At least she got her tubes tied after that."

"So there's a pretty big age gap between you two?"

"Ten years. Between the decade and the miles, it's been difficult to have any kind of relationship especially when our only common denominator is toxicity and trauma."

"I'm sorry."

"Nah, I've had a good life. I'm just a bit jaded, I suppose. What about you? Why aren't you married? Bad examples in your life, too?"

He tilted his head back and forth. "Yes and no. My parents have an amazing marriage. I've watched their friends and my friends get married and divorced and so it feels like what my parents have is so rare there's no point in trying to find it. If I ever get married, it's one and done. For life. I don't want to get married just to try it out. But I figure if I haven't found it by now, it's probably not ever happening and that's fine. Know what I mean?"

"I do. That's how I feel. Marriage is supposed to be a serious thing. It should be forever, and it doesn't seem like that's even possible in today's world. And this'll no doubt sound selfish, but I don't want to get married and end up stuck."

"It doesn't sound selfish to me."

"Have you ever come close?" she asked.

"Yeah." Way too close for comfort.

Allie's light arced upwards as she leaned her head back against the wall. "Me, too."

They sat in silence for a bit, lost in their own thoughts in the darkness.

Jake pushed the memories of his ex back where they belonged and hopped to his feet. "I'm calling it a day." He held a hand down to her. "You with me, Allie O'Malley?"

She grabbed his hand. "You know me so well, Mr. O'Malley."

They gathered their things and made their way out of the caves. Jake's knees hurt from crawling around the cave and then crawling out through the small spots in the tunnels. He climbed out of the hole and turned around to offer Allie his hand.

"Now what?" she asked. "Should we just leave? I feel like Selena will have something to say about us knocking off early."

"Do you think she'll even notice? We could just text William that we've headed out to meet with Charlie. Technically still work?"

She pulled her phone out of her pocket and sent a message to William. "Brilliant." She held her phone up and wiggled it. "You know, that's one upside to this little adventure of ours. I've been spending a lot less time doomscrolling social media. The only time I've been on my apps at all is to post pictures for Ralph."

"Definite upside." He strapped their packs to the ATV's rack. "The downside is that I've been missing the texts from my family."

"Do you text with them a lot?"

"Oh, yeah. We have a family group text and there's at least a dozen messages a day."

"About what?" Allie climbed on behind him and put her arms around his waist.

He was getting used to the feel of her arms around him, and wasn't sure if that was a good thing or a bad thing. "Nothing and everything."

"That's so great, Jake. I hope you know how lucky you are."

"I do." He started the ATV and drowned out any further conversation. The earlier conversation about marriage had dredged up some old feelings. He'd always wanted to get married and have a family, but no one had ever seemed to be the right fit into the puzzle of his life. He still wanted to get married, but he only wanted to do it once, and it had to be for life.

Chapter Twenty-Two

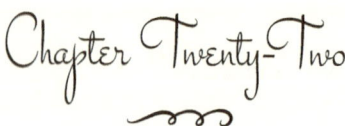

"Papi, I'm home!" Allie closed the door behind herself. The sound of Jake's rumbling truck grew faint as he drove away.

"Allie!" His voice came from the direction of his office. His cane clomped against the floor as he hurried through the mudroom and into the kitchen. "I wasn't expecting you until this evening."

She didn't have the heart to tell him that she and Jake were bored out of their minds. "I have three exciting things to show you as soon as I grab a quick shower and change, okay?"

"Of course. Did you have lunch? I can warm up some soup."

"That would be amazing, thank you." She already couldn't wait to get into her yoga pants and t-shirt, and the prospect of food made her move even faster.

A short while later, she sat at the kitchen table with her hair wound in a towel, blowing on a spoonful of tomato soup with an army of oyster crackers soaking up the liquid. A grilled cheese sandwich rounded out the meal.

"Okay, so we ended up with three things I want to show

you. Here's the first." She turned her phone to face him and tapped the button to play the first video.

Papi watched intently, nodding frequently and letting out several "Oh"s as if he was gaining context over things he'd been pondering.

When it was over, she said, "This one is just us exiting so you can see the complete loop." She played the second video.

"This is great. It really helps put all the pictures into better perspective." He sat back and drummed his fingers on the table. "Speaking of that."

She looked up and brushed grilled cheese crumbs from her lips. "What? Is there something else wrong with the pictures?" She steeled herself for more criticism.

"No, Allie-gator. There's something wrong with the way I acted about the pictures." He pursed his lips and took a deep breath. "I was feeling left out and I allowed myself to take that out on you. I'm sorry. I've been feeling terrible about it all week. I'm very grateful for all the photos and rubbings and all the attention to detail you put into capturing all the angles and sizes. I had no business criticizing, and I apologize."

Her hand froze halfway to her mouth. An oyster cracker teetered on the edge of her spoon for a long moment before it slid off and landed back in the bowl with a sploop. An apology? That was the last thing she expected.

"You're being so generous in doing this for me, and I haven't been nearly as appreciative as I ought to be." His mouth lifted in a half-smile. "I hope it hasn't been too tedious for you."

His attitude was a pleasant and refreshing surprise. "Yes and no. Jake and I got banished to Cave Three, which is horribly boring ninety percent of the time, but we did find something."

Papi's eyes lit up. "You did?"

She went to the living room to grab her backpack and brought it back to the kitchen. From one of the font pockets, she pulled out a plastic container and unscrewed the lid. "Here's the first thing we found."

He eagerly took the pottery shard from her and turned it every which way, examining every bit of its three-inch length. "Do you know what this is?"

"Pottery of some sort."

"It's from a clay cooking pot." He launched into an explanation of why this was so obvious to him, from the telltale glaze to the faint groove that she could hardly even see.

Allie half-listened to Papi describe what the rest of the pot would have looked like. It never ceased to amaze her how much knowledge he had stored in his head, and how he could glean so much information from something that looked completely insignificant to her untrained eye.

She finished her soup and sandwich as he talked and talked, to himself as much as to her. When he seemed to have run out of things to say, she interjected, "We found one more thing. This one was more interesting to me, but who knows. It might be nothing."

He sat up straight, waiting for her to produce the second something from the plastic container.

She pulled out the black triangle and handed to him. His brows scrunched inward.

She wanted to blurt out their guess, but she knew Papi well enough to know he'd prefer to make his own guess and then compare it to theirs.

He reached over to the junk drawer and rooted around until he found a magnifying glass. He studied the object in silence for the longest time. Long enough for Allie to wash her plate and bowl and refill her drink.

"Do you know what this is?" he asked.

"We had a guess. Do you want me to tell you?"

He nodded.

"We think it might be leather."

His head bobbed enthusiastically. "That's exactly what this is." He lovingly stroked the length of the piece. "Can you show me where you found it?"

It took her a second to realize he meant the video, not that he expected her to take him to the cave. Although if she suggested it, he'd absolutely go, no matter how bad an idea it would be. "Sure." She opened the lid of her laptop and connected her phone to transfer the video.

When it was done, she fast forwarded to the footage of Cave Three and paused the screen on the hole. "It was in here. Of course the hole was much bigger when we found it. Now it's probably from here to here." She pointed on the screen.

Papi nodded thoughtfully.

"Um, one thing, though."

"What's that?"

"We kind of didn't tell the rest of the team we found this. We showed it to William – Estelle's great-grandson – and her daughter Delia, but we thought it would probably be better to... I don't know, wait, I guess?"

He sat back in his chair and turned his attention to her. "How is the other team? Are they cooperative?"

"Most of them are. Piper and Aaron and Bess and Toby

are great. But Selena and Chip are in charge. I think she doesn't like the fact that I have to be there, so she assigned us to Cave Three to keep us out of her way. She's said several times that she doesn't think there's anything in that one anyway."

"Rupert and I both have some reservations about her, but her resume is outstanding, and she seems competent enough."

"I'm sure she's good at what she does. She's just lacking in the personality department."

"If I had a nickel for everyone I worked with who fit that description over the years, I'd be a very rich man."

His mention of money reminded her of their bills. "Speaking of rich, did you take care of the homeowners insurance?"

He froze like a deer in the headlights before frowning indignantly. "Of course I did."

"Papi."

"I'm sure I did. Pretty sure. I've been very busy." He pursed his lips. "Maybe I didn't. But I'll get to it."

Allie put the artifacts back into the container and screwed the lid on. "It's fine, I'll take care of it." She stood up and slung her pack over her shoulder to take to her bedroom.

"I think I'll go through this video again."

"It goes in the same order that I took the pictures in, so it should be easy to match everything up." She yawned. "I think I'm going to catch a quick nap before I tackle the grocery store and all that jazz."

"Have a good nap, Allie-gator."

Saturday morning brought a bright beam of sunshine into Allie's room. She stretched and snuggled back down under her covers. Her bed felt a million times more comfortable after sleeping on the mattress at the basecamp. At least she wasn't away on location and unable to sleep in her own bed at all for the month.

Her phone buzzed with an incoming text from Jake. A smile spread across her face. She leaned back against her pillow to look at his message.

> How was Charlie? Any complaints about the video?

She chuckled and typed her reply.

> He actually apologized for complaining about the pictures. He loved the video and was blown away by the stuff we found.

> That's great. What are you up to this weekend?

> Right now I'm still in my blanket cocoon.

> Lucky. I had to get up because the neighbor decided to start mowing at six.

She fluffed her pillow and leaned back.

> So rude. I should probably mow this afternoon so Papi doesn't try doing it himself this week.

I wasn't going to, but no way I can let his lawn look better than mine.

> LOL He issued a challenge. 😆

I'm going to raise the stakes and get some mulch.

> Ooooh, shots fired.

You know it. I'll see you tomorrow evening.

> Have fun with your yardwork.

You too.

She smiled at the phone, and was still smiling when she got out of the shower and got dressed.

She stopped smiling when she got into Papi's office and went through the stack of bills. It looked like he hadn't paid anything in the two weeks she'd been gone. Including the homeowners insurance, which, unlike several smaller bills, was not past due. Thank goodness. She logged onto the website and paid the bill, then wrote the amount in Papi's checkbook.

He was still a little old school, preferring a handwritten check ledger to anything electronic.

She logged into the bank account and skimmed down over the transactions and checks that weren't back yet.

Her eyes shot back up to an entry he'd written two days earlier.

"What the heck?" she muttered to herself. Papi typically sent a one-hundred-dollar donation check to the museum every month like clockwork. This time, his check was written for ten thousand dollars. That couldn't be right.

She grabbed the checkbook and went to the kitchen where Papi sat, eating a bowl of cereal and doing a crossword puzzle.

"Papi? What's this check? To the museum? It's supposed to be a hundred dollars but you wrote ten thousand dollars in the ledger."

He looked up and shrugged. "I wanted to send them more this time."

"Wait, so that's not just a mistake? You actually mailed them a check for ten *thousand* dollars?"

"Yes. Shell."

"What? Shell? What are you talking about?"

He rolled his eyes and went back to his puzzle. "A beach-comber's keepsake. Five letters." He carefully wrote the word into the crossword blocks.

"Papi."

"Don't take that tone with me."

"You can't be sending the museum this much money."

"I can and I did."

"Where did you get the money?"

"None of your business."

She smacked the checkbook down on the table. "It's absolutely my business when I have to clean up these messes. Where did you get the money?"

He crossed his arms like a petulant child. "You can't even tell the difference between Mayan and Incan artifacts, so don't act like you're smarter than me."

She squeezed the bridge of her nose. "Knock it off. I'm not smarter than you, but I *am* smart enough to know when you're trying to change the subject. Where did you get this money?"

He pressed his lips together.

"You know I'm going to find it, so you might as well tell me."

"I used one of those extra bank checks. The plain blue ones at the back of the drawer."

She snapped her mouth shut and forced herself to take a few deep breaths. "That's a cash advance."

"It's my money. I can do what I want."

"It's not your money. It's debt against the *house*, Papi. It's a home equity line of credit. It's only for emergencies like a new roof or something. You're not going into ten thousand dollars of debt just to make a donation to the museum."

"I know what it is, Allison Genevieve. I'm not stupid, and I'm not going to get myself in the same hole that you keep holding over my head. I, for one, am *grateful* to the museum for sponsoring this project. I want them to know that."

Oooh, he was annoyed if he used her full name. "Papi. First of all, they know you're grateful. Second of all, this isn't just for you. It's historically significant and important for the museum, even aside from their personal relationship with you. Third, I'm not holding it over your head, but you can't possibly blame me for not letting you go back into debt."

"I don't feel right that they're paying you," he snapped.

She took a step back. "Excuse me? I'm doing a job for them, why wouldn't they pay me for it? I might not be an expert here, but I'm working hard and the museum is getting value from my efforts. Just because I'm your granddaughter doesn't mean my work should be free."

"I'd do it for free," he scoffed.

"False. You'd do it for your personal reasons. You'd be gaining knowledge and closure, so you wouldn't be doing it for free."

"Oh, like you aren't gaining knowledge."

"Nothing relevant to my daily life." She held up a hand. "Okay. I'm done with this conversation. And by the way, the museum isn't paying me anywhere near ten thousand dollars."

She turned on her heel and went back to the office. Her stomach churned because she was going to have to make the most mortifying, embarrassing phone call of all time.

As the phone rang, she thought she might actually get sick.

"Rita, hi. This is Allie Quinn, Charles Scheffler's grand-daughter?"

"Yes, Allie of course. How are you?"

"Good. I'm glad I caught you. I figured I'd get your voice-mail on a Saturday morning."

Rita's voice was chipper and friendly. "Ten minutes from now, you would have. I just popped in for a few hours to get some paperwork cleaned off Rupert's desk. What can I do for you?"

"Well, this is horribly embarrassing, but my grandfather sent in a donation check."

There was rustling in the background. "Yep, it's in my stack of mail."

"Well, there's a problem with the check." She hadn't

168 · CARRIE JACOBS

expected to be speaking to a live person, so she had to come up with an excuse on the fly. "It's um—"

"Oh, dear." The rustling stopped. "Did he mean to send us this much money? This is very unusual for him."

"No, he didn't. And I'm so sorry, I know it's terribly inconvenient, but if you could—"

"Don't worry about a thing. Jake just came in. I'll mark it void and send it back to you with him."

"Oh." Oh, crap. Jake was the last person she wanted to get involved in this.

"Jake, I need you for a minute," Rita called, then spoke to Allie again. "All taken care of. I'll see you soon!" She ended the call before Allie could say anything else.

Great. Just when she and Jake had reached a nice level of almost-friendship, he was going to be inserted into Papi drama that he'd definitely have an opinion on. Perfect.

Chapter Twenty-Three

JAKE WAS STILL ANNOYED when he rolled into Charlie's driveway Sunday evening to pick Allie up. He knew it wasn't his business, but running into Lucinda at the grocery store still had him annoyed. All his old feelings about her and her ways reminded him how uncomfortable be was with Allie's controlling dynamic with Charlie.

At least he knew his personal situation was coloring his perception, so he vowed to keep his thoughts to himself.

He knocked on the front door. Charlie answered with a big grin. "Jake, my boy, come on in!"

Jake couldn't help but return the smile. "How are you? Did you check out the video tour of the caves?"

"Oh, that was wonderful! Allie did such a good job showing all the nooks and crannies. I was able to match up the drawings and carvings and get more perspective of the setup. How are you doing? Are you enjoying yourself?"

"It's interesting," Jake said. "I'm not a big fan of being underground, but it's been... interesting." He couldn't think of a better word. "What did you think of the leather we found? Shane thinks it's from a book of some sort."

"That's exactly what I think. Wouldn't it be wonderful if you were able to find more of it?"

"I'm not getting my hopes up. Who knows how far away that piece is from the rest of the book, assuming it hasn't just disintegrated into the ground after all this time."

"Probably." Charlie patted his arm. "But it's fun to dream."

Allie pushed her suitcase around the corner. "Ready?"

"Sure." He reached into his back pocket and pulled out the folded envelope from Rita. "I was told to return this to you." He felt a teeny, tiny, minuscule flicker of guilt about peeking into the envelope. It wasn't his fault it wasn't sealed when Rita handed it to him.

"Thanks." She took the envelope without any change in her expression.

Charlie's lips pressed into a thin line. He looked a bit annoyed, maybe, but not terribly curious or concerned.

Allie walked back around the corner and came back a moment later without the envelope. She gave Charlie a hug. "I love you, Papi-dile."

"Love you too, Allie-gator."

"See you Friday," Jake said.

"Have a good week. Find lots of buried treasure."

"We'll do our best," he said as he held the door for Allie.

She blew a kiss to Charlie, then wheeled her suitcase to the truck and put it in the backseat.

Jake tamped down his annoyance. Obviously Charlie knew about the check, but why did it have to be returned in the first place? Why was Allie meddling in the man's business and making a fuss at the museum? It was ridiculous.

But he held his tongue all through the drive back to base-camp and the walk up the stairs to the room they shared.

They went through their evening routine and climbed into their respective beds.

"You're really quiet this evening. Everything okay?" she asked.

"Yeah."

"Did you get your mulch and make your neighbor jealous?"

He couldn't quite muster a smile. "Yeah, I mulched the side of my house that faces his This evening when I left, I saw he had a new pile of mulch in his driveway."

"Nice. I guess we know what you're doing next weekend, rain or shine." She yawned. "I got our lawn mowed, but none of the neighbors care enough to get competitive about it."

He waited a beat, then said, "Well, good night." He flipped onto his side, facing away from her.

"Night," she said, but it sounded more like a question.

He fell asleep to the sounds of Allie's white noise app.

Monday morning he was still on edge after seeing Lucinda. She'd had the audacity to come over to him and wave a new engagement ring in his face like it was supposed to bother him. It didn't. Best of luck to that poor sap.

Allie was dressed and organizing her pack.

He fished a box out of his bag and tossed it onto his bed. "Those are for you."

She grinned and snatched the box. "Mixed berry! Thank you. You're the best temporary husband ever."

He turned away and forced a laugh. The way she treated Charlie, he didn't even want to joke about her being a great temporary wife. Thank goodness it wasn't real and when this was over he could go back to his life without her in it.

Allie put two of the bars in her pack.

A while later, they'd eaten a hearty breakfast, made small talk, and taken the ATV to the parking area with the rest of the group. As they walked to the cave entrance, Jake breathed in the fresh air that held the threat of rain. The warmth helped his mood a bit. The sky was overcast and dreary. Despite that, birds chirped and squirrels scampered to and fro, making a louder ruckus than their little bodies could account for.

They dropped into the tunnel one by one. His improved mood tanked as quickly as the light faded away. He turned his headlamp on and got on his hands and knees to crawl through the narrowest part of the tunnel. The darkness absorbed whatever positive energy he had left and he accepted the fact that he was going to be grumpy as long as they were stuck underground. Awesome.

Everyone else branched off to the main caves, but he followed Allie through the left fork to Cave Three. He was already missing the warmth from the outside. The caves were dry, which was nice, but they were a constant fifty-five degrees or so, which wasn't nice at all.

He had a long-sleeved shirt on under his safety-neon Ralph's t-shirt, but today he wished he'd brought a jacket.

In their cave, they hunkered near the hole that was slowly getting larger.

Allie adjusted her headlamp and leaned down to look into the hole. "Welp, nothing magically appeared over the weekend. No loose rubies, either."

He grunted a response.

She tried a few more times to engage him with small talk, but he wanted no part of it. He thought he'd succeeded in making her give up for the day when she put her shovel down and said, "What's wrong?"

"Nothing."

"Baloney. You've been moody all day. Was there a pea under your mattress?"

"What are you even talking about?" he barked with more force than necessary. "You're not making any sense."

"I was referencing *The Princess and the Pea*. Old fairy tale. I guess I know not to do that again. Geez." Now her scowl matched his. "What is your problem?"

He tossed his shovel to the ground. "I'm not the one with a problem."

She tilted her head and stared at him. "Care to elaborate?"

"No, I don't."

"Seriously? You're going to be grouchy and rude and insinuate I'm the problem, when clearly it's you. Nice."

"You *are* the problem. I don't want to be stuck here with you knowing how you treat Charlie." So much for holding his tongue.

"You don't have the first clue about how I treat my grandfather."

"Bull. I had to play delivery boy with evidence of your controlling financial bullying, remember?"

She yanked her gloves off and threw them in the direction of the hole. "You've got some serious nerve."

"What, you don't like being called out?"

"Not when it's by a loudmouth trying to mansplain something he has not a shred of a clue about." She got to her feet and planted her hands on her hips.

Jake scrambled up to stand, too. He wasn't about to have her looking down at him. "I have all the clues I need. He made a donation and you made him return it. It's his money."

"You sure about that?"

Her response caught him off guard.

"Come on, Jake, tell me where he got the money."

"I assume from his pension or savings or—no. You're not turning this around on me. I know it was his money because his name was on the check, and you had no right to stop him from making a donation."

She spoke slowly, enunciating every word. "That check was from a line of credit. It wasn't *money*, Jake, it was *debt*. Against his *house*. The house he almost lost to *foreclosure*."

Oh.

"Go ahead, Saint Jake, Patron Saint of Financial Irresponsibility, keep running your mouth about things you know nothing about. Nothing!"

Wait. Foreclosure? Charlie was a brilliant man. She had to be exaggerating. Or lying. Or both. "I have a hard time believing Charlie's house was anywhere near foreclosure."

"I don't care what you believe. You're nobody to us, Jake. You're just a wannabe-do-gooder security guard who has a soft spot for some old guy who comes into your museum, and you're so arrogant you think casual small talk ten minutes a month gives you some great insight into his life. Newsflash, it doesn't. You. Know. Nothing. I don't care if that hurts your widdle feewings, but it's the truth. You're a stranger, and you've got nothing but audacity and opinions, both of which you are free to turn sideways and shove."

They stood, glaring at each other for a long moment. Jake wanted to give a clever retort of some kind, but he couldn't think of anything.

"I need a break from you." Allie stalked to the tunnel.

Jake opened his mouth to say something, but a rumbling boom cut him off. His legs trembled and it took a second to realize it wasn't him, it was the ground. Another boom followed the first, then the horrible sound of stones tumbling somewhere in the tunnels.

Allie was frozen a few steps into the passageway.

Another boom shook the ground harder. The loud crack of a large rock hitting another rock spurred him to action. He leaped forward, grabbed her arm, and yanked her backwards just as the fourth boom shook the ground harder than the first three. A massive plume of dust billowed into the cave from the tunnel, right where she'd been standing. He spun around, keeping Allie in front of him, tight to his chest, and lurched toward the farthest side of the cave.

The cloud overtook them. Something beeped urgently. Jake's eyes stung and his next breath pulled dirt into his lungs. He coughed violently. Allie coughed, too. He waved his hand in front of his face, but couldn't see anything.

Allie was still against him. Her coughing subsided, but his didn't. He felt her turn. Her hands clawed at his shirts and yanked them up over his face. He immediately understood and covered his nose with the fabric. It felt like forever until his own coughing slowed and finally stopped. He squinted into the darkness, but still couldn't see more than a few inches in front of his face.

The shrill beeping continued, but the shaking and rumbling had stopped.

"What is that?" he asked, his voice muffled by his shirts.

"Air quality monitor," was her equally muffled reply.

That couldn't be good.

Chapter Twenty-Four

ALLIE HAD no idea how long it took for the dust to settle. She and Jake cowered, huddled together in the far corner, their lights doing nothing to pierce the darkness.

"Are you okay?" Jake asked through his shirts.

"I think so. You?"

"My throat hurts from the coughing, but I think I'm okay. What do you think happened?"

Her light bounced against the cloud that was still too dense for comfort. "Another earthquake maybe?"

"Do earthquakes boom like that?"

"I have no idea." That didn't make much sense. But neither did... "Explosives?"

"That's what it sounded like. It couldn't have been, though, could it?" He sounded as skeptical as she felt.

She shook her head. "Nah, of course not. Right?"

"Maybe thunder?"

"Could be." She held onto the idea of thunder. A raging storm brought on by nature. Because someone deliberately setting off explosives was unfathomable.

The air quality monitor beeping slowed as the dust settled. It finally stopped and the heavy silence was somehow worse than the incessant beeping.

Allie pulled her shirts away from her face and took a breath. It seemed fine, even though an odd chalky scent lingered in the air.

They sat still for a few more minutes.

"What should we do?" Jake asked.

"I guess we check the tunnel first." She dreaded doing it, because she already knew it would just confirm what they both already feared – that they were stuck.

Jake fished in his pack for the brighter handheld flashlight.

They slowly crossed the room, both of them kicking small stones out of their way, probably stalling.

He shined the light into the hallway. "We have a problem."

Allie gripped his arm and peered around him. Problem indeed. Instead of a tunnel, they were faced with rock. Nothing but rock. "Okay, let's see if we have any signal at all." She got her phone out of her backpack and lit up the screen. Nope. Zero bars. Exactly as she'd expected.

Her hand brushed the air quality monitor. She looked at the screen. It stopped beeping, so they shouldn't be in any danger from the air, anyway. A number caught her attention. "Jake? Look at this." She unclipped the monitor and stood.

"Yeah?"

"The humidity. It's at forty percent and climbing. It's been almost zero the whole time. There must be air coming in from the outside." Her heart leapt with a flash of excitement. "Turn off your headlamp."

"What?"

"Just for a minute."

He snapped his light off, and she did the same, throwing them into pitch blackness.

"Allie."

"Hang on." She looked upward, turning in a full circle. She could almost make out shapes above their head. "There! Do you see anything?"

"Hardly," he snapped.

"Look up." She felt for his arm and turned him. "There's some light coming from up there."

"Allie, that has to be fifty, seventy-five feet high."

"No problem." She looked downward and flipped her headlamp back on, then excitedly rummaged through her pack.

"What are you going to do?"

"I'm going to kiss Ralph for making us bring an anchor kit."

"Oh, no. No, you're not going to try climbing that."

"It'll be fine." She took the handheld flashlight and shined the beam upward about twenty feet. "See how the rock kind of disappears up there? It's probably a ledge. If I can get up there, maybe there'll be enough signal to make a call."

"Shouldn't we wait? Maybe there's already someone on the way."

"Or maybe everyone else is trapped, too." She hated giving voice to the thought.

He hissed out a breath. "Okay," he grudgingly relented.

She found the kit at the bottom of her pack and thanked her lucky stars she hadn't listened to the urge to leave it behind. She studied the wall, picked what she thought was the best path upward, and got to work, hammering the drill bit into the rockface to create a hole she could screw the anchor into. The first hole she wanted to drill was above her head, so her arms quickly got tired.

Halfway into the first hole, she had to stop and rest.

She sank to the floor. "Sorry, it's not a quick process."

"We've got nothing but time, right? Have a mixed berry bar."

"No, we should save them. We might be stuck here a day or two." Or longer, but that was all she was willing to admit to.

"Or just a few hours."

She highly doubted they'd be that lucky. "Maybe."

Jake sat on the floor beside her and leaned back against the wall. "Allie, look, I'm sorry for overstepping. I only want what's best for Charlie."

She gritted her teeth and slowly pulled in a long breath. "I can appreciate that you care about him. But I'm serious. You. Know. Nothing. You're not apologizing because you realize you've done anything wrong. You're only apologizing because we're trapped here and you don't want to be uncomfortable. I know this because you've apologized for overstepping before and then ten minutes later you're back to making unfair assumptions and being rude to me."

"Is it an assumption, though? You put a stop to his donation. That means you have power over his finances. That's a fact, not an assumption."

"Here's another fact, Jake. You arrogantly fill in the blanks, all to my detriment." She let her head fall back against the wall. Her helmet clunked when it contacted the rock. She'd never told anyone the whole truth about why she'd come home, not even her best friend. Why? To preserve everyone's high opinion of Dr. Charles Scheffler. Was he a great man? Absolutely. Was he infallible? Absolutely not.

Jake shifted beside her.

"I've idolized my grandfather. From the time I was a kid, he told me these amazing stories of things he'd done and places he'd been and people he'd met and it was all so exciting and exotic and wonderful. He was – and still is – my hero. You're not wrong that he's an incredible man. He is. But he's also got some pretty big flaws that nobody sees."

She wasn't sure why it was all threatening to spill out. Maybe because she hated that Jake had such a low opinion of her for all the wrong reasons. Maybe because it was dark and that made it easier to talk. Maybe because she was tired of having it all bottled up inside. Maybe because she was still angry that she had to uproot her entire life because of Papi's foolishness.

"A few years out of college, I got my dream job in Tucson. I worked my way up to AVP in a private transportation firm. We did a lot of work with high profile clients. Celebrities, politicians, royalty... Very elite, very expensive stuff. I was making stupid money and was this close—" she held her fingers an inch apart "—to my VP promotion when Papi fell and broke his hip. Obviously I took a leave of absence and flew home to take care of him. I came home from the airport and was greeted by a notice tacked on the door."

He shifted toward her, obviously surprised.

"It was the third or fourth notice from the bank. We had forty-eight hours to pay the arrears or vacate. I used the bulk of my savings to pay off that debt. *My* savings. It had to be mine because Papi had nothing. His checking account was in the negative, his credit cards were over-limit, and there was no savings. Thankfully he has a pension and Social Security, so at least there's some income to live on."

"I had no idea."

She ignored that. "He had some complications from surgery and had to have a second surgery, and then he went to a rehab facility. He had to outstay his insurance, so more of my savings went to pay for that."

"Allie... I—"

"Yes, I get impatient when he demands yet another trip to the museum after I've worked ten hours. Yes, I get angry when he implies *he's* doing *me* a favor by not charging me rent, after I spent more to save his house than I would have spent in rent for two years if not more. Yes, I get frustrated when he says I'm controlling because it's somehow my fault when his debit card gets declined. And yes, you better believe I get upset when I find out he's trying to go back in debt to make a donation with money he doesn't have just so he looks good. All while I get to look like the villain who's taking advantage of this poor, brilliant man. Love that part. It's super fun to make a horribly mortifying phone call to intercept a check and then I get to listen to my fake husband get all judgmental and righteous. SO fun."

"I'm sorry. I had no idea."

"I reject your apology."

"What?"

"You heard me. I reject your crappy apology. You've now spent way more time with me than you ever spent with my grandfather, but he's the one you give the benefit of the doubt to. You know I'm here for him. You know I'm giving up a whole month of my life for *his* dream, Jake. But you're still so anxious to believe I'm the bad guy." She jumped to her feet and jerked her pack open to pull out her bundles of rope.

"Allie."

"I don't want to talk to you any more right now. I'm going to work on the anchors. Why don't you keep digging or something?" She brushed her hands down the front of her pants and prepared to get back to work. Maybe he could spend the quiet time figuring out how to apologize for real.

After a long moment, he simply said, "Okay."

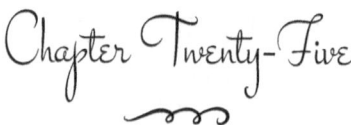

Chapter Twenty-Five

JAKE LISTENED to the metallic clank of Allie's hammer against the... chisel? Bit? Whatever it was, as he half-heartedly scraped his shovel around inside the hole.

It seemed easier to dig now, as if the thunder or earthquake or explosion had shaken the ground loose. Maybe it had. It kind of made sense.

The clanging stopped, so he sat back to see what she was doing. She made some fancy maneuver with her rope, making complicated knots and yanking to make sure they were secure.

"How can I help?" he asked. He wouldn't have been surprised if she completely ignored him.

"Um, I might need a little boost in a minute." She reached up and threaded the rope through a metal loop in the rock and tugged. "I'm basically going to hang from this anchor while I make the next one."

"Is that safe?"

"A fall from here," she tapped the anchor, "doesn't bother

me. It's when I get up there," she pointed upward, "that I'll start to worry."

He stood awkwardly beside her, watching her hands deftly whip the rope into different knots that probably served different purposes, but it was beyond him. He wanted to apologize. Again. But he wasn't sure she wanted to hear it. Again.

He felt bad because she was right. He'd spent more time with her than Charlie by now, and in a much more intimate situation. He'd witnessed her character as she interacted with the team, with the Hausers, and with him. But he still cast her as the villain when it came to Charlie. With no evidence. Or at least very little evidence. Which he could have been misinterpreting. He recognized that he was assigning motives to her that belonged to Lucinda, and that wasn't fair.

Allie made a sort of harness around her waist. "Can you hand me one of the big carabiners?"

Jake sorted through his pack and picked the largest of the clips. "This one?"

"Thanks." She clipped it to her harness and looked upward. Her light glinted off the metal anchor. "Okay. The goal is to boost me up to there. I'll clip onto the anchor and then I should be secure to get the next one drilled. From there, I'll need you to spot me."

"Does that mean holding the rope? Like at a rock climbing wall?"

"Exactly."

"Got it." He bent down and laced his fingers together so she could use his hands as a step.

"Ready?"

"Ready when you are." He pressed his palms against her

shoe and lifted until he was standing straight with his back against the wall.

"You okay?"

"I'm good." He could bench press at least twice her body weight, but the position was awkward and not as straightforward as lifting a bar.

"I can't quite reach."

"Step on my shoulder."

"Jake..."

"I'm serious. Step onto my shoulder."

She carefully placed the toes of her shoe on his shoulder and hoisted herself upward. "I don't want to kick you in the face."

"I bet you do."

She laughed at that.

He was glad he'd made her laugh again, even if it was at the idea of kicking him in the face.

The metallic clip snapped and her feet left his shoulder. "All good."

"Are you sure that's secure?"

"Yup."

He watched her maneuver the tools from her belt and begin work on the next anchor.

After a few minutes, she said, "I'm good. You can go back to digging."

He poked at the hole, digging out a few tablespoonfuls of gravel and dirt at a time and adding them to the pile they'd accumulated. He didn't know how much time passed before the metallic clinking stopped and Allie called down to him, "Jake? You ready?"

He jumped to his feet, ready to assist her however he could. "I'm ready."

"I need you to keep me up here. It's going to get really heavy, really fast." She tossed the end of the rope down and instructed him to put the giant loop over his head and down to his waist, then pull the end to tighten it.

"I'll try to catch you if I have to. Just remember that you tied the knot. I had nothing to do with it."

She chuckled. "Trust me, I won't forget. Are you ready? I'm going to unclip and then it's all on you."

"Got it." He braced himself, gripping the rope tightly and leaning back so he could counterbalance her weight. A few seconds later, he heard the click and felt the immediate tension on the rope, but it wasn't as drastic as he'd anticipated. "You good?"

"All good. I need you to pull me up so I can clip to the next anchor."

He carefully placed his foot and moved backwards, slowly hoisting her upwards. "How's this?"

"Perfect. Slow and steady."

He took more steps backwards, careful not to lose his footing on the loose stones, holding the rope taut, until he heard a click and suddenly there was no tension on his line.

"I'm secure."

"Should I—"

"OH!" Her excited word echoed off the walls.

"What? Did you find something?"

"I have two bars!"

Jake stayed still, listening to the rapid electronic clacking as she typed a message.

"I texted William and Delia." She'd barely finished the words when the familiar whoosh sound told Jake she'd gotten an incoming text.

"Is that them? Did they get the message?"

"It's William. Everyone else is accounted for. Hang on, I'm telling him about the light we saw."

His lungs forced out a relieved breath. Not only because everyone else was okay, but because they wouldn't be trapped here for long. He sent up a quick prayer of thanks and listened to the back and forth typing and incoming messages.

"They're going to hike around and figure out where we are from overhead. I'll just hang here until I hear something more from them."

He guessed more than an hour passed while Allie hung suspended a good twelve feet above him. His back and legs ached, so he could only imagine how uncomfortable she must be, but she wasn't complaining.

She gasped as a new little electronic whoosh sounded. "He thinks they're getting close."

Only a few minutes after that, Jake heard a muffled voice from far away.

Allie yelled, "In here! We're in here!"

The voice called again, and Allie responded. They went back and forth a few times, with the outside voice getting closer each time.

Finally, it was close enough for Jake to make out the words.

"Allie?"

"William!"

"Can you hear me okay?"

"Yes!"

"The explosion must have uprooted a tree. That's where we found the hole."

"Can we climb out?"

"Negative. The roots are tangled and right now the opening is barely the size of a cantaloupe."

"What do we do? The passage is completely blocked."

Jake didn't want to think too hard about what situation they'd be in if the tree hadn't fallen.

"Now that we have your exact location, Shane's going to check some things and make sure the ground is stable. Then we'll get some chainsaws and get these roots cut. That's the good news."

"What's the bad news?"

Jake held his breath, waiting for the answer.

"Uh, it looks like you're going to be in there for the night. Shane's testing ground thickness and all that to make sure we get you out safely. We don't want anything to cave in. The bad part is that it's going to take a few hours and by then it'll be too dark to start cutting the roots."

"Okay."

"How's your phone battery?"

"I'm at forty percent."

"Keep it off and only use it to text me if you need something, okay? We're heading back to basecamp to get Shane's equipment. I'm not sure if I can send anything down this hole, but if there's something you really need, I'll try."

"I think we're good. We've got some granola bars and water."

"Heck of a honeymoon, huh?"

Jake startled at the reminder that they were supposed to be married. Some husband he turned out to be.

Allie said, "I'm coming down."

He immediately got into position, holding the rope taut so he could absorb her weight when she unclipped from the anchor. "I'm ready," he said.

"Three... two... one."

He braced and slowly moved forward, letting her ease down the wall. As soon as her feet touched the ground, she cried out and nearly fell.

Jake grabbed her around the waist. "What happened?"

She gripped his arm, leaning heavily against him. "Must have been up there too long. My legs feel like jelly."

He eased her to sitting and helped remove her rope harness.

She grimaced and clenched her hands into fists.

"Allie?"

"It's fine," she managed through gritted teeth. "Pins and needles."

"Oh." He moved back, careful not to touch her legs. It was one of the worst feelings ever to have your leg fall asleep, and then when the feeling came back... ouch. And if you bumped something? Double ouch.

After a few minutes, she jiggled her legs and said, "Ugh, I hate it when that happens."

"You okay now?"

"Yeah." She got to her feet and stomped her feet a few times. "Except I have to pee. Bad."

"Oh."

"I was thinking the tunnel would be a good spot. It's kind of out of the way and it's lower so we don't have to worry about... uh..."

"Drainage?" he offered.

"Drainage," she agreed.

"Is it stable?"

"I guess we'll see." She walked over and mumbled, "Please

don't let me get crushed to death while I'm peeing."

Jake huddled, so subtly, at the farthest end of the cave, which wasn't nearly far enough away, suddenly fascinated with the blank expanse of solid rock in front of his face, so close his light only left a circle the size of a softball in his view.

"Can you maybe hum or something?"

For the life of him, he couldn't think of a single tune to hum, so instead he started belting out, "Row, row, row your boat, gently down the stream! Merrily merrily merrily merrily, life is but a dream!"

He sang the lines three times before Allie laughed behind him. "Thanks, I'm done."

His bladder demanded relief, too. "My turn."

Allie took his spot along the wall and laughingly sang the same song until he was done.

"Are you hungry?" he asked.

"Yeah."

"I'm confident we'll either be rescued tomorrow, or they'll make a big enough hole to send us food, so I'm going to eat my lunch."

Allie nodded. "I have two mixed berry bars, so we can save them for breakfast."

They both got their lunch boxes out of their packs and settled against the wall, sitting beside each other.

"What did you call this thing?" He tapped the sectioned container that held his food.

"A bento box," she said, popping the lid off hers. "It's very practical."

"It's very fancy," he said, eyeing the little crustless squares his ham sandwich had been cut into in order to fit neatly into one of the sections. The other sections held baby carrots, crackers, cheese cubes, and trail mix. "I'm more of a 'shove a sandwich into a plastic baggie and throw it in a paper sack with a bag of chips' kind of guy."

"Yes, but then you'd be eating a smashed sandwich and chip crumbs." She nudged his arm. "Admit it. You like the bento box."

"Fine. I like the bougie bento box." He extended his pinkies as he ate his sandwich. "All I'm missing is some Grey Poupon."

Allie laughed and covered her mouth with her hand. "That would be the *ultimate* in bougieness."

They finished their meal in silence. Jake ate slowly, working out the words he wanted to say. Hopefully an apology was still an apology if it was the tenth one.

Chapter Twenty-Six

ALLIE SNAPPED the lid onto her bento box and slipped it into her pack.

"How'd you go from almost-VP to working at Ralph's?" Jake asked.

She settled back against the wall. "I'm sure this will only reinforce your opinion that I have no patience for my grandfather, but in all honesty, I was going stir-crazy at the house. I was at Ralph's getting something, I don't even remember what, and Ralph and I got to talking. He was putting up a help wanted sign, and I said I needed something temporary and part time, and he hired me on the spot. Hired me back, technically. I worked there all through high school and my college breaks."

"Is it good? I mean, do you miss your other job?"

"Depends on the day," she answered honestly. Comparing the jobs was like comparing apples and airplanes. "What about you? How'd you end up being a security guard?"

"It's a long story, but here goes. I started out as a mall cop because I couldn't pass the exam to be a state police officer, which was my original dream. It was all very routine until one Black Friday. This super organized team dressed as Santa's helpers came in to rob the mall. We had to get all the civilians out, which was super hard. They took some hostages, including my daughter, the woman who ran the wig kiosk, and some filler hostages. My trainee and I tried to stop the criminals, but in a shocking turn of events, he was one of the masterminds of the operation! I basically had to ride my trusty Segway all over the mall to find codes, stop the bad guys, and rescue the hostages. My high school bully was in charge of the SWAT team trying to help us, and in a second shocking turn of events, *he* was working with my trainee."

Allie laughed, impressed with how he recapped the movie with a straight face. "Wow, let me guess. You solved the crime, saved the hostages, and the next day you were offered a position with the state police, but you turned it down, and you and the wig lady got married at the mall and rode a Segway off into the sunset."

"Whoa! It's like you were there the whole time."

"You had me for a minute. And fine, I apologize for calling you Paul Blart, mall cop."

"I've been called worse. Besides, Paul Blart is awesome."

"One of my favorite movies, actually."

"Mine, too."

She put her finger on her chin. "I wonder if Selena is the villain of our story."

Jake's tone turned serious. "Do you think she knows how to handle explosives?"

She thought about it. "It wouldn't surprise me. Don't they use a lot of explosives in underwater stuff? I feel like I saw them blowing stuff up underwater in some documentary."

They lapsed into a comfortable silence for a while.

Jake said, "My real story is a lot more boring. I wasn't sure what I wanted to do after college, a security guard position was open, I got hired for it, and that was that. I was promoted to Head of Security a couple years ago, which was nice. It's a solid job with good pay and great benefits, and I like it, so here we are."

"I bet you never thought it would lead to being trapped in a cave."

"I'm sure it falls under that nebulous 'other duties as assigned' part of the job description."

"Soooooo many things go under that heading."

"I really am sorry, Allie," he abruptly said.

She wasn't sure how to respond, so she just waited.

After a long moment, he said, "After my grandmother died, my grandfather was in bad shape. He had to move in with me, because my parents had already downsized and had no room at all, and my sister was on bedrest expecting her second baby. My fiancée at the time, Lucinda, started out being helpful but it all went downhill fast." The last word held a lot of venom. "There wasn't one big thing I can point to. It was a million tiny things that I didn't notice until there was too much to ignore, you know? Like if she ordered pizza, she'd 'forget' that he only wanted plain cheese. She'd get annoyed and tell him to pick the toppings off."

"I hate picking mushrooms off. You can never get them all."

"Exactly. Then she started researching care homes and suggesting we find one before the wedding."

Allie thought it was a fair conversation to have, but she didn't say it out loud.

"I can't even tell you some of the stuff because it's so petty. Like she quit buying the brand of toilet paper he liked for his bathroom. She didn't live with us, so I'd sound like an ingrate if I said anything that was even close to a complaint because she was helping me out by stopping at the store to grab a few things. Then I found out she was deliberately signing out of the streaming services because he couldn't figure out how to log back in, so he'd be home by himself all day and not able to watch television. She said it was for his own good because he needed to be active and not watch tv all day."

"Yikes." Encouraging activity? Sure. Blocking the tv? Yikes.

"Anyway, fast forward almost a year. It was three months before the wedding, and my grandfather went downhill fast. Like, he took the express train downhill. He ended up on hospice." Jake swallowed hard. "Lucinda called me on her way over and I asked her to stop at Pennywig's ice cream shop and get him some of their mint chocolate chip ice cream. It's all he wanted. Mint chocolate chip ice cream from Penny-wig's. He hadn't eaten a single thing for days."

Allie's light bobbed as she nodded.

"Lucinda showed up with a little carton of sugar free, low fat mint sorbet crap from the grocery store and said she didn't get the ice cream because it wasn't healthy." He shook his head, sending his beam of light back and forth. "I threw her out, threw the carton in the trash, and I got in my truck and I drove to Pennywig's myself. I... I didn't know if he'd still be alive when I got back, that's how close to the end he was, but I *had* to get him mint chocolate chip ice cream from Penny-wig's. I had to." His voice cracked.

She reached over and slipped her hand into his.

"I got back and when I tell you he gave me the biggest smile... He ate every bite of that mint chocolate chip ice cream and he told me about the first date he had with my grandmother. It was back in the fifties when Pennywig's was an apothecary with a soda fountain. Every year on their anniversary, they went to Pennywig's for mint chocolate chip ice cream. The funniest part? My grandfather hated mint chocolate chip ice cream. He only pretended to like it on that first date because it was her favorite and he wanted to impress her." He chuckled a little. "He said he only ate it with her on their anniversary and told her it was because it was so special he didn't want to have it too often."

Allie blinked back tears.

"I hadn't seen him look so happy since before she passed. I took the empty bowl out and put it in the sink and by the time I got back to his room, he was gone."

"I'm so sorry," she whispered. It suddenly made so much sense why he'd formed such a bond with her grandfather.

"I called Lucinda, and she was furious I told her to leave. I will never forget what she said. Her exact words were, 'It didn't make sense to spend fifteen dollars on ice cream then, did it?'"

Allie gasped.

"My sister came straight over. After the coroner left and the funeral home came to get him, we couldn't sleep, so we boxed up Lucinda's stuff and took it to her house and left it on the front porch. Jessie may or may not have also gotten dog poop out of Lucinda's neighbor's yard and smeared it on the handles and windshield wipers of her car. Details are a little hazy."

"If she did such a thing, and I'm not convinced she did, I would say it's completely justifiable."

"Anyway, I hope that explains a little bit why I've been so quick to defend Charlie. It doesn't excuse me by any means, and I'm sorry for painting you with the same brush. I hope you can see where I've been coming from, I hope you believe I know how wrong I've been, and I hope you can forgive me."

Allie wiped her nose. "Thank you for sharing that with me. I'm sorry you had a partner like that, and it does give me a better understanding of your perspective. Part of an apology, though, is not doing it again. If you call out my impatience with Papi, that's one thing. Assigning bad motives to me is another. I *am* controlling in some ways, because I have to be. He *cannot* send ten-thousand-dollar donations to the museum. But Jake, I hope you understand that I would move heaven and earth to get that man his mint chocolate chip ice cream."

Jake reached over and squeezed her hand. "I know you would. I promise I'll be a better temporary husband going forward."

"You've only got about twelve hours to make good on that promise, because after this, I'm tapping out. I'm done with this expedition." She hadn't fully made the decision until those words came out of her mouth, but it was true. One time of being trapped was quite enough, thank you very much.

"I'm with you. I didn't sign up for explosives."

"We should get some sleep." Allie dug around in her bag for the tiny compressed space blanket. It crinkled loudly as she unfolded it. She put her pack under her head and shifted uncomfortably on the ground. "You know how I said the mattress at basecamp was terribly uncomfortable?"

"Yeah?"

"I take it back."

Jake laughed softly as he got himself settled on the hard ground. "What I wouldn't give for a Ralph's branded sleeping bag right about now."

She giggled. "Or a Ralph's air mattress."

"Yeeessssss, that would be even better." He rustled around some more. "I wonder if Selena blew the other cave up with Ralph's C4."

Allie laughed loud at that. "I could totally see Ralph adding explosives to the doomsday prepper section of the store, and yes, it would one hundred percent be branded."

They both laughed and suggested more and more ridiculous branded items Ralph could carry until yawns became more frequent than words.

They turned their headlamps off and were pitched into total blackness.

After a few long minutes, Allie said, "Hey, temporary husband, this situation is kind of freaking me out a little bit. Do you mind if we maybe get a little closer?"

He scooched over and put an arm around her. "Good?"

"Yeah. Thanks."

Despite the creepy pitch blackness, unnerving silence, and being trapped, they both eventually drifted to sleep.

Chapter Twenty-Seven

JAKE WOKE up stiff and sore. He hadn't slept on the ground for a lot of years, and even then it had been *ground*, not solid rock. Hopefully it wasn't something he'd ever have to do again. His headlamp made even less of a dent in the blackness that usual, so he rooted in his pack for the replacement batteries and the handheld flashlight.

He tried to be quiet in case Allie was still asleep, but the package crinkled loudly in the small space and he froze.

She lay still, her breathing deep and even, so he changed the batteries and put his helmet back on. Since there was nothing else to do, he pulled on his gloves and pulled some more loose dirt out of the hole.

Something smooth caught his attention and he dug his fingers into the dirt with more enthusiasm.

He wasn't sure how long he'd been scraping at the ground when Allie quietly said, "Did you find something?"

"I'm not sure. I think it's another piece of pottery, but it's big."

"Awesome."

The metallic crinkling behind him suggested she was folding the blankets.

"I had to change the batteries in my headlamp," he said as he dug. "Yours probably need changed, too, so I put them beside your pack."

"Okay, thanks."

The more he dug, the more he uncovered. "It feels like a bowl. Or a cup or vase or something." He was glad for some excitement to break through the anxious mess they were in.

"Do you want me to take a turn?"

His aching back twinged. "Yes. Please."

They traded places. Allie got on her belly and reached into the hole under the wall while he stretched and did a few jumping jacks.

After a while, she sat up and put her hands on her lower back. "It feels like it's mostly intact. I bet you'll be able to get it this time."

Sure enough, after another ten or fifteen minutes of careful digging with his fingers, the ceramic object was free from the ground. Jake carefully pulled it out of the hole and they examined it together.

"Wow."

It was about ten inches tall, with a rounded base the size of a pineapple that curved into a narrow neck the diameter of a lemon. Three quarters of it was fully intact, but there was a big chunk missing from its side.

"I wonder if there was a handle here that snapped off or something?" Allie wondered.

That speculation was as good as any. "I'll see if I can feel anything else." He gave her the vase and went back to digging. After another hour, he hadn't felt anything except a new stream of air coming from the other side of the crumbling wall. He assumed the explosion had created more instability and holes than he wanted to think about.

"Good morning!" William's voice called from above. "You guys okay?"

"We're good," Allie called back.

"Everything is a go up here. We're going to start sawing the roots and getting this hole big enough to get you guys out. Probably two hours or so, okay?"

"Roger that," Allie yelled upward.

Loud buzzing from the chainsaws echoed around the room. Allie grimaced and put her hands over her ears.

There wasn't much they could do once they packed all their gear, so they sat and waited.

Small clumps of dirt rained down, bouncing off their hard helmets. There was nowhere in the room they could escape the debris.

Allie wrapped the vase in the space blankets and put it in Jake's pack. "I hope it'll be okay."

"It'll be fine." Jake wasn't so sure about himself. "Is now a good time to mention I'm afraid of heights?"

"Uuuuuhhhh." Allie's eyebrows disappeared under her helmet. "Okay, well, bad news, this is the only way out, so you're going to have to suck it up."

"I got that."

"Okay. We'll do it this way. You'll go out first. Then the packs, then me. Easy peasy."

"I don't want to leave you down here. That's not right."

She shook her head. "It's not a matter of chivalry, Jake. If you're afraid, it would be dangerous for you to freeze up if you're down here alone. Dangerous as in life-threatening. I need you to understand me when I say *dangerous*. I have no problem climbing. So we get you out first. I'm way more experienced, so I wouldn't go first even if you had no issues with heights."

It made sense when she put it that way. He pushed aside the panicky thoughts that threatened his peace. He'd be secure. They'd get him out to solid ground. This plan was best for Allie. She was the expert, and he'd gladly bow to her experience. William would be supporting him from above. Allie would support him from below. He could do this. Easy peasy, right? He repeated those things to himself over and over.

The buzzing stopped and William yelled down, "Looking good! We're going to work on enlarging this hole now!"

"Sounds good!" Allie answered. Quietly, she said to Jake, "I need to utilize the pee corner."

Jake immediately started humming 'Row, Row, Row Your Boat' and positioned himself at the far side of the cave.

After a few rounds, Allie said, "All done. Thanks."

Jake figured it was a good time to avail himself of the facilities as well, so he took his turn in the pee alcove. He finished his business and was just zipping his pants when from above came a frantic, "LOOK OUT!"

A split second later, Allie screamed and hit the ground as something crashed against the wall.

Jake's heart thundered in his chest. He leaped over a thick chunk of root and clambered over hunks of rock that had been knocked out of the wall to get to her.

Allie held her leg, her face contorted in pain. Blood streaked across her calf.

Jake shoved the debris out of the way. Pain radiated

through his knees when he slid on the gravel beside her. "Allie? Where are you hurt? Is it your leg?"

"Yes." She managed through gritted teeth.

"Is anything else hurt? Is your head okay?"

"Just my leg," she bit out.

"I got you. It's going to be okay."

"Allie! What happened?" William called in a fearful voice.

"Allie's leg got hit!" Jake yelled back. "Let me grab the first aid kit."

"The vase. Is the vase okay?" Tears choked her words.

He looked over his shoulder. "Both packs are fine. You're bleeding."

"It's fine," she sobbed.

He ignored that and went to dig the first aid kit out of the pack. Thank you, Ralph, for thinking of everything. He kneeled at Allie's side. "It doesn't look too bad," he said, greatly relieved. "A pretty nasty scrape, but it doesn't look deep."

She sucked a sharp breath though her teeth when the antiseptic wipe touched her wound.

"Sorry." He knew it must sting like crazy, but they didn't need any kind of infection. He cleaned her up as fast as he could, then cleaned his hands again to apply the antibiotic cream. He thanked Ralph again for the gauze and first aid tape that allowed him to cover her wound securely.

Allie sniffled and wiped her face.

"You okay?"

She nodded.

William called down, "Rope coming down!"

Allie struggled to stand. "I'll get you—"

"Sorry, boss, change of plans. You're out first."

"But—"

"No discussion. That injury trumps my nerves. I'm fine. I'll help you out, I'll send the packs up, and then the team can put their backs into it and drag my sorry behind out."

She managed a tiny smile that quickly turned to a wince when she tried shifting her weight to her left leg. "Okay."

Jake knew she must be hurting if she agreed to go first. He helped her secure the harness they'd sent down.

"You'll hold this," she said through gritted teeth as she handed him the rope. "You'll be steering."

He pulled her against him and squeezed. "I've got you, Allie." It was his turn to carry their team, and he wouldn't let her down, no matter what.

She hugged him back and nodded. "Are you sure you'll be okay?"

He held her tight. "I won't freeze up and panic. I promise." He let go and took a step backward. "Ready?"

She positioned herself at the wall and reached for the first anchor. "Ready."

"Ready!" Jake yelled. "Allie's coming first!"

"Roger that!"

The rope slowly became taut.

Allie used her arms and her good leg to leverage herself upward. The process was slow and steady until she disappeared out of view.

"Rope's coming down!"

Jake ducked his head and waited until the rope unraveled beside him. He tied his pack, containing the vase and yelled up, "First pack secure and ready to go!"

The rope jerked and the pack slid slowly up the wall.

Jake turned and took a last look around the room. It felt silly, but on a whim, he bent down to peek inside the hole, to say goodbye, maybe. The airflow was stronger, now that a huge chunk of the wall had crumbled. He almost turned away, but a shadow grabbed his attention.

Only... it wasn't a shadow.

Jake scrambled onto the ground and shimmied his shoulders into the hole, praying he wouldn't get stuck. He reached out and touched the shadow. Beside it lay a pile of crumbled rock.

He pulled it gently, not wanting to damage it, but also not wanting to be wedged under a crumbling wall. It came loose easily.

He eased himself backwards out of the hole and the air whooshed from his lungs. In his hands was a book. A leather-bound book. With the corner missing from the cover.

"Rope's coming down!"

The words were background noise against the blood pounding in his head.

He scrambled to his feet and put the book in Allie's pack. He secured it to the rope and tried to speak, but nothing came out. He cleared his throat and tried again. "Pack secure, ready to go!"

He watched the pack ascend up the rock wall and disappear over the corner.

Allie's voice came down to him. "Jake, you've got this. Double check your harness. Use your toes like you're walking up the wall and use your hands like I showed you. Be Spiderman."

"You got it, Lois Lane."

"She's with Superman."

"Oh. Yeah." Too bad he couldn't fly like Superman and get himself out of this hole.

A moment later, William called, "Rope's coming down."

Jake stepped aside and grabbed the rope once it was down. He swallowed hard and ignored the fact that his legs shook when he stepped into the harness.

"Tighten the buckles," Allie said.

There were three buckles. One around each leg, one around his waist. He secured all three and double checked the clips that held his harness to the giant knotted rope. Yeah, sure. This was great. No problem. What could possibly go wrong?

"You ready?" William's voice was calm. Reassuring.

"Ready as I'll ever be, I guess," was his definitely not calm reply.

"Breathe, Jake," Allie said. "Everything's secure up here. All you have to do is stay calm."

"Easy peasy."

"Easy peasy," she answered back.

"Pulling now," William said.

The rope grew taut. Jake felt like a ragdoll. He gripped the rope with one hand and held the other in front of his face so he didn't end up kissing the wall.

He inched upward, past Allie's first anchor, then the second. He focused on the third anchor when the rope jerked and he dropped a good six inches. The highest pitched scream he'd ever heard come from his own mouth.

"It's okay! You're secure, I promise," Allie called down to him.

His breathing shallowed and he felt the panic rising in his gut. "Tell me about Ralph's Outsiders Club!"

"Ralph has these great punch cards. They're mostly for the kids because the adult loyalty cards are kept in the system under the customer's phone number. Some of the adults still like the cards, but theirs are plain. The kids get really cool colored ones."

He breathed, listening to Allie's voice as he was pulled higher, inch by inch. His neck muscles ached from the sheer force of fighting the urge to look down.

The third anchor was at his waist. His knees. His ankles. In his mind's eye, he could see the floor dropping away, creating a gaping chasm into the depths of forever.

Don't look down. Don't look down. Don't look down.

He felt along the wall, knowing it was going to angle away from him any time.

"Even if they sit on the bench, they get a punch on their card."

The harness cut into the crease in his legs, harder with every inch he was raised. This was not a fun experience for his manly bits.

"Most of the time we give double punches with a little wink like they're getting something extra. The kids love that."

The wall angled sharply and there was light reflecting off the top of the rock. He found himself in a new tunnel, probably ten feet long, that rose steeply to meet the hole of light. In trying to find a place for his fingers to grab, he glanced downward and saw nothing but a yawning black pool of inky nothingness. He swore it reached for him. He fought every part of himself that was trying to launch into panic mode. He'd promised Allie he'd get out, and that's what he was going to do, no matter how scary this was.

His legs scraped against the rock as he scrambled forward.

"We'll do lots of yard games for the raffle prizes over the summer. The giant tic tac toe is always a big hit."

He grunted and lurched forward, crawling toward the light.

He surged past the rope, scurrying forward and clawing out of the hole with a screechy grunt like a deranged groundhog.

William and Shane grabbed him by the armpits and hauled him up out of the ground. His weak knees gave out.

"Are you hurt?" Allie asked, concerned.

He shook his head, reaching up to shove the helmet off. "Just... need a... minute..."

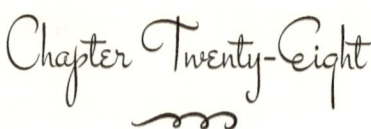

Chapter Twenty-Eight

THE PAIN in Allie's leg faded to the background as she tried to ascertain whether Jake was injured.

He rolled over to his hands and knees and dry heaved a few times.

She gave him a minute to collect himself, then put her hand on his back and rubbed soothing circles. "You good?"

He shuddered. "I was trying not to look down, but when the rock went like this," he held his hand at an angle, "I was trying to find a spot I could hold onto and I looked—"

"Got it. It's okay." She leaned closer and put her chin on his arm. "You did great, Jake. I'm so proud of you."

He tilted his head so his forehead rested on hers. "How's your leg?"

"'Tis but a scratch."

Shane walked over and said, "If you guys are okay to head out, we'll get you back to basecamp."

"Was it an explosion? How? Was anyone hurt?"

Allie was glad Jake asked again. William had already said

no one was hurt, but it's possible he didn't tell them the whole truth just to keep them from panicking.

"Yes, it was an explosion, and everyone's fine. We'll fill you in on all the details when we get back."

"Thanks for the rescue."

William's brow furrowed and he looked almost angry. "I'm just thankful you're both okay. At least nothing was hurt except the site itself." He turned a concerned expression to Allie. "Are you able to walk? It's a fair hike from here."

"I'm good, but I'll probably slow you down," she answered.

"Don't worry about that." William waved her concern away. "Take your time, and if we need to, we can take down some brush and get the four-wheeler back in here."

Allie picked up her backpack and slung it over her shoulder. She startled when Jake grabbed the strap and whispered, "Be very careful with your pack."

She wanted to ask why, because the vase was in his pack, but it was clear he didn't want to say anything in front of the others.

Shane and William each carried a chainsaw and a shovel and led them through the dense brush.

Allie looked around and was suddenly overwhelmed. They were in the middle of the woods, with no discernable landmarks. She put her hand on the trunk of a large tree to steady herself.

"Whoa, take your time. Is it your leg?"

She shook her head, unable to speak.

William and Shane set their equipment down and came over. "We'll start cutting some brush so you don't have to walk.

She shook her head again. As soon as she opened her

mouth to calmly tell them it wasn't necessary, that it wasn't her leg that was bothering her, she burst into tears and gestured to the woods around them. "I can't believe you found us. How did you know which way to go? I... I... We... We were so far away and, and, and—" A sob cut off her words.

"Hey, hey, hey," Jake murmured softly as he pulled her against him. "It's okay. We're safe now. It's okay."

While they were down in the cave, she hadn't realized how remote they really were, how far away from the entrance. How much danger they had actually been in. Even if they had managed by some miracle to climb out through the tangle of roots, they would have been lost on the mountainside. Especially if the others had been trapped as well.

Her chest seized with the realization of how easily they could have died, and how horribly.

"Allie, stop." Jake bent to look her directly in the eye. One hand stroked her hair. "Don't be chasing what if scenarios. We're out, we're on our way back to basecamp. We're safe now."

She nodded and sniffled.

William and Shane both patted her back.

"I look like an idiot," she mumbled.

"Not to us," William said. "Better to freak out after the fact and keep a level head during the crisis."

Shane added, "It's all that adrenaline letdown. Totally natural."

She wiped her eyes and nodded against Jake's chest. He gave her a squeeze and let go.

"Okay, I'm ready."

William and Shane retrieved their equipment and set off again.

It took a good forty minutes to hike back to the original entrance of the caves. Jake carefully secured their packs to the back of the ATV.

When William and Shane were done attaching their equipment, William pointed off into the woods. "Tomorrow I'd like to take you up there. There's something you need to see, but today we'll get you cleaned up, fed, and caught up to speed."

"What's up there?"

"What's left of Cave Two," he said somberly.

Allie had no desire to go back underground. But... William had pointed through the woods. Did the explosion open up the cave? What the heck happened here?

Back at basecamp, Piper, Bess, Kylie, and Delia rushed over and enveloped Allie into a massive hug. Piper looked like she had been crying. "We were so worried."

Aaron and Toby joined the guys and gave Jake those handshake-one-armed-half-hugs that men do.

"We weren't sure when you'd be back, so we made some sandwiches and cold food, but I can make you some soup or I think we have chicken if you want something hot," Piper offered.

"Thanks. I think I want a shower first," Allie said. "And sandwiches are perfect for me. Thank you so much."

Jake nodded. "Ditto."

A man she hadn't noticed in the commotion stepped forward and shook her hand. "Nathan Hauser. My mother insisted I look you over." He gestured to a black doctor's bag. "I'm a doctor. I normally don't make house calls, but what my mother wants, she gets," he said with an affectionate smile.

They trudged upstairs and Jake helped her take the gauze off her leg.

Nathan checked their vitals, made them follow a penlight with their eyes, and asked a few questions about how they were feeling. He examined Allie's leg, but agreed with her that it was nothing deeper than a nasty scrape, and would likely look much better after a shower.

It definitely did. He applied a fresh dressing and declared them both no worse for the wear.

"Don't worry," he said with a laugh. "I'm billing my mother for the house call." He winked and left them alone.

Jake turned his back so she could change out of the robe.

She dressed quickly, but took care to pull her yoga pants on without disturbing the gauze. "I'm decent."

He sat beside her on the bed. "In your pack—"

Her phone vibrated and she held it up. "William says Estelle just got here and wants to see us immediately."

He let out a long sigh that deflated his shoulders.

"Don't worry, go take your shower and change. I'll go down." She stood up and slipped her phone into the pocket of her hoodie. "You bring the vase so we can show it to them together."

"I—" He shrugged. "Okay."

It seemed like he had something to say, but it looked like it could wait. And not to sound terribly selfish, but she was really hungry. "Are you sure?"

"Yeah. Go down and see Estelle. And eat. Don't wait for me."

She appreciated his green light. Now she wouldn't feel guilty about inhaling a plateful of food before he even made it into the shower.

As it turned out, that wasn't too far from the truth. The rest of the team had already laid out a spread on the table. All she had to do was reach out and fill her plate.

"You guys are amazing. Thank you so much," she said, grabbing the first sandwich wedge and taking a big bite.

Estelle sat across from her. "How are you feeling? Did Nathan take check you over?"

"He did. I've got a nasty scrape on my leg, but it'll be fine with some ointment and gauze. No big deal. Other than that, we've got a handful of bumps and bruises typical for rock climbing, but we're fine. Just glad to be aboveground, and we're dying to know what happened."

Estelle's mouth pressed into a thin line.

Jake bounded down the stairs and joined her at the table. Once he had his plate full, everyone else sat and put lunch on their plates and started eating. Except Delia, who sat between Estelle and William, and began to speak.

"I'm sure you've noticed that Selena and Chip are absent."

Allie's head jerked up. She looked around the table. "Actually, no. I hadn't."

Jake shook his head. "I think we were more worried about getting cleaned up and fed."

"Understandable," Delia said with a warm smile. "Let me start over. Selena and Chip are not here. Actually, let's go back. As you *are* aware, we were hesitant to take on this project, but it seemed like a good opportunity at a good time, and with Rupert's enthusiasm, we moved forward, obviously."

Allie waited to see where the story was going.

"As it turns out, Selena and Chip Anderson are, in fact, brilliant archeologists and explorers for ARASNAC, who did discover a connection to M'yxnih from the *Santa Anna-*

Maria shipwreck." She gestured around the table. "Piper, Aaron, Bess, and Toby were recruited by Selena and Chip for their excellent work that at various points intersected with ARASNAC and their fieldwork. However, as it turns out, the folks who handled this particular mission were *not* Chip and Selena Anderson."

"What?!" Allie and Jake exclaimed at the same time.

"These two were actually Valerie and Rudy Billows, explorers in their own right. However, they are more treasure seekers than archaeologists, and their methods are somewhere south of ethical and in many cases, illegal."

Piper added some context. "None of us had ever met Selena or Chip in person, but since we've all done work with ARASNAC at some point, it wasn't weird for them to reach out to us about this project."

"How did they know about ARASNAC, though?" Allie asked.

Delia answered. "They did legitimate work for ARASNAC on several shipwrecks. They were fired and banned from the organization after they stole some valuable artifacts. The items were returned, so they decided to not press charges."

"Wow," Jake said quietly. His breathy tone reflected Allie's own shock.

"Long story short, apparently Rupert got a call from someone at ARASNAC on an unrelated topic, and when he updated them on our project, the person was extremely confused because Selena and Chip Anderson are currently diving near Rarotonga in the Cook Islands, which are in the South Pacific. Word got back to Valerie and Rudy and they decided to accelerate their plan to find the M'yxnihan treasure. Rudy has experience with explosives, and basically they waited until everyone was outside for lunch and blew a hole in the wall of Cave Two, which they probably expected would give them better access to the treasure they believed to be hidden there."

Shane shook his head angrily. "What they failed to consider was a..." He waved his hands like trying to find the right words. "Basically a tiny fault line running from the back side of Cave Two to the front side of Cave Three, where the tunnel is. Was. When they set off their explosions, they didn't consider that the blast would do anything more than put a hole in the wall. What it actually did was... here. Let me demonstrate." He pressed his palms together. "If this was solid rock, the blast might have done this, at most." He jerked both hands forward half an inch. "Objectively, it should have been a pretty small force. But what it did, because of the natural break, or fault, in the rocks, was this." He held his left hand steady and jerked his right hand forward several inches. "Which of course caused the wall to shift and seal the tunnel, and compromised the integrity of all the ground between Caves Two and Three."

Allie reached over and gripped Jake's hand. "So if the fault line was four or five feet closer to us..."

Shane shook his head. "Four or five *centimeters* would have—"

"But it wasn't," Delia said, cutting off his speculation. "The reality is bad enough, no need to consider even worse scenarios."

"We were all sitting outside, eating lunch, when we heard the first blast," Toby said. "We were going to try to get to

Selena and Chip when they jumped out of the hole, then three more blasts went off."

William picked up the story. "Shane and I went in and saw the tunnel to Cave Three was blocked. So we all headed back to basecamp to get the topography maps. We knew we'd have to hike aboveground to get to you two. At basecamp we realized Chip and Selena had hung back, so when Shane and I got back up here, we found them in Cave Two, digging through rubble to find the treasure."

"Where are they now?" Allie asked.

"On their way to jail," Estelle answered sharply.

William continued. "We hiked up to the topside of Cave Three, and thank goodness that tree uprooted. Made our jobs a lot easier." He rubbed a hand down his face. "While Shane was doing his ground tests to make sure it was stable enough to enlarge the hole under the tree, I hiked around to Cave Two. It was a lot closer to the surface than I expected, and their explosives basically ripped a giant hole in the roof of the cave. You can look down into the cave and see most of it."

"Is there any way to get to it? I mean, would it be possible for my grandfather to come see it?" As quickly as she'd said it, she gasped. "That means it's open to the elements. Oh, no."

Shane nodded somberly. "It's going to degrade quickly. That's why we want to hike up there first thing tomorrow so you can see for yourself and we can make a plan from there. We'll plan to head out around six."

Allie looked over at Estelle. "But... but he's widowed. He's not married."

Estelle smiled sadly. "I'll make an exception."

Piper came around and hugged Allie's shoulders from

behind. "I promise, we'll do our very best to preserve as much as we can."

Allie patted her arm. "Thank you."

"We have our stone saw, so we should be able to cut out some of the drawings and get them to safety. And as far as we know, Cave One is still intact."

It was little comfort. Her heart ached for Papi. Knowing that the caves existed, and now knowing that one torrential downpour would likely irreparably damage everything inside, was a heavy burden to bear.

Jake put an arm around her shoulders and squeezed her close to him.

She hoped against all hope that Papi would at least be able to make the trip to the cave and see that part of it with his own eyes.

Chapter Twenty-Nine

IN THE MORNING, Jake startled awake to Allie shaking his shoulder. "Jake. Jake! Come on, we're running late."

"Huh?" He pried his eyes open and cast a bleary look around the room, orienting himself. "What?"

"We slept through the alarms. It's after eight."

"Aww, man." He whipped his blanket back and hurried to the bathroom to get ready. He felt guilty as they hurried downstairs, but William and Shane were both sitting in the living room area. Neither of them looked concerned.

"Sorry, we set multiple alarms, but I guess we missed them all."

William waved a hand. "No worries. You both needed your sleep. How are you feeling?" he asked, looking at Allie.

"A little sore, but I'm good."

Jake put a hand on her back and gave her a little scratch with his fingertips.

"Grab some breakfast and then we'll get going."

"Where's everyone else?"

"Kylie and Delia are over at the house, and everyone else

is having a meeting with someone from ARASNAC to see if they're willing to step in and work on the project officially. It would make sense, since there is a definite tie between this site and the *Santa Anna-Maria*." William closed the lid of his laptop.

Shane asked Allie, "Have you talked to Dr. Scheffler?"

"Not yet. I wanted to wait and see what we end up with today. I'm hoping I can balance the news of getting trapped after an explosion with some good news about the site."

Jake saw her smile fall and guessed her mind was flipping between the optimistic chance of Charlie seeing a bit of the site with his own eyes and the pessimistic, or rather, realistic, reality that the site was now open to the elements and would not fare well for long.

When they got outside, Delia and Kylie were already at the ATVs, fastening their helmets. Jake secured Allie's camera bag to the rack of their vehicle.

They set off on a different trail than the one they'd used to go to the cave entrance. Jake followed the other two ATVs and made sure to pay attention to the terrain. Although the path was relatively smooth, it took almost an hour to get to their destination.

He parked beside the other two vehicles and waited for Allie to climb off from behind him.

Shane led them over to the brand-new massive gaping hole. It took a minute to get the bearings, but it appeared that it was the side of the cave farthest from the room's entrance that had exploded.

"I'm sure they didn't intend to make a hole this big," William said.

Delia agreed. "I don't think any of us realized the ceiling in that cave was so close to the surface."

Shane raised an eyebrow.

"Okay, any of us aside from Shane," she amended with a laugh.

Jake took in the scene before him. The hole was huge. Probably almost as big as Cave Three. The dirt and rock from the ceiling had caved in and landed in a pile in the room below. Which meant the floor was only seven – *eight?* – feet below where they stood. It surely couldn't be too difficult to come up with a makeshift ramp to get down in there.

Allie walked around the hole, snapping pictures. Jake followed after her, looking down into the cave. "You can see a lot from here."

"Yeah. I know he'd want to see this."

He felt her hesitation. "But?"

"I'm not sure he could handle an hour on a four-wheeler. I'm afraid it would aggravate his hip."

"Not trying to eavesdrop," Kylie said from a few feet away, "but the golf cart does get up in here. It's how William chauffeurs Estelle around the mountain."

"Did I hear my name?" William walked over to join them.

"I was just telling them we could bring Dr. Scheffler here on the golf cart. He wouldn't have to try riding one of the ATVs."

"Yeah, for sure. My grandmother rides all over the mountain in it."

Allie frowned curiously. "I thought golf carts were just for flat lawns."

"Ours is pretty rugged. No flat lawns here," he joked, gesturing to the woods surrounding them.

Jake jerked his chin toward the hole. "Do you think we can make some kind of ramp or makeshift stairs to get down in there?"

"Shane and I were just discussing that. Shane! Come here."

Shane walked around the hole to where they stood.

"What's your plan for accessing the cave?"

"Ladder," he said simply.

Jake knew there was no way Charlie could navigate a ladder. "What can we do that's more... accessible?"

Shane's brow furrowed, then immediately raised in understanding. "Ohhh, for Dr. Scheffler to get down in there." He rubbed his chin.

William produced a thick tape measure and extended it down into the hole. "Seven and a half feet straight down."

Shane nodded. "Okay, let's get back to basecamp and make a plan."

When they got back to basecamp, William said, "You might as well go home to see Dr. Scheffler. We'll figure out the logistics and get all the supplies together. The forecast looks good for the rest of the week, so we'll get the access built tomorrow, and tentatively plan on Dr. Scheffler coming out first thing Friday?"

Jake said, "I can help with that."

"Sure. I'll text you."

A little while later, he was opening the truck door for Allie. She slung her backpack into the back seat and he winced. "Be careful with that."

Her eyes widened. "We never told them about the vase."

"Get in." He hurried around the truck and ignored her curious stare until they were on the main road. "We can bring the vase on Friday. Along with the other thing I found."

"The shard? I left it there."

He shook his head and pulled over into the empty parking lot of a small church.

"What are you doing?"

He turned in his seat, putting his arm up on the back of the seat so he could lean toward her. "I found something else."

"What? When? How?"

"The piece of wood that came through the ceiling and hit you?"

"Yeah?"

"It knocked a chunk out of the wall right above the hole we'd been working on. After you got out and they pulled the first pack out, I—" He felt his face heat with embarrassment. "I got down to kind of say goodbye. Weird, I know. But then I felt air coming through and I saw a shadow, only it wasn't a shadow. I reached into the hole and I guess everything got knocked loose because it was right there."

"WHAT?! What was there?"

"The book, Allie. I found the book. It's a leather book with a missing corner. I put it in your pack and I've been trying to find a time to tell you, but it's been crazy since then and this is the first we've been alone except for crashing into bed last night and to be honest I was so exhausted I forgot. I was going to tell you this morning, but then we both over-slept. But yeah. I found the book. It's in your backpack."

She stared at him, slack jawed. Her hand slowly rose and covered her mouth. "The book," she whispered. "There's really a book?"

"Apparently so."

"And it's here? Like, right here?" She pointed toward the back seat.

"Yes."

"JAKE!" She reached over and grabbed his forearm. Her fingertips dug into him. "It's... Are you joking? Are you just messing with me?"

"No."

"Ohmygosh, we never showed them the vase. This is bad, isn't it? We're hiding evidence."

He chuckled. "Allie, this isn't a criminal investigation. I'm sure we're breaking protocol, but we're taking them to the expert to be examined. He's a legit member of this project."

"Yeah. Okay. All right." She gave a sidelong glance to the back seat. "I probably shouldn't take it out in here, right?"

Jake shrugged one shoulder. "It did okay being yanked out of a hole in a cave."

"But..." She trailed off, not finishing the thought.

He waited a few long moments, then said, "It's your call. We can look at it now, or when we get to your house."

She sighed. "Let's wait."

He pulled back onto the road and drove to Allie's house.

They carefully took both backpacks into the house.

"Papi? Where are you?" Allie called out as they went through the front door. She frowned, then said, "Oh. It's Wednesday. Physical therapy. He should be home around three."

Jake glanced at the clock on the wall. It was two forty-one. Before he could ask, Allie said, "I can't wait any longer."

He followed her to the kitchen table.

She unzipped her pack and her eyes widened. "Wow. I'm afraid to touch it. Hang on, let me get the gloves." She hurried from the kitchen and came back a few minutes later with two pairs of thin white cotton gloves.

The utter concentration on her face held him captive. He couldn't look away from her as she carefully lifted the book out of her backpack, despite the fact that it had been tossed there in haste. "Wow," she breathed, holding the book flat in her palms.

The book looked to be roughly six inches wide by about nine inches tall. It was probably two inches thick. The cover was blackened leather. He wondered whether it was originally black, or if it had been brown and darkened over time.

Allie carefully put the book down on the table and gingerly lifted the cover. A significant bunch of pages stuck with the cover, so she stopped and leaned over to peek inside. "I'm afraid of damaging it."

"It's really fragile," he agreed.

"I can see fancy scripty handwriting. I'm guessing it's in Portuguese? Like the slivers of paper we saw in Rupert's office." Her head bobbed this way and that as she tried to get a better look without opening the book any wider. Suddenly, she gasped. "Tesouro! I see it right there." She leaned back and pointed. "Right in the middle of the page, close to the edge."

Jake bent and looked inside the book. There it was, in neat, tight script. "Tesouro. Treasure."

"This *has* to be Fernando de Cabra's journal." Excitedly, she looked around the room. "Over there on the counter. Grab that tablet and pen."

Jake walked over and got the paper.

Allie read off some letters and he copied them down. When she was done, she opened an app on her phone and they were able to translate tesouro to treasure, semana to week, malvado to evil, and porco to pig.

"This week, the pig told us the treasure is evil?" Jake suggested.

Allie laughed. "Last week, the evil pig ate the treasure?"

"That probably makes more sense than a talking pig."

"Although a talking pig would certainly be considered evil."

"When were the witch hunts? I'd bet hearing a pig talk would be considered more evil than the talking pig itself."

"True."

The front door opened. "Hello?" Charlie called.

"We're in the kitchen," Allie answered. "We have a surprise for you."

"This is surprise enough. Why are you home on a Wednesday?" Charlie's voice got closer until he came through the doorway. "What's the—What's that?"

Jake pulled his cotton gloves off and handed them to Charlie, who took them without taking his eyes off the book.

"Bring it to my office," he said, his voice a reverent whisper.

Chapter Thirty

ALLIE FOLLOWED Papi to his office and set the book on the round table where he studied, across the room from his messy desk. It was the one surface in the house that was always – *always* – clutter-free when it wasn't in use. He pulled a lamp and magnifier over and sat. He pulled on the gloves and reached for the book, but his hands hovered without touching it.

She sat beside him, while Jake went around the table and sat on the other side.

Papi put his glasses on and carefully studied the entire binding. "We must take this to Rupert."

"Well, hang on. We've got a lot to tell you." She looked over at Jake. "And one more thing to show you."

Understanding her look, Jake left the room.

"It's been a crazy week. So much has happened." She started with Monday morning, leaving out the part where she and Jake argued over the donation check. "We heard a boom and the ground shook. Jake pulled me away from the tunnel just as the rocks crashed in and sealed it off."

Papi's mouth dropped open.

"I'm okay, obviously. Everyone's okay. There ended up being four booms that turned out to be explosives."

"Explosives! With part of the team underground! Unacceptable!" He pounded his fist on the table.

"I know. Let me go in order or I'll forget part of this."

Jake came back in the room with his pack and took his seat.

Together, they described the events of the past several days.

"So if you feel like you can handle an hourlong ride in a golf cart, you'll be able to at least see down into Cave Two with your own eyes. I know it's not the same as being down there digging yourself, but if you want to, we'll go."

"Of course I want to!" Papi's eyes shone with tears.

Jake said, "Hopefully—"

Allie shook her head at him. She didn't want to mention the remote possibility of William and Shane being able to make some sort of ramp.

"Uh, hopefully the golf cart ride is smooth. We'll take a chair along so you'll be able to sit if you need to, and the ground is pretty even in that spot."

She could tell he'd switched what he'd intended to say, and gave him a grateful smile. "We don't know what was found in the other caves, but we found the shard we showed you last week, the book, and this."

Jake unwrapped the space blanket to reveal the vase.

Papi took it and studied every inch of it, nodding or making an appreciative noise every so often. Finally, he nodded and set the vase on the table. "We need to take these to Rupert. He'll take care of the vase and get the archivist to examine the book."

"Do you think they'll be able to translate it?"

"I'm hopeful. Paper and textiles are a little outside my area of expertise, but it appears to me that the book has been very well preserved. I'm guessing it was compressed between those rocks until the explosions shook it loose, and the dryness of the air was certainly a good thing."

"I couldn't make much out, but I did see the word 'tesouro' in there."

Papi nodded thoughtfully. "Doesn't mean the treasure is there. It could be little more than a personal journal where he references the original treasure Princess K'nih carried with her from M'yxnih."

"Or it *could* say 'I buried the treasure right here.'"

Jake said, "I still think it says the evil pig ate the treasure."

Allie laughed. "It's the most logical assumption." She showed Papi the tablet with Jake's scribbled notes. "We were able to figure out a couple words."

Papi chuckled. "I did not have evil pigs anywhere on the bingo card for this expedition."

She snickered at Papi's comment. He was always trying out new lingo, with varying degrees of success. At least he'd only tried skibidy rizz once and thankfully never again.

It was after six o'clock. "How about we figure on going to the museum tomorrow afternoon?" She knew Papi would want to go first thing in the morning, but her leg hurt and all she wanted was a good night's sleep and waking up whenever her body was ready to.

Surprisingly, he nodded. "You're needing a good night's sleep, I'm sure."

"She definitely does," Jake said.

"I do. But first, I need food."

"Trista stopped so I could get myself a sub on the way home from therapy, and I'm afraid there's not much in the fridge. Why don't you two go get something? I'll call Rupert and let him know we're coming by tomorrow."

Jake stood and inclined his head toward the doorway. "Pizza?"

"Sold." Allie got up and leaned over to kiss Papi on the cheek. "We'll be back in a bit."

Papi said, "Did you take pictures of these?"

"No, I didn't have a chance." She followed Jake out to the truck. "I know what he'll be doing the whole time we're gone."

"No angle unphotographed." He started the truck. "I'm not totally set on pizza. We can get whatever you want."

"Pizza's fine. I'm skirting pretty close to hangry."

"Say no more."

She yawned and stared out the window for the short drive to Harry's Pizza Shack. There were only two other cars in the parking lot, which boded well for getting quick service.

Inside, they took a booth along the back wall and studied the placemat menus.

Allie tapped the menu. "I think I'm getting steak fries."

"That sounds good. I'm getting a combo sub and mozzarella sticks."

The server took their orders and brought their drinks.

Allie sipped her tea and sat back in the booth. "You said you like to read historical nonfiction. Anything in particular?" It felt like all their conversations in the caves had to do with the project itself, and aside from a few moments, they rarely got personal. She kind of wished they had, because now that it was over, she wanted to get to know him better. Funny how that worked.

"Lots of World War II stuff, and biographies of past presidents."

"So modern history, not, like, ancient Greece?"

He shrugged one shoulder. "If I found an interesting book on ancient Greece, I'd read it. A lot of the stuff I run across is really dry and reads like a textbook, so I give up pretty quick."

"You don't read fiction, right?"

"I do, but not nearly as much."

"What else do you do in your free time?" It felt like an interview, where she had a list of getting-to-know-you questions to check off.

"I spend a lot of time with my nieces."

"How old are they?"

"Five and almost two. They're a blast. I wish I had that much energy, though. Jessie has a big back yard with this massive swing set thing Brian roped me into helping him build. It's like a personal amusement park. There's two big fancy slides, monkey bars, a mini climbing wall thing, swings, of course, and a walkway that goes into a clubhouse. It's amazing, really. I would have killed to have one when I was a kid."

"I think I want one now."

"Right?" He leaned back as the server put their food on the table.

When they were alone again, she said, "It's so great that you have such a close relationship with your sister. You're very lucky."

He nodded. "I am. What about you and Anna? Is there a chance you could ever be close?"

She was surprised he'd been paying enough attention to remember she had a half-sister, let alone her name, since she was certain she'd only mentioned it once. "I haven't seen her since she was a baby. Mom brought her around and just when I got attached, she did her middle-of-the-night Houdini act and dumped Anna with her dad." She poked at her fries with her fork. "I was only ten, and even then I knew Anna was better off without our mom in her life. I guess I kind of thought she was better off without me, too, since I'd already messed up my grandparents' lives."

He scowled down at his mozzarella sticks. "*You* didn't mess anything up. Your mother's actions were the problem."

"I know."

"Does your grandfather have a relationship with Anna?"

"Sort of. Her dad's family limited contact pretty strictly, which was understandable, especially when Nancy tried popping in and out of her life like she did mine. Her dad wasn't having it, so Papi and Noni had a hard time developing a close relationship with her. I think they were afraid Nancy's parents would be as unreliable as Nancy and they didn't think it was worth taking a chance with Anna's well-being. They did allow cards and gifts and occasional phone calls, so there was a connection. Papi does still talk to her on the phone occasionally, but I think it's pretty surface-level stuff."

"That's too bad."

Allie dug into her fries and pulled a forkful out. "To be honest, I think we're probably both better off that Nancy did what she did. I don't think she's a bad person. I just don't think she was cut out to be a mother. Not everyone is, so good on her for recognizing it, I guess." She hesitated, looking at her food. "It would be nice to be friends, though. Maybe that's a possibility."

Chapter Thirty-One

JAKE FELT A PANG OF SYMPATHY, even though he was sure Allie wouldn't want it. He couldn't imagine his mother abandoning him or Jessie. He also couldn't imagine calling his mother by her first name, but he supposed Nancy hadn't earned that title with Allie or Anna. Even more, he couldn't imagine Jessie not being a huge part of his life.

And if he was being honest, it was unpleasant to think about Allie not being in his life.

He broke a mozzarella stick in half. The two pieces pulled apart with a long strand of melted cheese stretching between them. There was probably a metaphor in the cheese.

"What about you?" he asked. "You said you like to read thrillers, but what else do you like to do in your free time?"

"Hmm. I like gardening, which is going to be completely messed up this year. Originally I planned to work in the garden on weekends while we're doing this, but I haven't done a single thing except stare out the window and feel bad." She rolled her eyes and laughed.

He chuckled along with her. "My garden has been sad for the past couple of years. I always have these grand plans I sketch out over the winter and then when the weather gets nice, I find too much other stuff to do."

"Yup. Those gutters won't clean themselves."

"A few years ago I needed new gutters, so I splurged and got the ones with a guard. It's like a mesh screen on top so the rainwater goes in, but none of the gunk does."

"That's so smart."

He steered the conversation away from the fascinating topic of gutters. "What do you usually have in your garden?"

"Tomatoes are my big one. I have a whole row of giant canning tomatoes, and then a whole row of cherry tomatoes, which I usually snack on when I'm pulling weeds. Then more of the usual suspects. Lettuce, cucumbers, peppers, cantaloupe, watermelon. Beans. Lots of beans. Potatoes. I think that's it."

"Wow. That's ambitious."

"Well, this year's garden will be more like tomatoes and whatever seeds left over from last year fight their way through the stuff I haven't cleaned up yet."

"Survival of the fittest."

"You know it."

They lapsed into comfortable silence while they ate. It was nice.

Jake dredged the last bit of mozzarella stick across the last of the sauce and popped it in his mouth. "How were your fries?"

She held a napkin to her lips and nodded as she finished her last bite. "Perfect. They hit the spot. How was your sub?"

He gestured to the puddle on his plate. "A little too much oil, but otherwise it was really good." He took the check as the server slid it onto the table.

"How much do I owe you?"

"Don't worry about it. I got it this time." As he said it, he wondered if this would be the last time they spent time together except for occasionally seeing each other at the museum. He didn't like the thought. At all.

"Thanks, temporary husband, I appreciate it."

"No problem, temporary wife." He wasn't ready for their temporary arrangement to come to an end.

He drove them back to Allie's house. In the driveway, she said, "Are you coming in to see what Papi's gotten into?"

"Nah, I'm going to head home and mow my grass so the neighbor has to mow his tomorrow."

"So petty." She laughed as she opened the door.

"Is this it for us?" he asked suddenly.

"What do you mean?" She let go of the handle and the door drifted shut with a small click.

"After Friday. Is that going to be the end? We won't be going back to Hauser Mountain. At least not together, right?"

"No, after Friday, I'm done. If Papi wants to go back, and he probably will, he'll need to arrange it with the Hausers or the museum or something. Maybe I'm being selfish, but I feel like I've gone above and beyond to get him the answers he's been desperately seeking and we got more answers than I ever dreamed possible. Besides, my 'one near-death experience per adventure' quota has been met."

He knew he was risking making tomorrow's trip to the museum and Friday's trip to Cave Two the most awkward day in the history of awkward days, but he said it anyway. "Would you be open to anything else? After Friday?"

Her hair swung as she shook her head. "Not for a long time. After Friday I'm going back to my regular routine and my adventures will be limited to binge-watching *The Amazing Race* or *Survivor*."

"Not with the project, Allie. I mean with us."

"Oh!" Her eyes went huge.

Clearly they'd been having two completely different conversations.

"I thought maybe we could grab dinner every now and then or something."

She tilted her head. "Jake O'Malley, are you going to miss me?" Her tone was teasing.

"Eeeww, no," he joked, then said, "Maybe a little bit." He held his finger and thumb half an inch apart.

"I was going to say I'll miss you this much." She held her thumb and finger an inch apart.

"Whoa, that's twice as much."

"Yeah, but now that I'm thinking about it, it's more like this." She made the space a quarter of an inch, maybe less.

His heart thumped in his chest. "Would that be enough to maybe, I don't know, see me sometime?"

"See you? Are you asking for a date?"

"Sure. I was thinking we could go backwards. Since we're already temporarily married, we can date after that."

"Ooh, like a Benjamin Button scenario. But by that theory, we'd have to be engaged, too. Married, then engaged, then date. And then at some point we meet."

"I guess I didn't think it through all the way. I didn't even shop for an engagement ring."

She held up her left hand and pointed to her silicone band, then wiggled her fingers. "I think a ruby would look great with this. A big, giant, six carat ruby just like all the red treasure we haven't found. Or garnet, or red topaz, or any other expensive red gemstone since we don't actually know what stone the treasure might be."

"Maybe I'll just buy all the red stones and then if we ever find out, we can swap them out."

"I like the way you think. The more the merrier."

He looked down at the gear shift and fixated on a stray crumb that was stuck on the edge of the cupholder. He'd put the idea out there, now he'd let it be for now and maybe broach the topic again on Friday.

"I think that would be nice," Allie said quietly. "After all... this." She waved her hand in a circle, encompassing everything ever. "We can try something normal."

He couldn't contain his grin. "No monthlong excursion to scale a mountain with a pack full of Ralph's branded gear?"

"Absolutely not. I'm adventured out for a while."

"Me, too. How about dinner? And if we decide to go really wild, a movie."

"Whoa, whoa, slow down there, Indiana Jones. Let's not get crazy."

"Sorry, I was getting ahead of myself."

"We can iron out the details tomorrow or Friday?"

"Sounds good."

She opened the door again. "And now I'm going to go listen to Papi talk about his impressions of the book and vase until I can gracefully extricate myself and crash into bed."

"Sounds like a plan. Sleep well."

"I intend to." She hopped out of the truck and waved before she dashed up the sidewalk and into the house.

Later, as Jake crawled into bed, he couldn't stop grinning into the darkness. The conclusion of the project didn't have to mean the end of him and Allie after all.

Chapter Thirty-Two

ALLIE DIDN'T GET to sleep until noon like she'd planned, but ten was good enough. She stretched and reluctantly tossed the covers back. She contemplated curling up again, but her bladder had other plans.

She took her time in the bathroom, carefully removing the gauze from her leg and inspecting the scrape. It was still red, but healing nicely. She showered and took care to pat the scrape dry before deciding that loose yoga pants would be the outfit of the day and since the gauze was mostly to keep the ointment from getting on her pants, she could forego the bandage.

When she finally emerged from her bedroom after eleven, Papi was at the stove, stirring a pot of soup. "Morning, Allie-gator."

"Morning, Papi-dile." She went behind him and peeked over his shoulder to get a look at his homemade vegetable soup, made mostly from their garden bounty and canned last fall. "Smells delicious."

"Rupert said the archivist is actually going to be on-site today, so we'll be able to give her the book."

"That's great. I'm really hoping we'll be able to get some significant stories translated from it. It'd be amazing if it told us exactly where the treasure is."

Papi grinned but shook his head. "It's never that simple."

"Nothing ever is. Do you want me to make some sandwiches?"

"Sure."

She untied the bread bag and got the deli meat and cheese from the fridge. "I was thinking of letting the Hausers know we're going to the museum with some finds, if they'd like to join us."

"That's perfectly fine with me. Rupert said one thirty would be ideal."

Allie texted William and slipped her phone back into her pocket.

Soon after they finished lunch, Jake's truck rumbled in the driveway. Allie let him in and said, "It's easier for Papi to get in and out of my vehicle, so we'll take it."

"Yeah, I figured he might not be able to climb up in the truck."

Before long, they were on their way to the museum. The parking lot was full, so Jake had her drive around to the employee lot and utilize his spot. Once they got inside, he swiped his badge and they rode the elevator to the fourth floor.

"Jake!" Rita beamed at him. "You'll have to talk to Tom. He's had his hands quite full this week."

"What happened?"

"We had to put up the metal barriers around Ella and Levi again."

"Another school group?"

"Good guess, but no." She smirked like he'd never be able to guess the real culprit.

"Teenagers."

"Closer. No, this time it was a grown adult man trying to film a stunt for social media. Said his plan was to ride the T-rex. Tom almost got to use his stun-gun."

"You're kidding."

Allie shook her head. It might sound funny, but if the dinosaur was damaged, the entire exhibit could be closed for repairs. Not cool. She could see Jake's jaw muscle jump as he gritted his teeth, and she was doubly sorry for making light of his job. He was helping protect and preserve history for future generations.

While Rita dramatically described how the police took the man away in handcuffs, Delia and Estelle came through the doorway.

Allie rushed over and whispered, "I didn't mention the possible ramp, just that he could see down in. Don't want to get his hopes up."

Delia winked and matched her volume. "Don't worry, he will definitely be able to get up close and personal with Cave Two."

In her normal voice, Allie addressed Estelle. "I'm sorry I didn't tell you about the things we found until now. We weren't trying to hide anything, but the whole situation with Selena or Valerie or whoever happened so fast. We weren't sure if we should share with the rest of the team around, so here we are."

"Understandable. I'm not thrilled, but I trust you're not keeping anything from us."

"Not at all. We found the vase after the explosions, and Jake pulled the book out of the hole literally minutes before he got out of the cave. Those are the only two things we found. Well, except for the piece of leather and other ceramic shard we found early on."

Rupert's office door opened. "Good afternoon! Come in, come in." He patted Jake's shoulder as he walked past. "I trust Rita filled you in on Ella and Levi's latest adventure."

"Unbelievable. You expect it from an impulsive eight-year-old, but adults should know better."

This time, instead of chairs placed in a semicircle in front of Rupert's desk, he pointed them to the round table in the corner of his office, which had twelve chairs surrounding it.

Jake placed Papi's case on the table and slid it in front of the seat Papi chose.

The case was a well-worn leather briefcase that opened from the top. It had seen many artifacts on many continents.

Everyone took a minute to get situated. Rupert sat beside Papi, then Estelle, then Delia. Allie sat on Papi's other side, with Jake beside her.

Just as Papi opened the case, Rita rapped sharply on the door and opened it. "Dr. Cooper is here," she announced.

Rupert stood. "Oh, yes, yes, please come in. Everyone, this is Dr. Zoe Cooper, our brilliant archivist."

She smiled and waved a hand. "Call me Zoe. And please do not call me 'doctor' because I'm the last person you want trying to save you in a medical crisis." She took a seat on the other side of Jake.

Rupert introduced everyone and briefly described their

role in the current situation. He looked at Zoe. "Your timing is perfect. Charles was just about to show us the artifacts."

"Wonderful."

Papi carefully pulled the vase, wrapped in bubble wrap, from the case. "First, we have this incredible specimen. These markings are strikingly similar to what we encountered in M'yxnih. You can see the striations around the lip here."

Allie's mind wandered as he described, in excruciating detail, each of the markings on the vase and their significance. Her gaze slid around the room, toward the window behind Rupert's desk, but the large manilla envelope under his wire outbox caught her attention. The envelope that held their marriage license. It was in the same spot they'd left it in three weeks earlier.

She wasn't sure how she felt that in a few more days, they'd close this chapter and come back here and shred it. No, she definitely wasn't ready to be married to Jake, but she wasn't prepared to not have him in her life, either.

He'd surprised her by asking if she wanted to go out, which suggested he might be feeling the same way.

A nudge on her arm pulled her attention back to the meeting.

Papi was handing the vase to her.

She took it and looked it over before handing it to Jake.

Once everyone had inspected the vase, Papi pulled in a deep breath and a slow grin spread across his face. "And then we have this." He put on a pair of white cotton gloves and pulled the book out of a nest of acid-free, archival-safe tissue paper.

Zoe and someone else gasped.

"Allie, Jake, why don't you tell us about your discovery?"

Allie looked at Jake. "This was all him."

Jake cleared his throat and gave the short version of pulling the book out of the hole moments before being rescued.

"Fascinating. May I see it?" Zoe asked, pulling on a pair of her own cotton gloves.

"Certainly."

Zoe got up and went over to Papi to retrieve the book, then took her seat again. She carefully examined the outer part of the book, then produced a loupe to magnify it. When she'd looked at every inch, she gingerly opened the book. "Oh, this is remarkably well preserved."

"Do you think you'll be able to translate it?"

She shook her head. "Not me personally. I don't read Portuguese, but our team will certainly be able to."

Allie wanted to ask how long it would take, but she didn't want to seem impatient.

Fortunately, Rupert had other motives for asking. "Are you able to ballpark how long that might take? I'd like to be able to provide ARASNAC with an estimated timeline."

"Obviously it depends on a lot of factors. It could be anywhere from a month to a year. I know that's a massive range, but I really can't be more specific until my team gets a look."

Rupert nodded and wrote something in his notebook.

Allie balked at the wide timeline, but kept quiet. It didn't seem to faze anyone else. Jake reached over and gave her hand a squeeze.

Finally, the meeting adjourned with Estelle issuing a blanket invitation for everyone to come along to the exposed cave the next day.

"I would love to, thank you so much," Zoe said enthusiastically. "I rarely go out in the field, so this will be a nice treat."

Allie side-eyed Jake. He returned her expression, obviously on the same page wondering about Estelle's "no unmarried people" policy, which seemed to have exceptions. She glanced over at Zoe's left hand, which did sport a silver wedding set, so maybe it wasn't contradictory after all. Or maybe it was a loophole because they weren't actually working on the property. She wasn't sure exactly what the parameters were.

Papi's excitement was evident. He talked to Rupert with animated hand gestures and facial expressions.

Allie followed Jake out into the hallway to wait.

"He's really excited about tomorrow, isn't he?"

"Tonight he'll be like a little kid on Christmas Eve, I'm sure."

"And you?"

"Like a parent on Christmas Eve. I can't wait to see his reaction tomorrow, but I'd like to get some sleep tonight," she said with a laugh.

"I think tomorrow will make all of this worthwhile."

"I think so, too."

Chapter Thirty-Three

As it turned out, Jake didn't get much sleep himself and Friday dawned way too soon. He was anxious to see how Charlie reacted to seeing the carvings and drawings firsthand.

He met Allie and Charlie at their house and scrunched his legs into the back seat of Allie's SUV for the trip to Hauser Mountain.

They arrived and found a parking spot in the crowded parking area at basecamp. A group was congregating around the ATVs off to the side.

Jake and Allie walked slowly along with Charlie.

William introduced Charlie to the team members he hadn't met and pointed toward the waiting ATVs. "I'll be your chauffer today. You, Grandmother, and Rupert will ride with me in the golf cart. If you have any discomfort, let me know and we'll take a stretch break, because it's about an hour to get up to the site."

Charlie nodded once and climbed into the back passenger seat of the golf cart beside Rupert, leaving the front for Estelle. Kylie drove a second golf cart with Zoe as a passenger and lawn chairs and a cooler and other miscellany in the back seat.

Jake and Allie took a regular ATV, as did the rest of the pairs – Piper and Aaron, Bess and Toby, and Shane and Delia.

The parade set out into the forest with Shane in the lead.

The path had obviously been trimmed back since Wednesday. Jake went slowly, following the three ATVs in front of them. The golf carts brought up the rear.

The trip was slow but uneventful. The air grew warmer, but it settled in the mid-seventies and the slight cloud cover kept the sun from being a nuisance for the day.

The sudden silence was jarring when the last ATV was turned off and they all gathered at the edge of the clearing.

Allie wrapped her hand around his arm and leaned up toward his ear. "What is that?"

He looked where she was staring and saw something wooden sticking out of the hole. "I'm not sure. I guess we'll find out."

When everyone was on their feet, they gravitated toward the hole. William turned and gestured to the wooden structure. "Lucky for us, there wasn't a lot of depth to contend with, so we were able to get some of the cousins up here yesterday and build a ramp so we can all access the floor."

Charlie was a few yards away, stepping closer to the edge. He stopped and put his hand over his mouth. Jake was sure he was trying not to cry.

"Will you give us a hand?" Shane asked.

"Of course." Jake followed him to the back of the golf cart, where a crate of safety equipment had been strapped.

They worked to hand out hardhats and safety vests. Bundles of rope lined the bottom of the crate, just in case they were needed.

When everyone was outfitted, they formed a haphazard line to walk down the ramp into the cave.

Allie grabbed Jake's arm and squeezed. She said, "I want you to go with Papi. If he trips, I'm not strong enough to prevent a fall."

"Of course." He went over to Charlie and was immediately impressed with the ramp. The cousins William referenced must be involved in construction, because the ramp, while on the steep side, looked solid, and had sturdy handrails on both sides.

"I'm going to walk ahead of you. Grab my back if you need to. We'll go nice and slow."

Charlie must have been anxious to get down in there, because instead of putting up any kind of fuss, he nodded. "Let's go."

Jake braced himself with both handrails and moved forward, slower than necessary, but Charlie stayed steady the whole time and reached the floor safely, which was all that mattered.

"Be careful, the ground's uneven," Jake warned.

Charlie ignored him and went over to the wall. His weathered fingers traced the lines of a beetle carved into the surface of the rock.

"What's with all the beetles?" Jake asked him.

"Could be a million reasons for them," Charlie answered. "Most civilizations I've studied revere all things in nature. Animals, plants, weather, insects, everything. It's no surprise they would choose a particular item from nature to revere above all others. A mascot, if you will." His voice trailed off.

Jake stepped away, giving him a moment alone with the place he never thought he'd see in this lifetime. He watched Charlie over the next few hours on his feet, moving along the wall, closely examining the carvings without ever saying a word.

Before he knew it, it was lunchtime. Jake helped Charlie walk up the ramp while William and Shane set the lawn chairs in a circle. As everyone settled into a seat, Aaron handed out bagged lunches and Toby followed with cold bottles of water for everyone.

As they ate, Jake noticed Charlie kept looking over at the cave. Probably itching to get back down there.

"What do you think?" he asked.

Charlie's face was the happiest he'd ever seen it. "It's beautiful. I'm so thankful to be here."

"It's a shame it happened like this, though," Piper said.

"Indeed."

Bess added, "And it's a shame we'll never know where the treasure is, if it even existed. That would have been fun."

"Oh, there's a treasure," Charlie said confidently. "And I know exactly where it's buried."

Everyone froze, watching him expectantly.

He grinned, deliberately put his trash into his paper bag, and said, "Did we bring a shovel?"

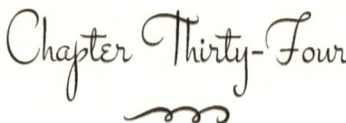

Chapter Thirty-Four

ALLIE HELPED GATHER up the trash and stow it in the empty cooler. When the area was clear, the group headed back down into the hole and followed Papi.

She was familiar with his stance. Professor Charles Scheffler was in the house, and he addressed his captive audience with authority.

"Over here, you can see why Selen—er, Victoria? Whoever. Anyway, you can see why they selected this wall to detonate their explosives. Can anyone tell me why?"

Piper raised a hand. "Because of the X?"

"Precisely. We've all grown accustomed to thinking that X marks the spot. A single carved X in any given location, in isolation, could certainly be an indication of hidden treasure or other significance. A directional marking, perhaps, with each point of the X indicating north, south, east, west. However, I believe in this instance that the X is a decoy. There is precedence for this, where certain civilizations were aware of the European penchant for X marking the spot, so they would place an X in a different location."

"We encountered that in Peru," Bess said. Toby nodded in agreement.

"Very good. If you look around, you'll see where the treasure is buried."

All heads swiveled, looking at the cave walls, but Allie watched Papi. He was in his element, excited that he was here, excited that he was able to educate and impart his knowledge with a willing audience, and excited that there just might be a treasure after all.

"This?" Piper took a few large steps over to the wall and touched a carving. It was four symbols. Two vertical lines about six inches long over a horizontal line of similar length, over a round groove.

"Explain your reasoning," Papi said.

Allie knew Piper was correct by the way Papi beamed and shifted from foot to foot.

"Well, a horizontal line can mean something is being concealed under something, right?"

"Yes! Well done!"

Aaron said, "So the dot symbolizes the treasure and the line means it's under here."

"Not quite," Papi explained as he carefully walked over to the spot. "But close." He touched the circle. "This would be the treasure." He moved his finger up to touch the horizontal lines. "This would mean it's under something. And this," he moved his finger up and tapped the vertical lines, "symbolizes opposite, or mirrored. Basically, 'Look over there' instead of here." He pointed straight across the cave. "Dollars to doughnuts our treasure is buried over there."

Shane and Delia exchanged a look, and Shane excitedly said, "That's exactly where we detected a small void."

Papi shrugged one shoulder, unsurprised.

Even though no instructions were given, there was a flurry of activity as shovels and brushes and bodies moved around the area.

Almost an hour later, Allie caught Papi wincing as he leaned heavily on his cane. She motioned to Jake. They went up to grab chairs and bottles of water for Papi, Estelle, and Rupert.

"How's your hip?"

He waved her concern away. "I'm fine."

The excitement on his face both concerned her and made her happy. She loved seeing him so excited, but she was afraid his disappointment would be crushing if there was nothing here. "Papi, no matter what—"

"THERE'S SOMETHING HERE!"

He sat forward in his chair, any aches or pains forgotten.

Toby, Aaron, and Shane were all on their knees, carefully scooping handfuls of dirt out of the hole they'd dug.

Bess passed a few brushes down to them.

"I can't believe it!"

"Careful!"

"Almost there!"

The excited phrases went back and forth for the better part of an hour as handfuls of dirt flew, until finally, all three men sat back, triumphant.

Papi gripped the armrests of his chair and leaned so far forward Allie was afraid he'd fall face-first onto the ground.

Aaron stood and bent down, lifting something out of the hole. He turned and Allie gasped. A box, the size of a shoe-box, wooden, scraped and chipped, but looking rather pristine considering its age, rested in his hands. He carefully walked over and set the box on Papi's lap.

Papi's cane fell as he released it and put both hands on the box. He felt over every inch, running his trembling fingers along the carved grooves along the edge – carvings that matched the ones on the vase they'd found. He choked out a sobbing breath.

Tears leaked from Allie's eyes and rolled down her cheeks as she watched him.

Someone said, "How many rubies do you think that box could hold?"

He touched a carving on the top of the box. A beetle, exactly like the ones carved on the cave walls.

"Does it open?" Estelle asked, her voice barely above a whisper.

Papi's trembling hands worked at the lid for a few minutes until the top of the box seemed to give way.

Everyone held their collective breath as he manipulated it and with a final pop, the lid was free from the base.

He sniffled and tears ran down his face.

"Okay, let's see this red treasure," Rupert said reverently.

Papi held the lid with one hand, and steadied the base on his lap with the other. He pulled the lid up and away and let out a strangled noise that was part sob, part shock, part relief. The noise quickly turned into laughter. Soul-deep laughter that wracked his entire body.

Shane held the base of the box to keep it from spilling off Papi's lap.

Allie peered inside. It wasn't empty. It was also definitely not full of rubies. Hundreds or even thousands of tiny translucent husks filled the box. "Is that... are those... beetles?"

Papi couldn't stop guffawing. He managed to nod.

Rupert looked into the box and also started laughing. "Red treasure indeed. We should have known."

They laughed while everyone else looked at each other, confused.

Papi finally calmed enough to wipe his eyes and set the lid back onto the base. He laughed a few times as he explained. "Cochineal. The treasure is a supply of cochineal beetles."

"To make dye," Piper said.

Papi nodded and was finally able to speak without chuckling. "Cochineal was a valuable commodity in the late fourteen, early fifteen hundreds. Our arid-climate friends had discovered that the beetle could be crushed and used to dye fabrics, to make paint, et cetera. They grow on the underside of certain cacti, and some communities farmed them. As expected, the Europeans wanted the ability to make red dyes that were difficult or impossible to attain at that time."

Estelle said, "So the king of M'yxnih really was sending a red treasure."

"Indeed." Papi patted the top of the box. "In the fifteen twenties, Spain even tried to raise their own cochineal, but the climate is not suited for the beetles, so they set to importing them. It's a fascinating story, and most people don't realize cochineal are still used today, even in food dyes." His eyes sparkled with mischief. "All of you have eaten these little guys – girls, actually, as the dye comes from female beetles – without even knowing it."

Zoe nodded, agreeing with his information. "Cosmetics, too."

Allie didn't want to think too much about crushed beetles in her food and makeup. She kept an eye on Papi, wondering if he was at all disappointed, but he certainly seemed pleased. Perhaps finding that there truly was a treasure was more of a reward than anything the treasure could have been. Of course, a five-hundred-year-old wooden chest was nothing to sneeze at. Especially when it all validated the dream he'd been chasing for more than half his life and even more importantly, it proved that M'yxnih had existed and would be more than a historical footnote with an asterisk. Even if it was filled with bugs.

"Let's go to basecamp," Estelle suggested. "We can collect the rest of the artifacts and make a plan to move forward."

Allie looked up at Jake. "Other artifacts?"

He shrugged.

Delia was standing nearby and must have heard them. "They found some pottery in Cave One. We hadn't found anything in here."

"Would it be possible for me to see Cave One?" Papi asked.

Allie didn't love the idea, but they were here now, so there wouldn't be a better time. She thought the tunnel connecting Caves One and Two were flat enough, but to be honest, it all kind of blended together and she couldn't swear which hallway led where at this point.

William said, "We'll take a quick walk over and Allie can see if the tunnel will be safe enough for you."

She nodded. "We'll be right back."

The walk connecting the caves was easy enough. There was only one pinch point that might be a little tricky for Papi to navigate sideways, but she knew he was motivated enough to make it through.

When they got back to Cave Two, she gave Papi two thumbs up. He grinned and got to his feet. Estelle declined the walk, so all the Hausers except William stayed behind with her. The rest of the original team, Rupert, and Zoe followed William to Cave One. The pitch blackness was broken up by the beams of light from their hardhats.

Allie and Jake brought up the rear and hung back a bit as Piper excitedly explained what they'd found, and where, in this cave.

"I know I shouldn't be glad they blew a hole in the cave and nearly killed us, but it seems to have worked out," Jake said.

"I'm torn. It's such a shame the site will start degrading now that it's exposed to the elements, but I've never seen him so happy, and that makes me happy."

"I'm not sure what's better for him: finding the treasure, or talking their ears off." He jerked his chin toward the group surrounding Papi, listening to him with rapt attention.

"Definitely a tie."

"Are you going to miss this?"

She looked around at the unending darkness and cold stone walls. "Not even a little bit."

He chuckled softly. "Good. I thought I was the only one."

"In fact, I think he's in good hands, so I'm game to head back into the sunshine."

"I'm with you."

Allie walked over to William so she didn't interrupt Papi's excited lecture. She quietly said, "Jake and I are heading back over to Cave Two."

They made their way through the dark tunnel and back into Cave Two, which was empty. Voices floated down from the surface, so Allie gladly went up the ramp and out of the cave. They put their helmets and safety vests in the crate on the golf cart and joined the Hausers in the circle of lawn chairs.

"Your grandfather and Rupert are having the time of their lives," Estelle said with a smile.

"I can't think of anything that would make Papi happier than this. He's over the moon."

"Well. I am sorry I denied access until now."

Allie shook her head. "We wouldn't have been able to do anything without the ARASNAC team coming along anyway. I certainly wouldn't have been any help without an experienced team to assign me some kind of task."

"Same," Jake said.

"I'm not sure if you were updated, but Rupert said that ARASNAC is legitimately willing to participate, even though this sort of retroactive agreement is highly unusual. Because the site is related to their discovery of the *Santa Anna-Maria*, they felt an exception was in order."

"That's great. I was hoping the team wouldn't be penalized and maybe go without pay. They're an amazing group of people."

Estelle waved a hand. "I told Rupert I would cover the salary they expected to receive if ARASNAC chose not to get involved. It's not their fault those other two were criminals."

"What's going to happen to them?"

She shook her head. "We don't know. It could be a slap on

the wrist and a fine, it could be serious jail time, or anything in between. We won't know until we know."

"That's frustrating."

"The wheels of justice turn slowly," Delia said with an eyeroll. "I'd like to see them spend some time in jail. It was reckless endangerment at the very least."

Chapter Thirty-Five

JAKE SAT BESIDE ALLIE, zoning out as she chatted with Estelle and Delia and Kylie. Shane sat on the other side of the lawn chair circle on his laptop.

His silicone temporary wedding band rolled as he rubbed his thumb over it.

"—moon, right Jake?" Estelle was speaking to him.

"Huh? I'm sorry, I was in my own little world."

"I was saying you'll be glad to have your free time back so you can work on planning your honeymoon. Where are you going?"

He wracked his brain. They'd told everyone they were going somewhere, but he couldn't remember.

"Cruise," Allie blurted out. It sounded like she couldn't remember the details, either.

"Yep, a cruise. It's nice because they handle all the arrangements. We just have to show up."

Estelle said, "I've been on several cruises."

"Which was your favorite?" Allie asked, turning the focus back to Estelle and off their fake plans.

"Alaska was stunning, as was the Mediterranean. I'm afraid I can't choose between them."

"Did you get to see whales on the Alaskan cruise?"

"We did. Oh, they were magnificent animals. We were very fortunate that a humpback whale came close to our boat. Normally they're farther out in the water so you need binoculars to see them clearly, but this one swam right alongside us. We also saw some orcas, which was an absolute delight."

"That sounds amazing. I'm hoping we get to see some dolphins on our cruise," Allie said.

His memory jarred. Yes. Tropical cruise. Something about the Caymans and Bermuda? Bahamas?

"Most cruises have dolphin encounters as excursions. I did one of those when I was much, much younger."

"I think I saw something about that in the information packet they gave us." That felt bland enough to be believable without inviting a ton more questions.

Estelle smiled at him. "Which travel agency are you using?"

Oops. "Uhhh, oh here comes the rest of the team." Jake jumped up from his chair and almost ran down the ramp into the cave to meet the team so he could escort Charlie to the surface. Lying was something he couldn't tolerate and here he was, lying to Mrs. Hauser left and right. Not cool.

Charlie was happily talking about the markings that were undoubtedly on the pottery they'd found, and when someone on the team confirmed it, he nodded like it was the only answer he'd expected.

"Watch your step," Jake said. He immediately got behind Charlie and stayed close as the old man slowly navigated the upward slope. He noticeably favored his left side.

At the top of the ramp, Jake caught Allie's eye. She made a bit of a grimace, watching her grandfather limp across the lawn.

Delia was beside Allie. "Hey Shane, how about we take our guests back to basecamp and come back for the equipment?"

He looked around. "How about you take Mom, Dr. Scheffler, and Dr. Cresswell now. Jake and Allie can go with you. It shouldn't take long for the rest of us to pack up." He looked at Zoe. "If you want to head back, too, we can—"

"No, I'll help pack up," Zoe said, waving his suggestion away.

Jake helped Charlie into the back passenger seat of the golf cart. He couldn't miss the wince of pain as he got himself situated.

"You okay?"

"Don't tell Allie. She'll make me take one of those horse pills and put me to bed."

Jake didn't answer. He probably wouldn't have to tell Allie anything, because the pain was written on Charlie's face.

"Promise me."

"Uh, there's nothing to promise."

Jake was taken aback by the glare burning from Charlie's eyes. His voice was low and irritated. "She's not *really* your wife, you know. You don't have to cow to her demands."

What demands? Jake let the comment go without responding.

"Everything all right?" Estelle came alongside Jake to take her seat in the cart.

"Um, yeah. Yes. Just getting Charlie settled."

"That's Dr. Scheffler to you," Charlie grumbled.

Rupert got in the other side of the back seat and gave Jake a curious look. Jake shook his head once and stepped back from the cart. He was a little stunned, but quickly realized he shouldn't be. This was exactly the sort of Jekyll/Hyde disposition Allie tried to describe to him, and he hadn't totally believed her.

Allie had put her helmet on and taken her spot on the back of the ATV's long seat.

"What's going on?" she asked as he approached.

"Hmm? Nothing. Just helping him get ready to head back to basecamp."

She snort-laughed. "Let me guess. He told you not to tell me he's in excruciating pain, like it's not obvious. And when you didn't immediately agree to hide it from me, he turned on you and got nasty."

Jake climbed onto the four-wheeler with a sigh. "You were right, I was wrong, I owe you a steak dinner."

She laughed again and put her arms around his waist. "You owe me way more than a steak dinner."

When everyone gathered back at basecamp, Charlie was in a slightly better mood as he examined the pottery the other team had uncovered. He talked about the markings on the pottery and was beyond excited to see a fully intact bowl. But his speech was slower and quieter.

Allie had already asked him twice to head home, but each time, he shook his head and went back to the pottery.

Jake settled on the couch beside her. They were alone on that side of the room. "What are you thinking?"

"I'm thinking he's overdone it and he's going to be miserable for the next few days."

He put an arm over the back of the couch.

Allie settled her head into the crook of his elbow and sighed. "I'm glad he got to see everything, but he needs to get home and get ahead of the pain."

"At least he's sitting now, right?"

"Eh. It's a hard chair, so it's probably not helping much."

"What if you bribe him? Tell him if he wants to come back, he needs to listen to you?"

"That might work. I can tell he's already hurting. Look at his face."

"I know." He dropped his hand to stroke her hair. "What should we do about that steak dinner?"

"That depends on what you mean by a steak dinner. Are we going to the city and getting a two-hundred-dollar Wagyu steak from a Michelin star restaurant? Or are you grilling supermarket steaks for me?"

He looked down into her eyes and smiled. "Whichever you want."

"Really." She sounded skeptical. "If I say I want to go to the fanciest restaurant in the state and get the most expensive steak, you're okay with that? Really?"

"Yup. It's not something I'd do every weekend, but yes, I will take you to any restaurant you want and you can order anything you want, including appetizers and dessert and fine wine."

"Why?"

"Because there's nothing I wouldn't do for my temporary wife."

She grinned up at him. "Get Papi in the car and we'll call it even."

"I'll get him in the car, but you're still getting a steak

dinner." He bent his arm to pull her close and kissed her forehead.

She gave a little gasp and looked up at him, surprised.

Truth be told, the gesture was just as unexpected to him, but it felt so right in the moment. Thank goodness she seemed pleased.

He said, "Let's get him home. I'll hold him down while you give him his pill."

She laughed and covered her mouth with her hand. "Just like an angry cat."

"You got it." He looked over and caught Charlie wincing again, so he reluctantly left Allie and got up.

Even though Charlie was in obvious pain, he stubbornly refused to leave. The cat analogy was so apt Jake was afraid he might have to take him by the scruff of the neck to get him out the door.

Fortunately, Estelle stood and announced that she'd had enough for one day, and they could resume on Monday.

The instant Charlie reluctantly agreed, Jake grabbed the back of his chair and said, "Alrighty, thanks for everything." Jake helped him to his feet and ushered him toward the door.

Allie grabbed their packs and followed him out.

The whole way, Jake was trying to plan his date with Allie. He didn't know of a Michelin restaurant in driving distance, but he did know of a of a little dive bar that had amazing steak. Ambiance? Two out of ten. Food? Twelve out of ten. He might not have known Allie well for very long, but he was confident she'd like great food even if the surroundings were questionable.

His hopes of taking Allie out that evening were dashed

when they got back to her house and Charlie stumbled getting out of the car.

"I'm fine!" he barked when Allie grabbed his arm.

"Don't start giving me attitude," she snapped back. "You knew this was going to be a tough day. Don't take it out on me because you overdid it."

He grunted a little and gave her a side-eye, but allowed her to help him into the house.

Jake followed them through the mudroom into the kitchen. He hooked her pack on the back of a chair.

Charlie sank down onto a chair while Allie filled a glass with water. She opened a prescription container and put a pill and the glass in front of her grandfather. "Take that. It'll help."

"You see how she treats me? She's a tyrant." Charlie swished his hand and flung the pill off the table.

Too bad for him, he was slow, and Jake had excellent reflexes. He caught the white tablet in midair and set it back on the table beside the glass.

Charlie glared at him.

"Papi, it's for the pain and inflammation."

"I'm not in pain."

"Okay." She sighed and turned to the sink.

Jake sat across from him. "Hey, you'll feel a lot better if you stay ahead of the pain."

"What would you know about it?" Charlie snapped.

"My grandpa was the same way."

"Bully for him."

Jake ignored the comment. "He didn't like taking medication, but sometimes he just had to suck it up and quit being difficult."

"Difficult? *I'm* not difficult. *She* is. That's why she never got married for real. Too difficult."

"Huh-uh, nope, that is unacceptable." Jake shook his head. "You owe her an apology for that."

"Apology," Charlie scoffed. "She's my granddaughter, I'll talk about her however I want."

"Yeah, she's your granddaughter. You should talk about her better than anybody else in the world."

Charlie glared some more, but he put the pill in his mouth and washed it down with most of the water.

Jake held his gaze steady and cocked an eyebrow, but said nothing else.

During their standoff, Allie came over and put another pill in front of Charlie. "Blood pressure. Don't even think about arguing over this one."

Charlie picked up the pill and grudgingly admitted, "I shouldn't have argued over the last one." He struggled to his feet.

Jake itched to help him, but he knew it wasn't just about standing up. It was about independence and pride. Pride that had been poked a bit when Jake called him out.

"Do you want some hot tea?" Allie asked.

"Yes, please." His voice was strained. He braced his hands on the table and nodded at Jake. "I think I'm going to lie down for a little bit."

"Okay, Papi, I'll bring your tea in a minute." She put a tea bag in a stainless steel travel mug and filled it with hot water from the coffeemaker.

Charlie limped gingerly out of the kitchen and into the hallway.

Allie put a little sugar in the tea and stirred, put the lid on, then put a handful of crackers in a small plastic zipper bag. "He's going to be in bed for the night, but I'd bet money he'll wake up around midnight and be hungry."

Jake's own pride was poked a bit. He'd made a lot of bad assumptions about her, and that was every bit as unkind as Charlie's comment had been. At least Charlie had the excuse, albeit still a poor one, of being in pain when he lashed out.

Jake was glad Allie had given him the chance to find out how wrong he was. She may not have the patience of a saint, but she was the kind of woman who would drive to the ends of the Earth to find Pennywig's mint chocolate chip ice cream.

Chapter Thirty-Six

ALLIE PUT the tea and crackers on Papi's bedside table.

He sat heavily on his bed. "I'm sorry, Allie-gator. I never should have said that. It was hateful and just plain stupid, and I didn't mean it."

"I know." She got his pajamas out of his dresser. "Do you need a hand?"

"Nah." He hooked his cane on the nightstand. "I do that a lot, don't I?"

"What?"

His shoulders slumped. "I say unkind things to you so often it's just normal, isn't it?"

Allie wasn't sure how to navigate this. Yes, he'd always gotten a little snappy when he was hurting or sick or tired, but she'd long since learned to let the comments roll off her back. She fluffed his pillows. "Let's just say this wasn't the first time, and it wasn't a shock."

"I am truly sorry. I promise I'll do better."

"Okay." She didn't doubt his sincerity, but wouldn't hold

her breath that it never happened again. "Are you sure you don't need some help?"

"No, I've got it. Thank you."

She leaned down and kissed his cheek. "You're welcome." She closed his door on the way out.

Jake was still at the kitchen table, scrolling on his phone. "You ready for that steak?"

She glanced back the hallway. "I don't think I should leave, sorry. He's in a lot of pain, so I'd feel better if I stayed here. Raincheck?"

"Of course."

She assumed he'd get up and head for the door, but he didn't.

Instead, he looked up from his phone and said, "No mushrooms, right?"

"What?"

"Pizza. Is that okay? Did you want something different?"

A warm feeling filled her chest with the knowledge he was staying. "Pizza's great. I like pepperoni and green pepper."

"I'm getting breadsticks, too. Anything else?"

"Oooh, see if they have one of those warm chocolate chip cookie dessert things."

"What's the house number?"

She told him and a minute later he said, "Should be here in thirty minutes."

They were settled on the couch, scrolling through a catalog of movies to stream when the food arrived.

Jake opened the pizza box while Allie grabbed paper plates and napkins from the kitchen. She curled one leg under herself and blew on her slice of hot pizza. "You didn't have to stay."

Jake shrugged one shoulder. "I figured I'd better take advantage of still having a temporary wife and have a conversation with someone other than my roommate."

She startled and sat back. "I had no idea you have a roommate. I can't believe you didn't tell me that."

"I forget about him a lot."

Something about the way he said it made her think he was joking. "Mmm hmm."

"His name is Horatio. He's a very good listener, doesn't make many messes, and never uses my stuff without permission. If I ignore him too long, he gets kind of droopy and I pay him some attention."

"Droopy. What exactly is your roommate?"

"Horatio is a Christmas cactus. But he seems to prefer New Year's, because that's when he usually blooms."

"Ah. Yes, I bet he is the ideal roommate."

"Much less cranky than yours," he joked.

She laughed and almost dropped her pizza. "Thank you, by the way. That was very sweet of you to stand up for me."

"I know he was hurting. The pain was all over his face. But I couldn't ignore the way he lashed out. He really went below the belt. Reminded me of some of the things I've said."

"You might be a good influence. He actually apologized to me when I took him his tea."

Jake smacked a hand over his heart. "Did you really suggest I'm a good influence?"

"I said 'might be.'" She tossed half of a pizza crust into the box and settled back against Jake's arm. "Don't let it go to your head."

"Too late."

They quieted, watching the action hero on the screen making his plans to go after the bad guy and avenge something or other.

Allie yawned and the next thing she knew, the credits were rolling. She stretched and rubbed her eyes. "I must have fallen asleep." Snuggling against Jake had been cozy. She liked it. A lot.

"Yeah, the chainsaw noises gave it away," Jake teased.

"Ha, ha, very funny. I must be more tired than I thought."

He stood and put his hands on his lower back and leaned backwards until his spine cracked. "No wonder. It's been a crazy week."

"And next week is sure to be just as bananas." She stood up, too.

Jake pulled her in for a hug. "Steak tomorrow evening?"

"As long as Papi's feeling okay."

"Of course."

"I'll text you." She walked him to the door.

Only a few minutes later, she crawled into bed and was back out like a light, wishing she was still cuddled against Jake.

Chapter Thirty-Seven

SATURDAY CRAWLED by until it was finally time to leave to pick Allie up. Jake looked in the mirror for the millionth time. He wasn't sure why he was so nervous. It wasn't like this was a first date. Or was it? Despite being together for weeks, it felt an awful lot like a first date. Whatever it was, he couldn't wait to see her.

He ran a hand over his hair and straightened the collar of his casual blue button-down shirt. He tucked it into his jeans, then untucked it.

Then tucked it again.

According to the mirror, he didn't look half bad. He was freshly showered, shaved, and dressed in something that lacked Ralph's branding across the chest. He finally quit primping and got in the truck.

By the time he pulled into her driveway, his mouth was dry. It felt like prom night without the wrist corsage and fake ID.

Allie didn't wait for him to come to the door. She came out and his feet froze to the concrete. She wore a blue floral sundress with a matching solid blue sweater and chunky sandals that gave her a good four inches of height. Her dark hair was loose, with one side tucked behind her ear. An assortment of silver bracelets caught the late afternoon sunlight.

He hurried to open her door. "You look amazing," he said as she climbed in.

"Thanks. You look pretty good yourself."

He couldn't help but steal glances at her as he drove. Her skirt skimmed her knees, and the scoop neck on her dress was a whole different vibe than their Ralph's shirts and khaki pants that were suitable for crawling around caves. Two silver hoops, one large, one small, dangled from each earlobe.

"What is this place?"

His smile was more of a grimace. They were probably overdressed for the location. "I'll warn you, it looks sketchy, but the food is totally worth it. We're almost there."

He turned down a side road and a few minutes later, turned into a gravel parking lot full of cars.

"The Rusty Bucket. At least my tetanus shots are up to date."

The small nondescript building looked like a whole lot of nothing. No neon beer signs, no shutters on the windows, no decorations except the faded, chipped, hand-painted name of the restaurant on the glass of the front door, and a generic rectangle sign listing the hours of operation.

"It must have great word of mouth to be this busy with no signage or anything."

"Every time I've been here, it's been packed."

He second-guessed himself the whole way across the parking lot, until he opened the front door for her and the music and laughter and aroma of really good food floated out like a cloud.

"Smells really good," Allie said, breathing deeply.

Inside, he felt a little better. Patrons were dressed all the way from filthy guys who'd just gotten off a construction site to several people who were dressed similarly to Jake and Allie.

A smiling hostess led them past the bar area, though a short hallway into a large dining area, and seated them in a corner booth.

They perused the menu for a few minutes.

Allie snapped her menu shut. "I'm getting the surf and turf with shrimp."

"Same." He put his menu on top of hers.

"I'm not a big fan of lobster."

"It's okay, but I like crab legs a lot better."

"Shrimp is my number one, but crab legs are a close second." She tapped the menu. "I might get a cocktail. I don't expect you to spend twelve dollars on a drink, so I'll give you cash, if that's okay."

"Absolutely not. This is on me, and you can get a dozen cocktails and ten desserts if you want."

"I'm definitely not getting a dozen cocktails, but I might hold you to those ten desserts."

Conversations and clinking silverware and the jukebox music piped in through the ceiling was just loud enough to have a regular conversation with enough background noise that it would be difficult to overhear any specific talk.

Their food and drinks came out faster than either of them expected.

"If this tastes half as good as it looks or smells, this might be my new favorite restaurant."

Jake dredged a shrimp through cocktail sauce and popped it into his mouth. "It does."

Allie took a bite of her steak and her eyes closed. "Mmm. I want the recipe for whatever marinade they're using."

They ate in silence for a while.

"How do you feel about the whole temporary marriage being over?" she asked.

He shrugged one shoulder. "I didn't think I'd feel anything one way or another, but I don't like it."

"Me, either. I feel kind of guilty."

"Guilty?" He didn't expect that.

"Yeah. I guess because marriage is something sacred, and we pretended to use it so the dig could move forward. That and lying to Mrs. Hauser just makes it all feel icky. But on the other hand, I don't think it was a reasonable requirement. I mean, obviously she can have whatever rules she wants for her own property and who's allowed on it, but I feel like my hands were tied."

"I agree. A lesser of two evils situation. Tell a little lie so the project can happen and your grandfather gets some closure, or let a massive opportunity die and he never gets any answers. Or worse, the site degrades over time and is lost to history. I'm not happy about lying either, but was worth it."

"For the greater good," Allie said wryly.

"I know you hate that phrase, but it's accurate. One lie, and Charlie got his closure, M'yxnih is getting its rightful place in history, and the legitimate members of the team will get some recognition. It's all a net positive."

"What about us? How do we move forward if we started out on a lie?"

Jake shook his head. "We didn't. There were no lies between us, Allie. We both knew the score from the start. I'm more concerned that we started out on a bad foot because I was being a judgmental doofus. How do we move past that?"

"I think we already have."

"What do you think a future would look like for us? If we were married for real?"

"Eeww," she said with a laugh. "No, I'm kidding. It wouldn't be the worst thing in the world. We share a lot of the same values and priorities. I think being trapped in the cave showed that we work well together as a team. There are way worse foundations. That's a pretty deep question, though. What are you thinking?"

"I think the past month has shown me that I like it when I'm with you a lot more than I like it when we're apart."

Allie put a hand over her heart. Her voice was quiet. "Me, too."

Hope fluttered in his chest along with a healthy dose of fear. They could be really good together. Their time in the caves proved that out. They could end up falling madly in love and living happily ever after. But it could also go spectacularly wrong and hurt them both.

Something in her eyes, though, convinced him it might be worth the risk.

Despite their earlier declarations, they were both too full to order dessert. Jake paid the check and held the door for Allie. She slipped her hand into his as they crossed the parking lot and his fingers curled around hers.

Music piped from a speaker to the bar's deck.

"I like this song," she said.

"Me, too." Jake put his free hand around her waist and they swayed with the music.

She laid her head against his chest. "Slow dancing in a bar parking lot. Unconventional, but this definitely goes in the net positive column."

Jake latched onto a sudden burst of bravery. "And how about this?"

When she looked up at him, he leaned down, hesitating an inch from her lips to wait for her signal that this was okay.

She tipped her chin and met his lips with hers.

Chapter Thirty-Eight

ALLIE WAS STILL SMILING on Monday morning. She'd floated home on a cloud after her date with Jake. They'd spent all day Sunday texting each other the most random things, and now she couldn't wait to see him again.

She drove Papi to the museum and Jake met them in the parking lot. He greeted her with a massive grin. "Good morning, Allie O'Malley, at least for the next few hours."

"Good morning, temporary husband." Temporary husband, official boyfriend? Ugh, they were too old to be boyfriend and girlfriend, weren't they? Wait. She was getting ahead of herself. *Slow your roll, Allie.*

Jake's hand was warm on her back as they rode the elevator to the fourth floor and walked to Rupert's office.

He rushed over to them. "Good morning, good morning! We're actually going down to the basement. There's so much to see."

Allie glanced over to Rupert's desk. The manila envelope was still on the corner of his desk, under his wire outbox, waiting to expire in another four days. She didn't mind waiting to shred the certificate. Even though it wasn't anything more than symbolic, she hated the idea of destroying it.

In the elevator, Rupert swiped his badge to access the lower levels of the museum.

They followed him down a long, brightly lit corridor, to a smallish room that was mostly empty except for a row of stainless steel tables that took up most of the space.

Strewn along the tables were all of the artifacts from the caves, with little cards and handwritten notes near a few of the pieces.

Allie leaned closer to Jake. "I didn't realize there was so much."

He shook his head. "Neither did I."

On the tables were the box full of bug carcasses, the mostly-intact vase Jake had found, one complete bowl, and one mostly-intact bowl. Along with those were three or four dozen pieces of pottery and a handful of large chunks of the wall holding carvings and drawings that had survived the explosion. The book was with Zoe and her team.

"This is so neat to see it all in one place," she said. "It's going to make an incredible exhibit."

Jake nodded in agreement.

Papi was at the table, excitedly looking over each artifact. He and Rupert spent a long while examining the vase.

"Exciting enough to hang out here all day?" Jake asked quietly.

"Nope," she answered.

"Would you like a private tour of the museum?"

"That sounds amazing."

He tilted his head toward the two men. "Should we tell them we're leaving?"

She went over and said, "Papi, we're going for a walk."

"Okay," he said without ever looking away from the piece of ceramic in his hand.

"I guess he doesn't mind," she joked as she walked back over to Jake.

They walked down the hallway and he swiped his badge for the elevator. It opened a moment later and let them out into a back hallway on the main floor. Jake led her to a door that opened to the main lobby.

"And this is the entrance. You can see the visitor station over there to the left, and if you go through the arch on the right, you'll be in the gift shop."

"I haven't been in the gift shop for ages."

"We should rectify that right now." Jake steered her across the lobby and into the gift shop.

A few minutes later, Allie laughed as Jake paid for a stuffed dinosaur. "Everyone should have a dinosaur."

She accepted the bag. "Thank you. I have the perfect spot on a shelf in the living room."

"A place of honor."

"Of course."

"And now let's go meet our resident dinosaurs."

They started across the lobby and nearly ran into Rita, who was hustling toward the front door. "Oh!" She stopped short and looked extremely flustered. "Jake! Allie! Don't worry about a thing."

Allie opened her mouth to ask what she meant, but Rita was already speed-walking away from them.

"What was that about?"

Jake shrugged. "I have no idea. Let me check with Tom and see if he knows what's going on." They went back into the gift shop and he used the phone under the counter to call the security office.

Allie watched Jake nod a few times, then hang up.

"Tom checked all the monitors and didn't see anything. Charlie and Rupert are still in the basement looking at artifacts, so it didn't have anything to do with them."

"Good. I was afraid maybe they were up to something."

"Beats me. Shall we continue?" He offered her his elbow.

"By all means." She hooked her hand around his arm.

"Over here we have the natural history section, with our welcoming committee at the doorway. This big guy is Levi. He's a T-rex the museum acquired in nineteen ninety-two. His velociraptor buddy here is Ella. Despite the liberties taken by a certain dinosaur movie franchise, Ella and Levi would have both lived during the Cretaceous period. Their Stegosaurus friend over there, Milton, is the one who would have lived during the Jurassic period."

"Fascinating."

"I still love the movies, though."

"Me, too."

They walked through the rest of the first floor, then the second, and finally the third, ending at the Aztec display. Somewhere on the second floor, in front of a display about clouds, Jake had reached for her hand and she'd laced her fingers with his.

He asked, "Should we go back down and see if they're done looking at the pottery?"

She reluctantly answered, "Yeah, maybe we should get the certificate shredded before we leave."

Jake swiped his badge in the elevator and they went back down to the basement level. Papi was no longer standing at the table. He was sitting on an uncomfortable molded plastic chair.

Allie rushed over. "Are you okay? What happened?"

He shook his head wearily and waved an annoyed hand, gesturing to the room. "Stood too long on this hard floor. My hip's killing me, and my knee's not far behind."

"That's enough for today, then. Let's get you home."

Jake moved in front of her and hooked Papi's arms to help him stand. They slowly made their way to the elevator. Outside, Jake stood with Papi while Allie jogged across the parking lot to get her SUV.

She drove around to the sidewalk and got out to help Jake get Papi settled in the front seat. Once the door was closed, Jake quietly said, "Sorry about the wheelchair comments. You were right. Again." He grinned. "I guess you're stuck with me another day."

"Could be worse," she joked. "It could be *two* more days. Eww."

Jake scrunched up his face. "Eww indeed. Nobody wants that."

They both laughed and he headed for his own vehicle.

"You feeling okay?" she asked Papi when she got back in.

"I'll be better when I can get home and put my feet up." His voice was strained.

When they got home, he struggled to get out of the car. Allie helped him get to his feet and offered her arm as support. He gripped it tightly as they walked into the house.

She settled him on his recliner with a glass of ice water and one of his pills for pain and inflammation. "I'm not taking you back to the museum tomorrow. You're going to need to rest a day or two."

He nodded and took his pill without complaint, which let her know he was in a fair amount of pain.

"I'm only off through Thursday. Then I'll be working pretty much four solid days for the Memorial Day sale. So I'm going to have Trista check in on you."

He nodded again but didn't answer. His eyes drifted shut.

She leaned against the door frame separating the living room and kitchen and watched him. His chest rose and fell steadily. It was hard to admit he was getting older, and they were awfully close to the point where she wouldn't be able to handle all of his care herself.

Chapter Thirty-Nine

JAKE PULLED into Allie's driveway Tuesday morning. He was happy to see her, but not happy about their mission. He knew it was all a ruse from the beginning, that they were never *really* married, that they were just starting to date and it was way too soon to plan a future anyway, but... the idea of shredding their marriage certificate kind of hurt.

It felt wrong somehow. Even though their "marriage" was fake, it felt more real than it should, and since he'd always been adamant that marriage should be forever, it felt even more like they'd been making a mockery of it.

He also fully realized it had been his own big mouth that had gotten them into this situation. And even though he felt a little guilty, he was glad they'd done it. So much good had come from the project that he couldn't be too mad at himself for doing what they did, even though it was kind of sketchy. And who knows where they might be able to go from here.

Allie bounded out of the house before he'd stopped the truck. She jumped in the passenger side.

"How's Charlie this morning?"

"Good. He overdid it yesterday, but he actually listened to me and took his medication and stayed hydrated."

"He must have been feeling pretty bad if he did as he was told."

"No kidding." She snapped her seatbelt into the buckle. "I'm hoping it'll dawn on him that when he listens, he feels better faster, but I'm not holding my breath."

"That sounds a little unrealistic."

"I was thinking, how should we celebrate the end of our temporary marriage?"

He pulled out of the parking lot onto the main road. "I don't know if I'm feeling like it's something to celebrate."

She put a hand on his arm and gently squeezed. "I do. That chapter of our story was written on the dreams and requirements of other people. I want to celebrate starting fresh and being together because we both want to be."

"I like that perspective. A lot." He glanced at his speedometer and lifted his foot slightly from the gas pedal. "I'd say it should involve food of some sort."

"I'm not sure how you're going to top that steak. It was one of the best steaks I've ever had."

"Told you so. Now we need to find the best wings."

"That sounds like the perfect celebration. Wings, a bucket of ranch dressing, and a stack of wet wipes because the best wings are horribly messy."

"Sold. We'll go in search of wings after our shredding ceremony."

She laughed. "Shredding ceremony. Clever."

He groaned. "I didn't even realize I made a joke."

"Here's a critical question for you: drums or flats?"

"I'm definitely team flats."

"Ooh, I'm team drums. Does this signal incompatibility?"

He shook his head and slowed to turn into the museum parking lot. "On the contrary. In any given order of wings, drums and flats are generally evenly distributed. Which is great news for us, because we can just divvy up the wings and not be fighting over the same kind."

"Hmm. What about sauces?"

At the back of the building, he pulled into his parking space and turned the truck off. "I've got a few favorites, but I'm open to negotiation."

They walked into the building through the employee entrance and headed for the elevator.

"My favorite is garlic parmesan," she said.

"We can work with that. It's in my top five." He looked upward as if contemplating something deep and serious. "Actually, it might even be in my top three."

"Sounds like we're celebrating with garlic parmesan wings and a ton of ranch."

"Whoa, hang on. I'm actually team bleu cheese."

She scrunched up her nose. "I think that really might signal incompatibility. Who wants to eat moldy cheese dressing?"

He pressed the button for the fourth floor. "I'd say lots of people since it's offered just as often as ranch."

"Okay. We split an order of garlic parmesan wings, and we get our own dressing."

"The perfect compromise." He leaned down to steal a kiss before the doors opened.

As they walked down the hall, he said, "Coke or Pepsi?"

Allie shook her head. "If we don't agree, that's too big of a discussion to start now."

"Good point."

They walked past Rita's empty desk. Jake knocked on Rupert's office door and opened it when Rupert called out for them to come in.

"Hey, Rupert."

Rupert stood behind his desk with his hands clasped. Concern was written all over his face. "Please close the door."

"What's wrong?" Allie asked.

He let out a long breath. His brows pinched inward. "Please. Sit down."

Jake dropped into one of the chairs facing the desk. "Rupert? What's wrong? Are you okay?"

"Oh, I'm fine. I'm fine." He was paler than usual and looked like he might be sick.

Allie slowly sat down. "Rupert?"

He sank into his own chair. "I don't know how to tell you this."

"Is it the project? Is there a problem? Oh, please don't tell me this wasn't related to M'yxnih after all, please," Allie pleaded.

"No, no, no, nothing of that sort."

"Is it the book? Rupert, what's going on?" Her voice rose on the last word.

"The project is fine. The artifacts are fine. Everything is fine. Except..."

Jake wanted to shake the words out of him. "Except?" he prompted.

Allie gasped. "Where is it?"

Rupert's eyes drifted shut.

Jake had no idea what she was talking about, but Rupert clearly did. "Anyone care to fill me in?"

Allie grabbed his arm and pointed frantically to the wire outbox on the corner of Rupert's desk. "The envelope. It was right there. I saw it yesterday, and now it's gone."

"Envelope?" He was not following.

"The *envelope*, Jake. That had the marriage certificate. It was right there. It's been right there all month and now it's gone."

Everything clicked into place. "Oh! Oh. Oooooh. Rupert? Where's the certificate?"

He let out a heavy sigh and pressed his intercom. "Rita, could you please come in?"

There was a single knock on the door before it opened. Rita poked her head around the door, then came inside and shut the door behind her.

Rupert's lips pressed into a thin line and his brow furrowed with concern. "Rita and I had... a miscommunication."

Rita addressed them. "Jake. Allie. I need to apologize. Rupert's usually so meticulous about his paperwork, but for some reason, your license got put *under* his outbox instead of *in* his outbox. I saw it yesterday when I was cleaning off his desk, and when I opened to check what it was, I saw it was the marriage certificate and, oh my goodness, it was almost set to expire! I personally took it to the courthouse and handed it to them myself. Just under the wire, too. I'm so sorry. I don't know how we overlooked that."

Allie's mouth hung open.

Jake looked back and forth between Rita and Rupert. Rupert rubbed a hand down his face. Rita wore a sincerely apologetic smile.

Now what? They should have shredded it as soon as Mrs.

Hauser got a copy. He opened his mouth to speak, but snapped it shut. He couldn't say anything that would alert Rita to the fact that the whole thing was a fraud.

"I was simply horrified when I saw it there, so I had to immediately make sure it was filed properly. I hope you're not terribly upset."

Allie shook her head, but still didn't speak.

"No," Jake managed. "We're not upset at all." Yes, they were. They were very upset. But Rita, always efficient Rita, was just doing her job. None of this was her fault.

"Are you sure? It was an honest mistake, I promise."

"Yeah, yeah, of course." He felt bad for her. She wrung her hands and looked back and forth between the two of them.

"Thank you, Rita," Rupert said gently.

"Oh, dear. You both seem upset." Her chin quivered.

Jake shook his head. "No, no, not at all, Rita. We had no idea, so we're just... surprised. That's all."

"Yeah. Surprised. Thanks, Rita," Allie said. Her fingers dug into his arm. "This whole project has been one crazy surprise after another."

"Is there anything else I can do?" She trailed off.

"No. Thanks for letting us know what happened," Allie said.

Rita gave them another uncertain smile, then left the room.

They all three sat in silence for a few minutes until Rupert cleared his throat and said, "There aren't words sufficient enough to tell you how sorry I am. I imagine it would be possible to get an annulment, but the only grounds would likely be fraud."

"Or we need to get a regular old-fashioned divorce," said Allie. Her voice was flat.

They could. Jake hated the thought even as the germ of a new idea spawned. What if they... didn't? It was crazy to consider, but his last wild idea got them to this point, and that turned out okay, didn't it? Maybe this impulse could work out, too.

Rupert nodded.

He was going to throw it out there. Shoot his shot. There was nothing to lose, right? "Or," Jake said, "we could see how it goes."

Allie's jaw dropped. She stared. And stared. And stared.

Jake willed her to say something. Anything. Of course it was a ridiculous suggestion. For Pete's sake, they'd had one date. One. Of course she wouldn't want to jump into marriage. That would make her just as crazy as him.

After a long stunned silence, Allie flashed a huge grin. "We should discuss our options over wings."

Wings? She was smiling. Did that mean... Oh, wow, they were doing this, weren't they? "Celebratory wings? Are you sure?"

"I'm sure." She stood up and held out her hand.

Rupert cocked his head in confusion. "What is happening right now?"

Jake grinned and took Allie's hand. "Rupert, I believe we're diving headfirst into our next adventure."

He nodded at them and smiled. "I expect you'll find treasure in this one, as well."

Epilogue

ONE YEAR *later*

Allie took one last look in the mirror. She smoothed down the front of her black gown with a delicate black lace overlay. In some ways she couldn't believe it had been an entire year since their M'yxnih project, and in other ways she couldn't believe it had *only* been a year.

"You ready?" Jake asked as he came into the room, adjusting the cufflink on the starched white shirt of his black tuxedo. He stopped short. "Wow. Allie. Wow."

She felt her face heat. "Oh, stop."

"No. You look amazing."

She took in his fitted tux. "You don't look so bad yourself."

He straightened his sleeve and held a hand out. When she took it, he spun her around. Her skirt twirled, brushing against his legs, and she laughed. "I'm ready when you are."

"Almost. I have something that might look good with your

outfit." He walked over to the dresser and pulled a black box out of the top drawer.

"What is it?"

"Open it."

She eagerly took the box from him – her forever husband – and lifted the hinged lid. "Oh, Jake," she breathed.

A silver necklace with a ruby heart caught the light and glinted up from the black velvet.

"You finally have your red treasure."

She wrapped her arms around him. "My treasure was better than anything red."

Jake took the necklace from her and fastened it around her neck.

She touched the gemstone. "But this is pretty awesome. Thank you."

"A treasure for my treasure," he said with a grin. "We should probably get going."

They drove to the museum and found a spot in the mostly-empty parking lot. The gala to unveil the brand-new M'yxnih exhibit wasn't going to start for another two hours. And when it was over, they were heading to the airport for their honeymoon – a two-week trip to Yellowstone and a detour through Montana, where Allie's half-sister Anna had invited them to visit.

Allie had Jake to thank for that. He'd encouraged her to reach out to Anna, and over the past year, they'd formed a really nice friendship. She couldn't wait to meet her sister and her family.

Inside, Jake swiped his badge for the elevator and they rode to the third floor. Papi, Rupert, the Hauser family, and their former teammates from the project were dressed in formalwear and gathered around the glass cases displaying the artifacts they'd found. Rows of chairs were placed in a semicircle facing the display, which Papi would introduce with a speech to kick off the gala.

Rupert lifted an arm in their direction. "Ah, Jake and Allie are here. Everyone, please have a seat."

Jake and Allie joined him in front of the case holding the book.

Papi patted the seat next to him, but Allie shook her head slightly and couldn't help but grin. Butterflies swarmed in her belly. She couldn't wait to make this all official. Like *officially* official. For real.

When everyone was seated except them, Rupert addressed the group. "We've asked you to be here early not just for the exhibit unveiling, but for a very special surprise. Allie?"

Allie looked up at Jake, then at their friends. "This has been a wild ride. Papi has spent his whole life chasing the treasure of M'yxnih, and we certainly found it, didn't we? I never expected that the red treasure would be bugs. I also never expected that searching for Papi's treasure would lead me to mine."

Jake squeezed her hand.

"As you all know, sorry again Mrs. Hauser, Jake and I weren't actually planning a wedding. In fact, we didn't even like each other all that much. But during the M'yxnih project, we kind of grew on each other and had started building a nice foundation for a relationship. As we got to know each other better, we decided maybe we should try dating. Then Rita threw a monkey wrench into our plans and all of a sudden, our fake temporary marriage was all too real." She looked up at Jake. Try as she might, she couldn't pinpoint when she started to fall in love with him. It might have been the first time he asked her to describe the Outsiders Club. Or when he covered her to protect her from falling rock during the explosion. Or when they slow danced in the parking lot. Those few weeks had a thousand little moments it could have been. And the year since had a million more little moments that made her fall in love again and again.

He picked up where she left off. "We decided to go with it. See where it took us. And it's brought us here. Technically we've been married for a year, but this is the day that counts. Since you've all been a part of our journey, we wanted you to be a part of our wedding. And since searching for the treasure of M'yxnih brought us together, we thought it would be most appropriate to exchange our vows here, in front of Fernando de Cabra's journal that chronicled the treasure that was the love he and Princess K'nih shared."

Allie glanced to Rupert. "Even though we haven't done anything the traditional way, we've decided to exchange rather traditional vows. And since Rupert already signed our marriage license, we figured we'd give him the chance to do the ceremony part, too."

He chuckled and stood in front of them. He opened a worn leather book and recited some passages, then looked at Allie.

"Allie. Do you take Jake to be your lawfully wedded husband? Do you promise to love and cherish him, in sickness and health, for richer or for poorer, for better or for worse, for so long as you both shall live?"

She blinked back the tears stinging the backs of her eyes and looked at Jake. "I do."

"Jake. Do you take Allie to be your lawfully wedded wife? Do you promise to love and cherish her, in sickness and health, for richer or for poorer, for better or for worse, for so long as you both shall live?"

A tear slid down his cheek. Allie reached up and wiped it away with her thumb.

"I do," he answered.

"May I have the rings?" Rupert asked.

Jake pulled a two silicone bands out of his jacket pocket.

Allie's head dropped back as she laughed. "This is so perfect," she murmured as Jake rolled the silicone band onto her finger.

Finally, Rupert said, "You may kiss your bride."

Allie lifted her chin and looked into Jake's sparkling eyes.

He whispered, "Meu tesouro."

The museum filled with people dressed in tuxedos and gowns. The lighting in the lobby was lowered, creating a calm and serene atmosphere. Uniformed servers threaded through the crowds carrying trays of champagne and fancy hors d'oeuvres.

People naturally gravitated to Papi, who was loving every second of the limelight.

When Rupert announced it was time to move to the third floor, the crowd moved toward the staircase.

Laughter, conversation, and the rustling of fabric filled the air.

Allie hung back at the edge of the crowd, just watching.

"What are you thinking?" Jake asked. He stood behind her with his hands on her shoulders.

"It's been a crazy week."

"That's an understatement."

The day before, they'd gotten word that Valerie and Rudy Billows had taken a plea deal. The real Selena and Chip Anderson had traveled to Hauser Mountain after their project in the South Pacific wrapped up. They strongly encouraged ARASNAC to continue funding a complete excavation of the site, especially after a second diving expedition to the *Santa Anna-Maria* was authorized. They eagerly employed Papi as a consultant for the duration of the project.

The ultimate goal was to display the findings from the shipwreck alongside the M'yxnihan discoveries.

"I have an idea," he said quietly next to her ear. He slipped his hand into hers and tugged.

She followed him away from the staircase into the deserted hall of natural history and put a hand over her mouth to stifle a laugh. Someone had put bowties on the dinosaurs. "Did you have anything to do with this?"

He shrugged one shoulder. "It's a formal event."

The noise faded behind them as the first floor cleared and they were mostly alone. It was nice to walk around the museum when it was still and quiet and the lights were low.

"I have a surprise for you."

She looked up at him. "Another one? Jaaaake, why?"

"Wait here." He produced his badge from his jacket and swiped the pad beside a door hidden behind a display. A moment later he came back with a thin rectangular gift and handed it to her.

"What is it?"

"Open it." He put his hands in his pockets and waited.

Allie untied the silver ribbon and carefully peeled at the seam on the black wrapping paper. "It's so mysterious."

"Just like me."

She gasped when she pulled the paper back. "Is this? How did you?" She ran her fingers gently across the front of the black leather book in her hand. Stamped in silver leaf was a title: *The Love Story of Princess K'nih and Fernando de Cabra.*

"I worked with Zoe's team to get a complete copy of the translation, and then I pulled some strings – and by that I mean I groveled and begged – my friend who's an indie author to make it all pretty and get it printed. Happy anniversary, forever wife."

"Oh, Jake, this is amazing. Thank you." She leaned up to kiss him. "Happy anniversary. I feel bad that I didn't get you anything."

"Allie, you give me mint chocolate chip ice cream every day of our lives."

She sniffled and looked up at him. "Kiss me before you make me cry."

He put a finger under her chin and rubbed his thumb along her jaw. "I can do that."

She jerked back. "Wait. Your grandfather didn't like mint chocolate chip ice cream."

He chuckled. "I know, but it sounded better than beetles."

"It does sound better than beetles."

"Forever with you is better than beetles *or* ice cream."

"Better than buried treasure." She lifted up on her toes to kiss her forever husband.

Also by Carrie Jacobs

HICKORY HOLLOW (Can be read in any order):

Drunk on a Plane

Caller Number Nine

The Boy Next Door

Luck of the Draw

Cat Burglar

Mending Fences

Two Tickets to Paradise

Bad Advice

Where There's a Will (novella)

STAND ALONE:

The Bucket List

Unexpected Treasure

WILLOW CREEK:

#1 Everything's Under Control

#2 Recipe for Disaster

#3 Forget Me Not

For details about all of my books, visit my website. For exclusive sneak peeks, behind-the-scenes information, and much more, sign up for my newsletter at carriejacobs.com.

Author's Note

Dear Reader,

Lucky Number Thirteen!!

It surprises me every time, and once again I can't believe you're holding my thirteenth published novel!

It will come as no surprise to anyone who knows me that I had Rick and Evie O'Connell in the back of my mind as I wrote Allie and Jake's story. While I didn't take them to Egypt or make them run from mummies... although now that I think about it, maybe I should have. (*Files idea away for a future novel in a much different genre.*) Rick and Evie are the ultimate in adventure couples.

If you haven't read the book yet, go back and do that before you finish this note, because there's a pretty major spoiler ahead.

Last chance, I'm going to start talking about the spoiler.

Here we go...

In addition to Rick and Evie, one of my inspirations for this book was Josh Gates. I love watching Josh Gates on *Expedition Unknown*. It was during an episode of this show that I first learned about cochineal beetles and their value in Mesoamerican civilizations and how these little beetles became quite the hot topic during the Spanish colonial area.

The details I included about cochineal are true. (Yes, even the part where they are still used today in food dyes and cosmetics. Ewww.)

I loved getting to know Allie and learning why her exterior was so tough, and why she lost her patience with Papi on a regular basis.

Papi was a joy to write. Brilliant, charming, devoted... and flawed.

Jake was adorable, despite his initial (unfair) assumptions about Allie. I'm glad he came around. 😊

And yes, the earthquake I referenced from 2011 was a real thing. We were sitting in our offices when the whole building shook and we looked around at each other wondering what the heck just happened. (Believe me, earthquakes in Central PA are not a typical occurrence!) No damage done, but it certainly gave us plenty to talk about! (And I think a shifted rock is a plausible consequence of even the mildest earthquake.)

Now that I've finished another book, I think it's time to go rewatch *The Mummy* and *The Mummy Returns* for the 9,847,396th time. (And maybe binge a few episodes of *Expedition Unknown* or one of Josh's other awesome shows.)

To keep up with all the latest updates and news, be sure to sign up for my newsletter at carriejacobs.com! You'll get exclusive sneak peeks, behind-the-scenes info, notice of upcoming releases, and all that jazz. You can also follow me on Facebook facebook.com/carriejacobsauthor for updates, notice of my upcoming events and more importantly, pictures of my furry editorial assistants.

If you enjoyed *Unexpected Treasure* and have a moment

to spare, leaving a review online would be very helpful to me. (Even if you didn't buy it online, you can still leave a review.)

Until next time ∼ cherish your treasures!

Best,

Carrie

About the Author

Carrie's love of storytelling began in early childhood and never wavered as time marched onward. She reads in pretty much every genre imaginable, but found her writing happy place in small town contemporary romance and romantic comedy.

From that love came Hickory Hollow and the town next door, Willow Creek. Both towns are a mashup of her home-town and places she's either visited or would like to. Her favorite part of her fictitious locations? The residents don't have to drive an hour to get to Target, like she does in real life.

Carrie lives in beautiful central Pennsylvania with her very own romcom hero and thoroughly spoiled furry editorial assistants.

Connect with Carrie through her newsletter or social media!

Website: carriejacobs.com

facebook.com/carriejacobsauthor

instagram.com/carriejacobsauthor

goodreads.com/carriejacobs